*This book is dedicated to Michelle,
first, foremost and forever.*

Disorder

GERARD BRENNAN

No Alibis Press

First published in 2018
by No Alibis Press

Printed and bound by TJ International, Padstow

All rights reserved
© Gerard Brennan, 2017

The right of Gerard Brennan to be identified as author
of this work has been asserted in accordance with Section 77
of the Copyright, Designs and Patents Act 1988

*This book is sold subject to the condition that it shall not, by way of trade
or otherwise, be lent, resold, hired out, or otherwise circulated without the
publisher's prior consent in any form of binding or cover other than that in
which it is published and without a similar condition, including this condition,
being imposed on the subsequent purchaser*

A CIP record for this book
is available from the British Library

ISBN 978-1999882204

2 4 6 8 10 9 7 5 3 1

BOTTLE IT

A protest. In Belfast, it's a warm-up to a riot. Civil disobedience. Disorder.

Vic Wallace followed his cousin through the crowd; practically stepped on the larger man's heels as if he was afraid the red, white and blue sea of bodies would drown him if he fell too far behind. The cousin, Big Clark Wallace, slapped and clapped backs for attention. Bared teeth to match smiles and snarls when people turned to greet or challenge him. A killer whale among a school of fish. Not even the same class of vertebrate.

"All right, ball-bag?" Clark's thunderous voice startled a blocky man who was too busy eyeballing and threatening the cops to notice his approach. "Watch your back there. Haf'ta lead from the front, what?"

The man kowtowed, his hard-earned bulk stripped from him mentally by one of Clark's monster grins. Cheeks pink from roaring faded to ash grey. Amped up but unwilling to tackle Clark, the block shoved three men and a woman deeper into the crush to make room. Clark tapped the peak of his baseball cap with an extended index finger. Just a gunslinger greeting a cowboy.

"Hiya, Clark," the man said. "Head on through. Heard somebody asking for you."

"Who?"

The man shrugged. "Don't know him."

"Well, I'm here now. Whoever wants me can form an orderly queue, you know what I mean?"

"Aye. Hundred percent, Clark. Get stuck in, mate."

Vic attempted to make eye contact with the square man on his way past. "Hiya."

A rosy flush reclaimed the man's cheeks. "Fuck off."

Vic looked away. He inched closer to Clark and managed to kick his Achilles tendon. Clark half-turned and looked down on his cousin.

"Fuck's sake, are you trying to ride me, Vic?"

"That juice-head cunt you were talking to pushed me. Fuck is he, anyway?"

"Can't remember." Clark winked at him. "How you getting on there, wee cousin?"

"Buzzin'."

"Ach, here, you're not on something are you?"

"What? No, fuck. Remember when we used to say we're buzzin' cousins?"

Clark looked like he was working out long division in his head.

Vic yammered on. "I mean, I'm a bit pished, but that's it, like. Just excited."

"Good." Clark exhaled. His shoulders lowered. "No time for any of your usual shite right now. You can get off your tits on whatever you fancy tonight, right?"

"Except I've no money, like."

"Stop yapping about money, will you? We'll get you sorted soon enough."

"We who?"

Clark shoved forward another couple of feet. "Can't hear you, mate. Just stick close."

"What am I supposed to do with this?" Vic held an empty WKD bottle over his head.

"Come on to fuck. We'll talk at the front."

"When are we supposed to cover our faces?"

"When we get to the front."

A wee girl, barely out of her teens, jumped at Clark and shinnied up his torso. She chomped on air before shrieking. "Isn't this mad?"

"Aye, love. Fancy a buck later?"

"Maybe. So long as you don't get arrested, Clark."

"Making no promises. If you want it, come find it."

Clark mashed his lips against the girl's. Her cheeks bulged as he forced his tongue into her mouth. She slid her hand from the nape of his neck to the band of his baseball cap then jerked her head backwards to break contact. Made dreamy MDMA eyes at him.

"I love you, but it's still a maybe, Clark."

"Aye? Fuck you, then."

Clark slid his hands under her armpits and heaved her upwards. She flew. Screamed. Landed on top of the densely packed crowd.

"Jesus, Clark," Vic said. "You could have killed her."

"My hole. She's fine, look."

"Can't see her."

"I can send you after her to check for sure."

Vic laughed. Clark didn't.

"Nah, you're all right. I tried that crowd-surfing at an aul' illegal rave once. Didn't think much of it."

"We're nearly there, Vic. Mouth shut, eyes open."

Vic pulled the neck of his T-shirt up over the bottom half of his face. He clamped it in place with his teeth. Clark hooked the edge of his scarf to the end of his nose – the only real use for a scarf during a rare Belfast heat wave – and pulled the brim of his cap down an inch. Then they were through to the front line. Clark pulled Vic in tight and squeezed his neck in an aggressive one-armed hug until Vic had to swat his cousin's beefy arms for mercy.

PSNI Land Rovers were parked side-by-side to create a buffer between the protesters and the riot police. There was enough room between each vehicle to allow two men to walk shoulder-to-shoulder. These gaps would soon be plugged by riot shields and the injured. The tang of nervous sweat polluted the air. Two water cannon trucks had been called in already. They trundled to a stop behind the riot cops and grumbled threats, pumps primed. Both groups advanced a couple of inches each; plate tectonics in motion.

Clark grabbed Vic's upper arm and hauled him from the front line into no man's land. Vic stood still, his WKD bottle held behind his back, and stared at the police. Clark danced along the middle ground like a mascot, fist-pumping to the cheers of his fellow protesters. The clamour of encouragement soon swelled to a bloodthirsty communal yowl of profanity and violent promises. Clark spread his arms in an unconscious Christ-like pose, his back to the Land Rovers. A megaphone crackled.

"Please maintain a safe distance from the PSNI Land Rovers."

Clark abandoned his messianic affectation to mime masturbation. He'd have earned a standing ovation if his audience had been seated. As it was, they contented themselves with a burst of punk rock pogo jumps. Drummers to one side of the barely restrained protesters rattled out a beat; militaristic, aggressive, out of sync.

Vic drew back his right arm and tossed his WKD bottle over the line marked out by the armoured vehicles. It arced through the cool air, tumbling base over neck. Orange light glinted off the glass. The drums beat harder, faster, louder. Vic and Clark, stranded in no man's land, stood statue still.

The WKD bottle descended on a cluster of helmeted cops. Two of them had raised their visors to chat. Officer McAllister gave Officer Greene a cheeky grin. He returned it to her.

"At least the overtime will pay for Christmas," McAllister said. "Well, most of it."

"How many kids have you now?"

McAllister's grin faltered slightly, "Still two. And no plans for more. Couldn't afford…"

Greene's head snapped back and he toppled over, his nose instantly bloody. McAllister fell to her knees by his side.

"Oh my God, you all right?"

"What the fuck happened?"

McAllister looked up. A small audience had formed around them, casting shadows over the fallen Greene. One of the other riot cops, his visor in place, handed McAllister the WKD bottle. His voice was slightly muffled, but his words rang clear:

"It's starting."

McAllister pulled her own visor down then reached into her hip pocket. She took out a small packet of paper tissues and handed it to Greene. The bloodied cop snuffled, snorted and spat out a crimson gob before he ripped open the little plastic packet and pressed half the tissues to his nostrils.

"I think it's broken," Greene said.

McAllister nodded. "Aye, looks bad. It came out of nowhere."

"Fucking bastards."

McAllister held out the bottle. "You want a souvenir?"

Greene snatched the makeshift projectile out of her hand then sprang to his feet. He dropped the blood-soaked tissues on the road and pushed through the protective wall his colleagues had formed around him.

"Greene, come back!"

But Greene ignored McAllister. He marched towards the protest, the bottle swinging by his side. "Fucking bastards," he said again.

Other cops called his name but Greene's heavy footsteps didn't falter. He picked a target, drew his arm back and sent the bottle back to where it came from.

Clark had dropped the impression of a statue just before Vic. He stared at his smaller, skinnier cousin, his eyes narrow slits above the edge of his scarf. Vic smiled at Clark. His T-shirt fell away from his face.

"Did you see that? I dropped a cop, Clarky boy!"

"You stupid—"

The WKD bottle bounced off Clark's beefy shoulder. He turned on his heel to glare at the cops as the bottle bounced along the tarmac. Vic chased after his empty and snatched it up before it rolled into the mass of protesters. He traced a finger along the half-peeled label on his way back to his cousin.

"I think it's the same bottle, Clark. How the hell's it not smashed?"

"Look at this cheeky cunt," Clark said.

Vic looked to where Clark pointed. Officer Greene,

his visor still up to display his injury, stood between two Land Rovers with his right hand in the air and his middle finger extended. Protesters on the front line went for their phones, but Greene's colleagues swamped him before he could become the focal point of their amateur photography and a social media sensation.

Clark created a makeshift megaphone by cupping his hands around his mouth.

"I'll remember your face, dickhead."

"Sure it was covered in blood," Vic said.

Clark pushed his cousin into the crowd. "Fuck up, you."

The crowd shoved Vic back into no man's land. He tripped over his own feet and fell on his side. The WKD bottle thumped the road, and again, managed to stay intact, though a roadmap of cracks spread out from what remained of the label. Vic gathered himself up and rose to his feet slowly, his head bowed and his back to the jeering protesters. He looked to the police line. Cops filtered through the spaces between the Land Rovers and formed a line, their clear plastic shields overlapped.

"It's starting," Vic said.

"I wasn't done messing with them, cuz. Could you not control yourself?"

"Didn't know we were working to a timetable, like."

"Next time, wait for my word."

"Sorry, Clark."

"And cover your fucking face, you wank dog."

"Ach, shite." Vic pulled the T-shirt back up over his lower face. He spoke through clenched teeth. "I'm scooped for sure, now."

"Should have bought a scarf off one of them wee lads on the sidelines."

"I've no money."

"Told you to shut up about money. I'd have bought you one if you'd asked."

"Will you buy me a wee candyfloss too?"

Clark jutted his chin, aiming to intimidate the smaller

man. Then his lips parted in a begrudged smile.
"No surrender, Vic."
"Aye, for God and Ulster, Clarky boy."

LITTLE BOY BLUE

Tommy Bridge sat cross-legged on the floor in a stoop-shouldered bastardisation of the Lotus position. Barefoot and topless, he wore a pair of checked pyjama bottoms. His knees supported his upturned wrists and a smartphone rested on his left palm. In his other hand he clasped a Glock 17. The Japanese sleeve tattoo on his right forearm pulsed each time he tightened and loosened his grip on the automatic pistol. Worry lines formed tiny waves on his forehead, swelling and breaking on the ridge of his brow. His twitching jawline was partially concealed by an unruly, grey-streaked beard. It had grown longer than his close-shorn sugar-dusted hair.

The smartphone chimed and its screen lit up. Bridge opened his left eye and watched his thumb go to work. A text message from 'Dev' popped up:
At da door.
He tapped out a reply.
Haven't showered yet.
Can I come in?
Nope. Meet u in ur car, 10 mins.
10 mins my arse.

Bridge smirked slightly. He unfolded his legs and set his Glock on the floor beside him to free up a hand. His fingers sank into the arm of a two-seater sofa and he hauled himself to his feet. Bridge arched his lower back and allowed his head to flop forward. Three deep breaths swelled his muscled chest before he crouched to retrieve his gun from the floor.

He crossed the small living room in three quick steps to stand in front of a false fireplace. His reflection in the mirror above the mantelpiece imitated his head-jerking search for something. Then he had it. A little bottle of eye-drops was tucked behind a photograph of a teenage girl. The girl stared out from her crystal frame with eyes as brown and soulful as Bridge's. He didn't pay the picture a second glance. The drops were put to work and Bridge blinked away artificial tears. His shining eyes met those of his reflection. He sneered.

Bridge turned on his heel. A fist-sized anarchy symbol, tattooed between his shoulder blades, flashed in the mirror. He left the room and dragged his feet down the short length of a gloomy hallway. A door at the end of his unenthusiastic jaunt led to a bathroom lacking in natural light. Bridge set his gun and phone on the toilet lid then opened a tiny window before activating an electric shower unit at the tap-end of a small bath. He laid a hand towel on the floor and threw a larger one over the shower curtain rod before stepping out of his pyjamas and into the stream of steaming water. He washed quickly, paying most attention to his armpits, crotch and feet.

Sudsy water gurgled down the plug hole after Bridge pushed the shower unit's off button. He stepped over the side of the bath onto the smaller towel and wrapped the big one around his slim waist. Then he retrieved his gun and phone. Only a few drops of water hit the linoleum as he left the bathroom. He shouldered open the door to his bedroom, kicked it shut from the other side with his heel, and sat on the edge of his bed. Then he checked his phone. Two missed calls and a text message. He selected the text message.

2 more mins and I'm coming in.

Bridge's head snapped up at the sound of a door slamming shut. He set his gun and phone on top of his bedside cabinet and called out. "I'm still getting dressed, Dev."

"And what?" The answering voice was feminine with hints of a country upbringing and an Antrim whiskey dependency. "Do you need me to play home help?"

"Aye. Give us a bed bath, sure.'"

"Inappropriate, Bridge."

"Says the model of professionalism. How's the head this morning?"

"None the better for you giving me a stress headache

on top of the hangover, you cunt." Dev's voice got louder as she got closer to Bridge's bedroom door. "Get your cock out of your hand and into your trunks."

One half of Bridge's mouth twitched. "The call only just came in."

"Aye, and we were told to shift our holes."

"So stop melting my head and let me get dressed, will you?"

"I'll knock you out, boy."

"Make us a coffee first?"

"Instant? No. I need filter coffee. Thick as tar and twice as strong. You've held us up for long enough and I'm gasping. Ten seconds before I drag you out. Fair warning."

Bridge's eyes widened. He snatched a pair of boxers out of his bedside cabinet drawer and stood to pull them up under his towel, like a kid changing his togs at the beach. The door swung open. Dev swept in and snatched the towel from his waist. She dropped it on the carpet and looked him up and down. Settled her gaze on his black boxers.

"No luck, eh?" Dev smiled.

Bridge didn't. "Seriously, like? This is a bit much, even for you."

Dev planted her hands on her wide hips. Her stout farm-girl frame dwarfed Bridge's lean build. She looked down from her noticeable height advantage. "Hurry. Up."

"Dev? I don't remember giving you a key."

"You didn't."

"If you've broke my lock—"

"Bridge, if you don't know that door was unlocked you need to have a good look at yourself. Where's you sense of self preservation?"

Bridge moved to the foot of his bed and pulled open a built-in wardrobe door. "Fully tuned-in to you, Dev. Would you go sit down or something? I can feel your eyes in my cavities."

"Aye, you're that good looking, aren't you? If only you were a foot taller, eh?"

At five foot seven he was an inch shy of the old RUC height requirement.

"Why are you in such a rush to get into the middle of this stupid fucking thing, Dev?"

"Nobody told you?"

"No." He shoved his tattooed right arm into a black shirt.

"We've been given the go ahead to lift Vic Wallace."

"Vic?" Bridge buttoned the front of his shirt deftly and reached into the wardrobe to produce a pair of dress trousers. "And what about Clark?"

"Vic first. Then we'll get the other cunt."

"Vic'll never tout on Clark."

"How'd you ever get to be a Detective Inspector, Bridge? This is pretty standard stuff. Go for the weak one first. Vic's cornered, and I've always got a rat vibe off him."

"What's the charge?"

Dev shook her head. "I'm starting the car. In one minute I'm taking off. You can come with me or you can get a taxi. Your choice."

She slammed the bedroom door *and* the front door on her way out. Bridge pulled a shoulder holster and suit jacket from the wardrobe. Seconds later he was fully dressed with the Glock tucked away and the phone in his hip pocket. He pulled open the top drawer of his cabinet and snagged a thin wallet, flipping it automatically to glance at his PSNI ID.

Detective Inspector Tommy Bridge allowed himself a few seconds to scratch his beard and stare into space. A car horn sounded. He hurried out the door.

PSNIRA

Clark draped his meaty arm over Vic's shoulders and pulled him close. "Won't be long until this thing really kicks off, cuz. It's going to be mental."

"Sweet to the beat," Vic said.

"Fuckin' right, kid."

"I want to slap a cop so hard his helmet comes off."

"Hah! That's how we roll, Vic. I'm going to get one of them batons they love to swing around. See how they like being on the wrong end if it."

"I'll buy it off you."

"With what? Sure you're never done telling me how skint you are. Just grab one for yourself."

"Aye, dead on."

"Here, look." Clark pointed at the police line. "The cop with the busted face is still there. That's the one I'm going for. Teach him he can't fire bottles at me."

Vic held the WKD bottle by the neck and slammed it into his open palm. "You want to hit him with this?"

"Nah, you hold onto that, mate. Toss it again when we get a bit closer. That's where you went wrong last time."

"Aye, sorry, cuz. Got a wee bit excited, you know?"

"I know. Just hold fire another wee minute. We're about ready to pop."

"Still waiting on your word."

Clark patted the top of Vic's bristly head. "Watch this."

The bigger Wallace started a slow clap. Three beats. Clap-clap-clap. Clap-clap-clap. Then a chant was born. First Clark:

"P-S-N. I-R-A. P-S-N. I-R-A. P-S-N. I-R-A."

Vic joined in immediately, and the protesters standing

nearest the Wallace men followed close behind. The small pocket of chanters spread like a malignant tumour.

"P-S-N. I-R-A. P-S-N. I-R-A. P-S-N. I-R-A."

The riot cops rocked back and forth, bounced on the balls of their feet, twirled batons intermittently to loosen up their wrists, elbows and shoulders. It was about to happen. The chants from the rioters, the eerie silence from the PSNI; their opposing haka. Adrenaline spiked and managed poorly.

Battle ready.

Jimmy McAuley couldn't have picked a worse time to dander along the shrinking no man's land separating the two factions.

THINK DIFFERENT

Jimmy McAuley, barely out of his teens and rocking the slick-quiff hipster look, looked up from his phone. He shifted his weight on the toilet lid that he used as a chair. The phone's display lit his lightly stubbled face like he was telling horror stories with a torch under his chin. He stared at Squinty Steve, a youngish man with a face hard-worn by time or bad luck. Jimmy double-blinked at stoner speed. Steve might have blinked back. It was hard to tell, since his hooded lids were so close to being shut.

Thirty seconds later, Jimmy said, "You know what? I'm going to delete my Facebook account, boy."

"Good lad. You can use my computer when we've burned out this spliff. It's quicker than messing about with the app."

Steve passed Jimmy the joint. Jimmy nodded and pulled hard. He smiled. "I'm going to feel so free without all that Facebook bullshit in my life."

"That's the spirit, man."

Jimmy nodded to himself, took another puff and passed the weed back to Steve. "This is really good gear, man."

"High grade. It's called Think Different."

"I don't feel stoned, but I do, you know?"

"Clarity, mate."

"Is that what that is?"

"Probably."

Jimmy closed his eyes for a few seconds. He breathed in through the nose and out through the mouth; once, twice, three times. Then his eyelids snapped open like hastily pulled blinds.

"Steve!"

Steve stood up so he could extinguish his roach in the sink. He sat back down and crossed his legs, his attention on

Jimmy like a laser beam. "What is it, our fellah?"

"I do feel stoned, you know."

"It's a slippery high. Hold tight to it."

Jimmy giggled. "What the fuck does that mean?"

"It means you're higher than a giraffe's ossicones."

"Ozzy..?"

"Ossicones. Them wee horns they have."

Jimmy laughed. "Giraffes don't have horns."

"I know. They're ossicones."

"You're making that shit up."

"Google it."

"Can't even spell it, Steve."

"And you a student too. I shudder for the future."

"I'm not studying to be a zoo keeper."

"What *are* you studying for?"

"I don't really know, boy. A *higher* education?"

"Right... well, let me know how that works out for you, our fellah."

Steve stood up and crossed the cramped quarters to unlock the door. He stepped out onto the landing and looked over his shoulder at Jimmy.

"You coming or what?"

"Yeah, yeah." Jimmy rose to his feet. "Right behind you."

In the shadowy bedroom, Steve had planted himself in front of his keyboard. The widescreen TV on the wall showed that he was trawling through an extensive mp3 collection. Jimmy hunkered down beside him and gazed at the primary source of light in the room.

"Wait 'til you hear these vibes," Steve said.

Squinty Steve hit the enter key then rolled the swivel-chair back from his desk. A high-hat cymbal whispered through the small speakers dotted around the room, linked by tangled cables.

"What's this?"

"A bit of Sabbath, our fellah."

"Ah, Jesus. I could do without the 'kill your granny, fuck your dog' shite."

"This tune's about pacifism. You never heard War Pigs?"

"It's so old."

"Classic."

"That's just another word for old."

"So's your ma."

Jimmy scratched his head. "Right."

Steve got off his chair and nudged it towards Jimmy. The castors caused a sizeable kink in the loose carpet.

"Right, Jimmy. Let's get you off this Faceshite."

Jimmy settled his backside on the creaking swivel-chair and Steve bent at the waist slightly to rattle some keys. On the TV, the screen split down the middle, the mp3 list on the left and Facebook's login screen on the right. Jimmy flexed his fingers and waited for Steve to get out of the way. But Steve had another quick batter on the keyboard before stepping back. Jimmy's Facebook account opened up.

"How the fuck did you do that?" Jimmy asked.

"I've got the mad skills, our fellah."

"You a hacker?"

"I prefer the term hactivist. Hackers are gremlins. What I do… it's something else. It's about justice." Steve nodded slowly then smiled. "But here, I didn't need to do anything fancy there now. You let the browser save your password last time you were here."

"Why didn't you frape me?"

"Don't use that word around me again, Jimmy. People shouldn't make light of rape."

"I didn't. I'm talking about Facebook hi-jacking. Everybody calls it frape."

"I don't."

Jimmy shrugged and rotated his wrists before taking control of Steve's computer. "Well… thanks, man. At least I know I can trust you."

"You don't know that, our fellah. You don't know what's going on inside anybody's skull. Trust nobody."

"Paranoid?"

"Fuck's sake. It's still War Pigs. Jesus, our fellah, you need a Sabbath education."

"I mean, are *you* paranoid? From the weed, like."

"No. The diazepam keeps that at bay. It's just common sense. You're on your own, mate. Never forget it."

"Must be lonely being you."

"Rather that than constant disappointment when my so-called friends let me down." Steve sniffed then pointed at the TV. "Here, what's that, man?"

"That? Ach, it's another one of those Facebook pages that take the piss out of everything to do with flag protests, riots and all that shite."

"Yeah? Cool. Here, don't scroll past it yet. What's that video about?"

"There's another protest down at City Hall right now. Something to do with marching, or not being allowed to march, or some shite. Could be the flag thing again, I suppose."

"Hit play, will you?"

Jimmy did as he was asked and leaned back in the seat with his arms folded. Steve shifted from foot-to-foot, standing seemingly as strenuous an activity as he was used to. On the screen, a shaky image of Belfast City Hall came to life. PSNI Land Rovers blocked access to the lawns and the mass of protesters prevented traffic from passing by the front gates. The cameraman was a fair bit from the crowd, the images boxlike and blurred from a poor zoom function. The owner of the camera phone was attempting a running commentary but his words couldn't compete with the chanting from the protesters.

"What are they saying?" Steve asked.

"Sounds like white noise to me."

"Will I turn down the music?"

"Don't think it'll help, boy. Fuck it. This is boring."

"I know. They're doing it wrong. You need to get closer to the action, maybe interview a rioter, or something."

"They're not rioting," Jimmy said. "That's pretty peaceful."

"For now."

"You know, if I nail this English degree, I might want to get into journalism."

"And what?"

"I'd be covering political shite all the time."

"So…?"

"Maybe I should get a headstart?"

"Wise up."

"I bet the protestors aren't even all that bad."

"That's the weed talking."

"I'm going down there."

"You'll be on your own. I've more friends calling by in an hour or so."

"Good, leave my Facebook page open. You'll be able to see my first video by then."

"I really don't think this is a good idea."

"Ach, chill out. It's Belfast not Bosnia."

"What happened in Bosnia?"

Jimmy shrugged. "Google it. I'm away on."

Steve put a hand on Jimmy's shoulder. "Wait!"

"Why? You coming?"

"Fuck no. But I'll roll you a wee takeaway spliff. I'll be there in spirit."

"Happy days."

WEAR BLUES

"Did you not get the same text as me, Bridge?"

Detective Sergeant Patricia 'Dev' Devenney pulled her car in behind a PSNI water cannon. Bridge glanced up from the brightly coloured puzzle-game he was playing on his phone.

"I'm sure I did, Dev. What are you getting at?"

"My text told me to wear blues."

"You're not wearing them."

"Aye, I know. But they're in the boot of the car, and they're a wee bit oversized since I started on the Slimming World—"

"Slimming World?"

"Nearly a stone off in a month."

Bridge shrugged. "Never noticed."

"Dick."

Dev got out of her Mitsubishi Lancer and stomped towards the rear. Bridge followed close behind, a smirk tugging at the corner of his mouth.

"So, before you rudely interrupted me..." Dev flipped open the boot, "I was saying that my blues fit over the top of my street clothes, so I can stick mine on at the drop of a hat. But you... you came in that lovely wee little-boy-blue suit of yours. Was that what you wore for your confirmation?"

"I was never confirmed."

"Whatever. And you didn't bring a bag with you."

"So...?"

"So, you were told to wear blues."

"If you think I'm going to wade in with the rank and file riot cops, you've maybe taken one too many bricks to the head, Dev."

The protestors filled the air with a thunder-rumble roar.

"Oh, is the DI too good to rub shoulders with the real

men?"

"Are there no female officers fighting the good fight out there?"

"A real woman wouldn't let you anywhere near her, Bridge."

Bridge's smirk morphed into a sneer. "Ha. Ha. Oh, and ha. You're funny."

"Wasn't intended as a joke, DI Dickhead."

Dev snatched a ball of dark blue material from the boot and shook it out. Trouser legs and sleeves unfurled. She stepped into one leg of her riot overalls.

Bridge raised his voice to compensate for a protest chant:

"*P-S-N. I-R-A.*"

"You haven't put on the fire retardant undies, Dev."

"Fuck that. I'll not be putting on the helmet either. Baseball cap all the way for me. If the petrol bombs come out, I'm jumping into the nearest Land Rover."

"My hero."

"At least I'm making an effort."

"If you could call it that."

"They won't need me anyway, not today. It's just for the look of it."

Bridge looked Dev up and down. "Plus you hardly want to add on four stone of equipment after you've just shaved a stone off your big arse, aye?"

"You might want to remember that the standard issue riot gear includes a baton that'd slide right up your hoop."

"How much do you charge for that?"

"DI Bridge? DS Devenney?"

Bridge and Dev quarter-turned to acknowledge the presence of a fully-garbed officer. His visor was raised and he tugged at his open-faced balaclava with a hooked finger. Sweat beaded his forehead.

Dev spoke to fill Bridge's deliberate silence. "Can I help you?"

"Thought you'd like to know we can confirm that Vic *and* Clark Wallace are in attendance. We're hoping to get word that we can extract them both from the crowd soon... ma'am."

"Good to know, Officer. Thank you."

Before the officer could leave, Bridge grabbed his upper arm. "Whereabouts are they?"

"Where else? Front and centre, just opposite the main gates of City Hall. Clark's wearing a hat and scarf, but you can tell it's him by the size and shape. Vic's even more obvious. All he's done is pull his T-shirt over his big gob. You'd spot his scabby suede-head a mile away."

Bridge turned to Dev, his fingers still dug deep into the messenger's bicep. "You made it out like you knew for a fact they'd be here."

"And I was right."

"But it's only been confirmed."

"Call it female intuition if you want. I just *knew* they'd have to get involved. They've been lying low for too long."

The officer wriggled out of Bridge's grip. "I need to get back to work here, sir."

"Be safe," Bridge said.

The officer nodded and jogged towards his squad.

"So, what do we do, DI?" Dev asked.

"Hang around like a couple of spare pricks, I suppose."

PHONE'S FOR YOU

Jimmy McAuley's phone was held high, filming the scene, sweeping the shot from one side to the other. A joint burned in one corner of his mouth, his eyes pinker than a white rabbit's.

"What the fuck is this?" Vic said, and pointed out the grinning kid with the slick quiff, phone and spliff.

Clark's mouth opened and closed a couple of times before his brain and vocal cords caught up with the new development. "Is he videoing this?"

"Looks like it, cuz."

"The fuck?"

"It's all right. Our faces are covered."

"Aye, but... cheeky cunt, what?"

"I know. Thinks this is some kind of joke."

"Probably going to post it on one of them Taig-loving websites, isn't he?"

"Aye, funny fucker." Vic slammed his bottle into his palm again. "You know what? He'll not be able to upload the video if he's no phone."

"What are you...?"

But Vic didn't waste any more time. He bolted from the safety of the crowd.

Jimmy McAuley watched Vic Wallace come at him and smiled.

"Just making a wee movie, sir. Hope you don't—"

"You wee stoner prick. Come here 'til I take the head off you!"

Vic threw a haymaker, loaded with a clutched WKD bottle. Jimmy watched the base of the bottle breeze past his nose. He barely flinched.

"What are you doing, man?"

Jimmy and Vic locked stares. For a few seconds it looked like they were going to laugh with each other. Then Vic grunted and lashed out at Jimmy with a backhand swing. Jimmy had used up all his luck with the first miss. This time the bottle landed flush against the side of his face. The already weakened glass smashed. Drops of blood rained down on the tarmac along with the jagged shards. Jimmy staggered backwards, raised his empty left hand to the right side of his face and snatched it away again when his probing fingers further angered the wound.

"You fucking glassed me. Uncalled for, boy."

"Give me that."

Vic pointed at the phone in Jimmy's right hand with the remains of his broken bottle. Jimmy didn't move. His eyes were glued to the bloodied weapon in Vic's hand.

"I can't believe you did that," Jimmy said.

Vic lunged at him, the broken bottle leading the charge, and aimed for Jimmy's chest. This time the student had the good sense to scramble backwards. As Vic overextended his attack he started to lose balance. Jimmy's survival instincts cut through the weed high. He brought his fist down in a hammer-blow. The fist was curled around his mobile. Jimmy's phone clunked the back of Vic's head. The phone popped out of Jimmy's hand like a wet bar of soap. Vic's face hit the glass-strewn tarmac. He screamed.

Jimmy watched his phone arc through the air. The sound of it hitting the road was drowned out by the clump-clump-clump of PSNI boots approaching. A tidal wave of riot cops knocked him over. Vic's prone body was buried under a second cluster of police officers.

The dam burst. Protesters ran to rescue their fallen comrade and slammed into riot shields.

Meaty thumps, obscene roars, unheard pleas for calm.

Jimmy was dragged towards the line of Land Rovers by two large policemen. The friction between the road and his heels popped one of his Converse trainers off. He didn't seem to notice.

"I can't believe that bastard glassed me, boy."

One of the cops spat a reply at Jimmy. "Don't know

what the fuck you were doing there anyway."

The cops dumped Jimmy at the feet of a pair of paramedics leaning against an ambulance parked amidst the police vehicles. One was grey-haired and stocky with a flushed face split by a guileless grin. The other was a younger man, skinny and scared.

"See if you can do something with this one's face, will you?" the cop who'd spoken to Jimmy said.

"Nasty," the elder of the paramedics said. "Glassed?"

"Aye. Got walloped with a bottle."

"Was it one of his own?"

"Look closer, aul' fellah. He's no protester. Just some fuckwit student, half out of his tree on drugs, no doubt."

Jimmy muttered. "Only a bit of weed, like."

The paramedic snorted. "They don't teach them much in the way of common sense, do they?"

"And yet he'll probably end up one of our bosses in a few years. Better get back to it here, mate."

"Dead on. We'll clean him up in no time. Just the start, eh? Getting rough out there now."

"I know. Just make sure you look after us lot before you tend to any of those rioting wankers that get hurt, will you?"

"Just you concentrate on staying safe, son."

The talkative cop rattled his baton off the side of his riot shield and turned on his heel. His partner followed him back towards the scrum. Neither of them seemed to be in any great rush.

"Right, you," the grey-haired paramedic said. "Let's get a look at the damage."

"What do you need?" the younger paramedic asked. He was poised to climb into the back of the ambulance.

"A fucking drink, kid. But for now, get me the suture kit."

"Am I going to die?" Jimmy asked.

"We all are," the paramedic said.

"Today?"

"Probably not."

PHONE'S FOR ME

Clark Wallace picked up the phone Jimmy McAuley had dropped. He thumbed the home button at the bottom of the handset and the touchscreen lit up. Hairline cracks webbed out from the upper-left corner, but other than that it was a perfectly functioning smartphone. Clark pocketed it before joining the tug-of-war.

A bunch of cops had Vic by the arms. The protesters were on his legs. Vic screamed and spat blood that had run from the left side of his face into his mouth. He looked worse off than the kid he'd glassed. His T-shirt no longer covered his face, but the bleeding cuts provided him with an effective mask. One eye rolled wildly, the other was swollen shut. His screams weren't for mercy. He was encouraging the protesters to pull harder.

"Come on to fuck! Don't let the bastards have me!"

Clark tried to help his side by wrapping his arms around a protester's waist and heaving backwards. The protester lost his grip and they both tumbled backwards. Clark cursed the weaker man and sprang to his feet. The cops were gaining ground.

Clark roared. "Fuck's sake!"

He rounded the losing team and flanked the cops. Then he charged, his arms spread wide, his head and shoulders lowered.

Clark crashed into the riot police and toppled four of them like dominoes. They lost their advantage and Vic slipped out of the cops' clutches. The protesters didn't give their comrade time to get to his feet. They dragged him across the street; his T-shirt hiked up and his exposed flesh skated tarmac.

"You're skinning me alive, you wankers!"

And then Vic was swallowed up by the crowd.

Clark used his size, strength and aggression to fend off

the riot police. Windmill punches and vicious kicks bought him a little breathing space. But rather than retreat, he attacked again. His bulky body sailed through the air and collided with a pair of riot shields. He bounced off and scrambled to his feet. Then he was on them again, a human battering ram. The cops took a couple of steps back. Clark laughed and closed the gap again. He reached out for the nearest riot shield and grabbed the sides of it. Started a new tug of war.

The unfortunate cop stumbled forward. He let his shield go in favour of holding on to his balance. Clark tossed the shield aside and threw a textbook right cross. It blasted the cop's visor and his head snapped back. The cop's colleagues tried to help him but they were held back by a fresh wave of protesters with blood lust.

"Separated from the herd, mate," Clark said. "No luck."

The cop brandished his baton. "Stay back."

"Give me your stick."

"Stay back!"

Clark didn't stay back.

The cop swung his baton. Clark covered his jaw with a raised shoulder. The baton thumped his upper left arm. Clark acted like it didn't hurt. He hit the cop's helmet with a tight right hook – palm open to protect his knuckles – then seized his arm. The cop flailed at Clark's back with his free hand. He may as well have swung at the sun. Clark attempted to fold the cop's arm the wrong way. Something popped and the cop's fingers loosened. Clark grabbed the baton and tried to run with it, but it was attached to the cop's wrist with a loop of braided leather. The riot cop fell to his knees, a high-pitched scream breached the gaps in his clenched teeth and the cracks in his visor. Clark threw a roundhouse kick that Chuck Norris would have approved of. The cop's helmet came off and his lights went out.

Clark knelt by the cop's side and with surprising tenderness he removed the baton's leather loop from his wrist. He patted the unconscious cop's balaclava-clad head.

"Cheers, mate."

Two protesters, not long out of their teens and built like sickly lurchers, sidled up to Clark. One of them spoke up, his accent so thick it was practically a speech impediment.

"Ye aw rye, Clarky? Ye wrecked that cap, dint ye? Majeek, so it wuss."

"Aye, he'll be sore in the morning, kid."

The kid nudged his silent mate. "Mon ta wah daunce on 'is 'ead."

They moved towards the unconscious man. Clark tucked his new baton into the waistband of his trackie bottoms, reached out and grabbed them by the scruffs of their necks.

"Don't be at it, youse 'uns."

"Wah's da prablam, Clarky? Sure, 'e's juss a cap."

"And he's unconscious."

"So?"

"So, you'd be a lot more fucking helpful if you went after one of the fuckers that are still on their fucking feet, right?"

"S'pose, like."

Clark roughly manoeuvred them towards the real action. They reluctantly joined the fray, ineffectively bouncing off the backs of their own side. Clark shook his head and turned to check on the fallen cop. He was coming to.

"You may hurry the fuck up and get seen to, mucker. There's lads here dying to 'dance on your head' and all."

The cop flinched then tried to focus on Clark. His glazed eyes betrayed him.

Clark stomped the ground like he was chasing a pesky cat from his doorstep. "Move your hole, dickhead!"

The injured cop stumbled towards the line of Land Rovers. Clark watched him until a band of brotherly riot cops broke from a fracas to envelope him and accompany him to safety.

"Some *craic* this, isn't it?"

Clark faced the source of the comment with a smile on his face. "Fuck me, is that Billy Andrews?"

"The one and only."

"And there's Caroline. Still knocking about with this ballix, are ye?"

"Hiya, Clark."

Billy and Caroline stood hip-to-hip, each with a hand cupping the other's arse. He had the injured cop's riot shield in his free hand and she was wearing the damaged helmet.

"You're looking well, like."

"Do you think the peelers would have me, mate?" Billy asked.

"You'd have a better chance if you were a taig, like, but after we get done with them today there'll be a lot of sick days to cover." Clark drew the baton from his waistband. "You see my wee souvenir?"

"Cracker, so it is," Billy said.

"C'mon, then. Let's get the use out of these things, aye?"

Clark traced a figure eight in the air with the baton then pointed it towards the densest pocket of disorder. They charged at it.

AMAZED GRACE

Grace Doran guided her cameraman towards one of the ambulances behind the PSNI Land Rovers. She wore a smart fitted blazer; beige cord with brown elbow patches. Under that, a dark green nehru blouse. The combination didn't quite match her blue jeans tucked into a pair of punky Doc Martin's that encased three-quarters of her calves. But the purple leather boots were a practical choice, as evidenced by the ease with which she skipped over riot detritus to get to where she was going.

"Come on, Andy, there's an injured civilian over at that one."

She flicked her long black hair over her shoulders and jutted her chin towards a bloodied young man with slick hair sat on the metal step at the back of the ambulance. He was smoking a cigarette along with a ruddy-faced, stocky paramedic.

When they got closer, Grace called out to the young man with a sweet singsong lilt.

"Hey there, sir. Would you be fit to chat to us for a wee minute?"

The young guy's eyes widened with alarm. "Me?"

"Yes, please. I hope you're not too badly hurt, mister...?"

He shook his head and swallowed air. "Jimmy."

"Mister Jimmy?"

"No. No mister. Jimmy McAuley."

"Thanks, Jimmy. Sure why don't you call me Grace, then?"

"Is that your name?"

"Oh, hey. You're one to watch, aren't you?" Grace turned to her cameraman and allowed her expression to slip from smiley to deadpan for a microsecond. "Can you get a good shot of him, Andy?"

"Looks like you're going to be on the telly, kid," the

paramedic said. "Maybe flick that fag, eh?"

Jimmy dropped his cigarette and crushed it under a Converse All Star. His other foot was encased only in a Spongebob Squarepants sock.

"Could you get him to stand, Grace?" Andy the cameraman asked.

Grace flashed her whitened teeth at him. "Would you be comfortable on your feet, Jimmy?"

"I'm missing a shoe, like."

"I can see that… it won't be for very long, though. Just watch where you set that foot, eh?"

Jimmy reluctantly pushed himself off the ambulance step and stood with his shoulders hunched. The abrasions on his face were patched up with paper stitches. One of the cuts was longer and deeper than the others. It ran from his cheekbone to the lobe of his ear. A thin line of blood still trickled from it.

"My goodness," Grace said. "That's going to leave a scar."

The paramedic cleared his throat. "He'll get stitches at hospital, love. A good doctor will minimise the scarring."

Jimmy smiled at him. "Thanks, mate."

"Yes," Grace said, her smile never faltering. "Thanks for your input, sir."

"We'll be leaving soon," the paramedic said. "Just waiting for the police to clear a path for us."

"I'm sure we'll be finished by then, sir. That's okay with you, Jimmy, isn't it? Just a very quick chat."

"What do you want to talk about?"

"Maybe we should start with your injury? Andy, are you rolling?"

"All set, Grace."

"So, Jimmy," Grace said, her voice half an octave lower and much less cheery. "What happened to your face?"

"Some scumbag hit me with a bottle."

"So it wasn't the police that did this?"

Jimmy shook his head. "The police saved me, actually.

If it wasn't for the PSNI, I'd probably have gotten it a lot worse."

"Thank goodness. But I'm a little confused here. Did one of your fellow protesters turn on you?"

"Fellow protesters? Do I look like one of those cretins?"

"That's rather strong language."

"I've already told you my name's McAuley. That sound like a prod name to you?"

"I didn't really..."

"I'm a Catholic, Grace. An innocent bystander dragged into this freak show."

"Surely you would have seen the disturbance from a mile away?"

"When I happened along it was still a 'peaceful protest'." Jimmy used his fingers to trace quotation marks in the air. "I thought it was safe enough to get a closer look."

"I hope you don't mind me saying, but that seems a little foolhardy."

"Is that right?" The hunch in Jimmy's shoulders disappeared as he puffed his narrow chest. "Do I not have the right to walk the streets of Belfast, then? Are these fuh..." He bit off the obscenity and nodded pointedly at the camera. "Excuse me. Are these louts and thugs going to dictate to all of Belfast where law abiding citizens can and can't go? We've given the Loyalist scum far too much leeway, yet again. What's that all about, huh? I bet if this were a Republican protest the water cannons would have been pumping gallons before the first poor Fenian looked a cop in his eyes."

"Do you really believe that, Jimmy?"

"Look at the statistics!"

"Which ones?"

"Any of them. I bet you pennies to pounds, the Catholics always come off worse. Equal rights my hole."

"I'm not sure I'm following you, Jimmy."

Jimmy's bloodshot eyes widened. He looked Grace up and down, pausing for a few seconds when he noticed her purple Doc Martin's. Then he fixed his gaze on the camera.

"I am so sick of these subhuman imbeciles hogging the limelight and making our country look like some sort of red-neck, backwater, inbred dung-heap. They're a genetically inferior version of Irish Catholics. Completely out of step with reality. Throwing their toys out of the pram over flags and marches? I mean, who even cares about any of that stuff these days? Let it go, morons! If you feel so hard done by, frig away off to Scotland and kiss Johnny Adair's arse. Do you think you'd be missed? Do you? Walk off the Earth, you dirty, rotten, brainless thugs. And take your children with you. Did you see the prams in that crowd? Babies, like. It's too late for those kids already. They can't be helped. Best they can hope for is a cot death."

"Jesus Christ."

Grace looked at the lens and drew the edge of her hand across her throat. Andy lowered his camera. He smirked.

"You didn't beat about the bush there, Jimmy, did you?"

Grace shot him a dirty look. "Shush, Andy."

Andy shrugged like he didn't care, but the smirk disappeared.

Grace looked to the paramedic. "Is he all right?"

"The police suspected drug use."

Jimmy sighed. "It was just a bit of weed, for Christ's sake. It's well wore off now. Nothing sobers you like a bottle in the face."

"Could I get your signature on a waiver form, Jimmy?"

"Fuck it, why not? You got a pen?"

"Yes, yes. Just a second."

Andy passed Grace a sheet of paper filled with small print from the battered leather satchel slung over his shoulder. Grace produced a gold-plated pen from the inside pocket of her blazer. She handed both to Jimmy. He signed the form quickly, using the flat surface of the ambulance door as a makeshift desk, and passed it back to her.

"This is nice, Grace."

Jimmy twirled the pen between his slender fingers. Grace watched it dance over and under his knuckles, her face slightly slack like she found it a soothing sight.

"Why don't you keep it, Jimmy?"

"Are you sure?"

"Yeah, I'm done with it."

Jimmy tilted his head. "This is engraved... 'Amazing Grace' it says. Is it not sentimental?"

"It was. Not anymore."

"Fair enough. Thanks."

Jimmy slipped the pen into his hip pocket. He stared at Grace for a few seconds. She shifted uncomfortably.

"I guess we'll see you later then, Jimmy."

"Oh, yeah. Dead on."

Grace looked around her for the next interviewee. "Let's talk to one of those police women, Andy."

"Spot on, Grace."

Jimmy raised a hand like he was waiting to be noticed in a classroom. "Em, Grace?"

"Yes?"

"What channel is this report going to be on? BBC NI?"

"I've a feeling your video might go beyond local TV."

"Fair enough. Don't really know anybody who watches the news on TV anyway. The internet has all the best stuff."

Grace flashed her whiter than white teeth again. "Well, maybe you'll go viral."

"That'd be some *craic*, wouldn't it?"

VIC'S WICK

Clark had lost his baseball cap, but his lower face was still covered by his red, white and blue scarf. He clutched the baton he'd snatched from a riot cop in his right hand and used his left to shove protestors out of his path. None of the people he manhandled complained. Below a receding widow's peak hairline, his forehead and the bridge of his nose were a mess of cuts and scratches, though the fine red marks were superficial. The blood had clotted already. He swayed as he strode through the battle zone, visibly exhausted, but he held his head high and scanned the crowd with widened eyes.

"All right, Clarky?"

Clark barely glanced towards the source of the question. "Seen our Vic?"

"Nah, mate."

"Fuck's sake."

Clark moved on. Protesters instinctually made room for him as he cut through the crowd. He didn't acknowledge a soul. His gaze swept from side to side and every so often he muttered to himself. His words were lost in the white noise of the riot.

VICTIMISED

Vic struggled against three men. Two controlled his arms and the third tried to take the fight out of him with punches to the stomach and slaps to the face. The trio wore the same colours in slightly different combinations: red, white and blue. Vic – his face already coated red from his earlier injuries – attempted to reason with them between strikes.

"Stop it. Please. We're on the same side."

The man dealing out punishment took a break. He caught his breath then bared his teeth at Vic. "The fuck we are. You're scum, Vic. Only reason you've lived this long is because of Clark."

"Come on, Sammy. You haven't even told me what I did wrong."

Sammy slapped Vic's face again. Crimson droplets flew.

Vic renewed his struggle and almost slipped the grip of the two men holding his arms back. Sammy raised his hand and wrapped it around Vic's neck. Fading tattoos writhed on his forearm. He pushed while the other two dragged. Then Vic had his back against a redbrick wall. He gargled for help, but the narrow alley, mere yards from the action at City Hall, offered no cavalry. Vic spat and hissed and tried to kick out, but Sammy deflected those kicks with his shin and closed the gap between the two of them. There wasn't enough room for Vic to manoeuvre. He slumped. Accepted his fate.

"What's going on here, lads?"

Vic looked to the source of the question. Squinted at a silhouette cut into the daylight at the mouth of the alley. The silhouette approached. Details and features filled themselves in. Blue suit. Beard. Half a smirk.

"Bridge?" Vic's voice held a groggy, dreamlike quality.
"Hiya, Vic. You well?"

Vic smiled at Sammy. Blood dribbled down his chin. "You're fucked now, mate. He's a cop, so he is."

Sammy snorted. "Aye. I'm shaking."

"Bridge." Vic's voice got louder and higher. "These ones are trying to kill me. Get you gun out."

"Don't worry, Vic," Bridge said. "They've been told to keep you alive."

"You took your time," Sammy said.

"Getting through the crowd was a wee bit of a challenge. You got what I asked for?"

"Aye."

Sammy backed away from Vic and moved to a cluster of large commercial bins on wheels. He flipped the lid, reached in and extracted a beer bottle. Clear glass, Corona label, a wedge of lime still jammed into the neck. Sammy walloped the base off the brick wall close to the bins. Created a jagged weapon. He trotted back to Bridge and passed the broken beer bottle to him gingerly.

Bridge glared at Vic, the nasty end of the makeshift weapon pointed at him. "Looks like you've been glassed today already, Vic. Popular lad."

"You're a cop, Bridge, you can't do this." Vic's face became childlike with panic.

Bridge ignored the statement. "This'll be the last time it happens to you, though. I guarantee it."

"Bridge, come on. Stop."

"No chance, Vic. You know why this has to happen. Take it like a man."

"She wouldn't want you to do this. I loved her, Bridge. And she loved me."

"Don't you dare."

"I'm serious. It just went wrong."

"It just went wrong?" Blood flared high up on Bridge's cheekbones. His nose scrunched and his mouth pulled back into a rictus of rage. "Fucking *wrong*, Vic?"

"I'm sorry, Bridge. Swear to fuck. I loved her. Loved her to bits, like."

"I loved her first. You and Clark took her from me."

Bridge moved closer. Raised the bottle to Vic's jugular.

"Please. Please don't."

"It's happening. But if it's any consolation, you're getting it easy. Clark has a lot worse coming to him."

Vic went to talk again, but Bridge struck out, fast as a death adder. The words mutated into a horrific gargle. Bridge turned away from his handiwork. Met the amused gaze of Sammy.

"I need to get back to it, Sammy. You all set to get rid of this shite?" Bridge tilted his head backwards in Vic's direction.

Still propped up by the other two men, Vic continued to bleed out.

Sammy nodded.

Bridge passed him the murder weapon. "On your way, crush this up and kick the pieces down a drain or something."

"That's a lot of trust, Bridge," Sammy said.

"Nothing to do with trust. It's confidence." Bridge winked. "Confidence that you're not stupid enough to go against me after seeing that."

And then he left them to it.

COULDN'T WATCH HIM

Dev pulled open the driver's door of her Lancer. She knelt on her seat and reached across to open the glove box and snag a pack of cigarettes. With a grunt, she pushed herself back out of the car. Flipped open the box of Benson & Hedges. Her lighter was jammed into a space left by the cancer sticks she'd already consumed. Dev drew the light and a smoke, popped the filter end in her mouth and sparked up. Another cop in blue overalls and a baseball cap sidled up to her. His moustache twitched before he spoke.

"Spare us one?"

"Thought you'd quit, Reggie."

"I have. Made a deal with myself that I'd only smoke when I'm drinking, or when I'm at the scene of a riot. Pass the time a little."

"If you smoke when you drink *and* at every riot, you may as well just admit you're a smoker again. These rucks were like a daily occurrence over the summer, and there's no sign of them letting up yet. And the way you gargle? Sure your liver must be in worse condition than George Best's first one."

"Fuck off. Liver like Geordie Best? The cheek of it." He winked at her. "These bastarding recreational rioters, though... You think it's the heat wave, just?"

Dev snorted, a burst of smoke from her nostrils adding to the effect. "Who the fuck knows? It is what it is. We'll have to see what happens when the winter bites."

Reggie drew deep on his cigarette. "Where's your DI?"

Dev flicked her head back towards a Land Rover. "Over there having a cuppa and a yarn, I think."

"He's not, though."

Dev looked over her shoulder. Sure enough, there was no sign of Bridge. "Dickhead never tells me anything."

"Bit of an odd-bod that one."

"You're telling me. Fuck's sake. Just wish he wasn't so determined to make me look bad."

"I'm sure that's not his intention."

"Whether he means it or not is irrelevant. The prick hardly tells me a thing, but expects me to cover for him if anybody ever comes asking."

"Aye, you're doing a great job of that now," Reggie said. "Covering for him, I mean."

"Ach, he wouldn't give a shite what *you* thought of him. He just wants to prove himself to the uppers. Fancies himself as a high-flier, like. Reckons he'll be running the place in a few years, no doubt."

"Well, he's got the sneakiness for senior management, if he's as bad as you make out. Not sure he has the attitude for it, though. The man never smiles."

Dev eyeballed Reggie. She opened her mouth to speak. Closed it. Started again. "Right, I'm away to find him here."

"Good luck, well."

Dev took a final pull from her cigarette, stared at it lengthwise with a snarl. "Barely got a smoke out of this at all." Then she dropped it and ground the glowing cherry to grey ash under her boot.

Reggie called to her as she walked away from him. "Put on your helmet if you're going anywhere near the action, Dev."

She waved his concern away with the back of her hand as she stomped on.

"Andy, for fuck's sake, keep up, will you?"

Grace Doran's voice yipped and yapped like a pissed off Pomeranian's bark. Andy's doleful eyes rolled, but he didn't complain. The way he was breathing, in fits and gasps, it was possible that he couldn't reply, even if he wanted to. Grace moved fast and with confidence. She breezed past cops and rioters to lead Andy and his camera deep into the chaos.

"There's that bird off the telly!" A youngster in a Rangers FC jersey pointed at her.

Grace treated him to a quick, polite wave and moved on.

Andy worked hard to catch up with her. He sucked in a deep breath and spoke to her in a strained voice. "What are you looking for here, Grace?"

"I'll know it when I see it."

"It's a wee bit hostile, don't you think?"

"Everybody wants to be on TV, Andy. Your camera's safe."

"Maybe so, but what about me?"

"Man up, will you?"

Andy sighed, looked about him with the widened eyes of natural prey. He pushed on.

A big man with a shaved head wearing a white vest, blue jeans and enough chunky jewellery to keep him in cash-for-gold bailouts for the rest of his natural life sidestepped in front of Grace and held out a palm.

"Here, you off the news. Want an exclusive?" He grabbed a handful of his own crotch. "Because I've something here you might be interested in."

A small band of cronies made a good show of forcing their laughter. Grace barely flinched. She skipped to the left, turned on her heel and juked to her right. The baldy man bedecked in gold was two moves behind her. She breezed past him as he clumped to his right.

Big Baldy's complexion had gone an angry shade of red

by the time Andy tried to get by him. He caught Andy with a meaty slap to the back of the head.

"Fuck away off, then."

Andy barked and stumbled forward, bent at the waist. He forged ahead rather than risking a look back at his antagonist.

"Seriously, Grace, this isn't safe."

Grace whipped around, pointed her microphone at Andy. "Want me to carry the fucking camera for you? Is that it, No Balls? You too *afwaid* to do your job?"

"Are you too stupid to see that you're leading us up shit creek? Because I didn't pack any paddles."

"Ugh. How long have you been storing up that line? They're doing this for attention, Andy. Trust me. We're the safest people here. Without the cameras and the possibility of the whole world seeing it, what the fuck do *you* think *they* think is the point of all this stupidity?"

"Keep your voice down. You're drawing too much attention."

"Good! Maybe we'll get somebody to talk to us, then!"

"You're a melter, Grace."

"You love me really. Come on, Yellow Belly. When you're done pissing in your boxers, we've work to do here."

"Charmer."

"I'll buy you a drink later."

And she was off again. Neither Grace nor Andy noticed Big Baldy following them.

"Andy." Grace pointed in the direction she was headed. "Look at this man. Is he a politician, do you think?"

Andy squinted. Grace had spotted a bearded man in a blue suit. The man's hands were buried deep in his trouser pockets. His jacket was open and bunches of material spilled over either side of his wrists.

"Don't know the lad," Andy said. "But if he was a politician, he'd be talking more. Probably to us, no?"

"Come on 'til we have a wee natter with him."

"Can we get out of here after that?"

"Yeah, dead on. Whatever you want. Just get over there and put your camera in his face."

Grace grabbed hold of the camera lens and dragged Andy towards the man in blue. She set that Pomeranian pitch to work. "Excuse me! Sir! Sir? Sir! You in the blue. Can you look this way, please?"

DI Tommy Bridge half-turned to face Grace Doran. He smirked with one side of his mouth then looked beyond the newsreader and her cameraman and pointed. "Watch yourself!"

Grace turned in time to see Big Baldy coming. But that was all that those seconds afforded her. A glimpse of red scalp and glinting gold. Then a sharp slap closed her eyes.

Andy skipped back and levelled the camera, already rolling, on the assault. He caught a perfect shot of Grace stumbling over an errant brick. She landed on her backside. Hard. And sat there.

Bridge darted towards the man who'd slapped Grace Doran. Big Baldy barely saw him coming. Bridge closed in. Kicked a leg. Punched an ear. Elbowed a cheekbone. Headbutted an eye. Big Baldy hit the deck. Stunned. Bridge grabbed Grace Doran under one arm and hauled her upwards. She limped awkwardly but managed to keep up as Bridge bulled his way through the contracting ring of protesters. Bridge roared:

"That baldy bastard's a woman-beater! Skin-head hit a wee girl! That prick with the vest and the gold chains hit her! Scumbag! Scumbag! Rapist! Paedo!"

With each wild-eyed accusation, Bridge jabbed a thumb over his shoulder in the direction of Big Baldy. The man in the white vest and gold chains barely got to his feet before a bunch of have-a-go heroes rushed him.

Bridge growled in Grace's ear. "Get a move on, Ms Doran. It isn't safe here."

"Who are you?"

"Never you mind. Just come on for fuck's sake."

Bridge yanked Grace's arm and propelled her in the direction he'd picked. She dropped her microphone and her newly freed hand went to her lower back. Her wiggling gait became more pronounced, like she was dancing on hot coals. She whimpered.

"My tailbone must be cracked."

"Ah, shit one." Bridge said, his mouth still close to her ear as he pushed her into and pulled her away from confused protesters, rioters and spectators. "Broken arse? You'll not sit right for a couple of months."

Andy stepped on Bridge's heel. Bridge looked over his shoulder to find Andy's camera aimed at him.

"What the fuck?"

Bridge straight armed the lens. Andy's head movement was sharp and he whipped to the side to avoid a face-mashing.

"Could you not be more helpful, dickhead?" Bridge said.

"Keep rolling, Andy." Grace said.

"Drop the camera before I drop you," Bridge said.

Andy lowered his camera. It still rolled, but it no longer framed Bridge and Grace. Instead it pulled in a jerky, nauseating view of the rubble-strewn ground and a thicket of legs. Behind Andy, a karaoke queen scooped up Grace's microphone and belted out the first few lines of *God Save the Queen*.

PEEKABOO

Billy Andrews still held the riot shield and his missus, Caroline, still wore the helmet. They were taking a breather from the action and watched the chaos from a few yards back, careful to keep the mayhem between them and the riot cops. One cop got close, and they sidled, crab-like, away from him. Caroline saluted the law man with her middle finger and then he was dragged back into the melee.

"This is a gag," Caroline said, though in her accent it sounded more like 'geg'.

Billy chuckled. "I know. Beezer, so it is."

"Glad youse two are having fun, like." Clark Wallace's voice rumbled towards them. "Either of you seen our Vic?"

Billy and Caroline jumped and split; wobbled like nudged bowling pins. They turned to face Clark.

"You're a bit dinged up there, Clarky boy." Billy's voice wavered a little. He tried to make up for that with a puffed chest.

Caroline didn't try to act tough. She pandered to Clark's ego instead. "Look at you. You're like some sort of warrior. Braveheart or something. Aye, Braveheart. Wasn't he a Wallace too?"

Clark tilted his big head, the lower half still wrapped in a scarf. "That turncoat fucker from the Mel Gibson movie?"

"Aye. But in a good way."

"Fuck him and fuck you. Now, answer the question. Billy first. Have you seen Vic?"

"No," Billy said.

Caroline shook her head when Clark's stare landed on her.

"Well what the fuck use are you two?" Clark craned his neck to see over their heads. "Look at this wanker here."

Billy looked over his shoulder, but from his lower

vantage point he couldn't see anything apart from the mass of seething pushers and punchers. "Is it Vic?"

Clark held a hand up. "Shut up, fuck-nuts."

Billy chewed on his knuckles. Caroline put her hands on her hips and tilted her head back. Her helmet almost fell off. "Are you going to let him talk to us like that, Billy?"

"Fuck off, Caroline," Billy spat the words over the knuckles he'd been chewing and shooed her with his riot shield.

She fucked off.

"Make sure you put her in her place later, Billy."

"I will, Clark."

"Follow me."

"No sweat."

"Cover your face."

"With what?"

"Do I have to figure every fucking wee thing out? Jesus Christ, Billy. Just come on to fuck, will you?"

Clark tore around the closest pocket of violence as if he'd broken from a rugby scrum. Billy did his best to tail him but he was tackled by a couple of cops intent on getting the riot shield off him. He called out Clark's name, but the big man jogged on. Then Billy was gone. Mobbed and dragged away, stripped of his trophy.

Clark cupped his hands at either side of his mouth. "Bridge! Bridge! You're wanted! C'mere, Bridge!"

Bridge had navigated his way to relative safety with Grace and Andy still in tow. He winced when he heard his name called and turned to see a juggernaut make a beeline for him. The juggernaut's face may have been swaddled in a red, white and blue scarf, but Bridge had no problem identifying him.

"Ah shite. Not now, Clark."

Clark got closer. Fake-laughed loud enough for Bridge and his companions to hear.

Grace Doran tugged at Bridge's elbow. "Who's that?"

"Don't worry about it. Keep moving until you find some cops. Riot cops, I mean. They'll take you into a Land

Rover if they can hear you call for help."

"I have a job to do."

"If you want to help your mate pull a camera out of his hole, be my guest. But if I were you, I'd take my own broken arse to the sidelines."

Grace hesitated. Bridge didn't. He broke away from the newsreader and her cameraman and marched towards the oncoming threat.

Clark's voice boomed. "Good man, Bridge. Come to me, now."

"I want a word with you, Wallace."

Clark Wallace shook his covered head. "Who the fuck's Wallace? There's no Wallace here."

And then he was in swinging distance, a fair few inches further out than Bridge's swinging distance. Bridge took Clark's first haymaker on the side of the head before he'd a chance to raise his hands. He stumbled, tried to shake off the damage and get into the fight. But Bridge ate a jab. And another. He fell backwards before Clark could feed him his killer right cross.

"Bridge!"

Dev had tracked down her DI but she was too far away to help. She watched Bridge topple backwards. Then she ran towards him.

"Bridge!"

Clark turned to see Dev draw her baton. He'd raised his foot to stomp Bridge. Recognising the danger from an oncoming valkyrie in dark blue overalls, Clark lowered his leg. He stepped on a half-brick and went over his ankle. Wobbled.

Dev saw the stumble and tried to take advantage. She threw her baton like a tomahawk. It whirred towards its target, end over end, then thumped into Clark's chest.

The big man froze, as if confusion had overridden any sort of pain the launched baton might have inflicted. Clark looked at where the ineffectual missile had landed on the rebound. He watched it get swept up by one of a bunch of scrabbling hands.

Bridge had rolled away from Clark as well. He'd raised himself to his knees. Looked towards Andy for support and met only the cold stare of the camera lens.

"Thank fuck for Dev," Bridge said.

Bridge spat blood then bounded forwards. He didn't take a run at Clark, though. Instead, he attempted to intercept the DS. They connected like opposing rugby players. Bridge's arm snaked around Dev's waist. He was shorter and lighter than Dev but momentum and technique were on his side. He managed to nullify her reckless charge and forced her backwards. Many of the protesters, who only saw a man in a suit try to bull through a big cop in riot gear, cheered Bridge on. Dev spat and clawed with alley cat ferocity.

Behind Bridge and Dev, Clark hunched over in an attempt to look smaller and sidled towards the crowd.

Andy tried to follow Clark's departure with the camera, but his luck had run out. A chunk of rock, too rugged and mud encrusted to have come from anywhere but a dug-over garden, sailed into the all-seeing lens. Blinded it.

Andy blubbed. Grace latched onto him; her arm hooked through the crook of his, and she led him to the sidelines. Her broken tailbone wobble threw the pair's balance off.

"That drink I promised you, Andy?"

"Fuck you, Grace," Andy said.

"I deserved that. But if you'll let me finish…" She laid her head on his shoulder for a second as they continued their disjointed pilgrimage. "I was thinking we could maybe make a night of it? You're owed a wee bit more than a pint, I'd say."

"Like a new camera?"

"Ach, calm down. I'm sure it's insured. And the footage will be fine too, right?"

"Maybe."

"It better be."

"You're all heart, Grace."

"I know. Which is why, one time only, I'm offering you the choice of any bottle you can find in the first off licence we come across."

Andy waited a few seconds for a punchline. Grace treated him to an almost genuine smile. Andy sighed.

"It's not going to be a bottle of fucking Buckfast, Grace, I'll promise you that."

"And you from Lurgan? The folks back home would disown you."

"I'm from Lisburn."

"Same thing."

"It fucking isn't. And you're about to be stung for a single malt. Fuck wine."

"You drive a hard bargain."

"You're weighing me down. Can you not walk straight?"

"Ah, you're such a dick, Andy."

"If I said something similar to you, I'd get the sack."

"Depends what you mean by sack. And if you're man enough to test me."

Andy sighed. He didn't test her.

WASH AWAY THE SCUM

Dev huffed and puffed. She sat on the rear bumper of a PSNI Land Rover. Bridge stood in front of her; looked down on her for a change. His frame shaded her from the harsh light of the sun in descent.

"Do you want a smoke?" Bridge asked.

"You quit."

"It wasn't an offer. More of a reminder."

"Where the fuck were you?"

"You saw."

"I saw where you ended up. In the middle of mayhem wearing nothing but that ugly blue suit while half the city attempted to murder itself. Where *were* you?"

"It's not important."

"It fucking is."

"Have a smoke."

"*You* have a smoke."

"I quit."

"I fucking know. Now I always have to make sure I've a pack handy, you useless shitebag."

"You haven't forgotten that I'm your superior, have you, Dev?"

"How could I forget?"

Dev reached into the pocket of her overalls and pulled out a squished pack of Benson & Hedges.

"Doesn't look hopeful," Bridge said.

"Your fault."

She peeled back the torn and unfolded cardboard flap. Found a flattened cigarette that hadn't been snapped. The lighter was intact too. Her hands shook too much to keep the flame lit.

"Let me," Bridge said.

Dev jerked away from his outstretched hands. "You

want a slap?"

"I think Clark Wallace did enough damage, don't you?" Bridge angled his face from side to side to display the injuries Clark's fists had meted out. His nose bled a little and his lips were thicker. The bruises hadn't been given enough time to shine.

"It was him, then?"

"You saw the size of the beast." Bridge said. "Of course it was."

"Right enough. You looked like a Jack Russell having a go at a Rottweiler. But then, everybody looks big compared to you, don't they?"

"Funny."

"And you're funny looking."

"Want me to see if I can find a petrol bomb to light that thing for you?" Some of the playfulness had departed from Bridge's voice and demeanour.

"If anybody asks me, I can't account for your movements for the last half hour."

"Wise up. I wasn't away that long. And I was well monitored. Check with that stupid bitch off the TV."

"So it *was* Grace Doran?"

"Who else? But here, guess what. She broke her hole out there."

Dev honked like an asthmatic goose. "Hah! Serves the nosy bitch right."

"Think she might have got some footage of me going for Clark."

"I'd like to see that."

"The super won't."

"You care?"

Bridge didn't answer. He stepped away from the Land Rover they'd taken shelter behind. The roars, chants, crashes and smashes were overridden by a bass rumble of articulated lorry engines and the ear-piercing shriek of a fresh and further amplified blast of police sirens.

"That the water cannons?" Dev asked.

Bridge nodded.

"About time. Next riot, I'm going to see about getting my arse inside one of those things. How much better would that be?"

"I think you'd have to improve your driving."

"Shut up."

"I'm not joking."

"Neither am I. Shut. Up."

The water cannons sounded horns not unlike the kind a long haulage driver would yank on. Yelled insults from the strongest of lungs cut through the general clamour of indignation.

"Scum! Scum! Scum!"

"Black bastards!"

"Wankers! Youse are fuckin' cunts!"

Dev huffed cigarette smoke. "Did somebody call us black bastards?"

"Aye. Must be Catholic blood in them," Bridge said.

Dev smiled.

"Does that awkward looking grin mean you've forgiven me?"

"I still don't even know what you did, Bridge."

"Makes two of us."

"Will we go watch these rats get drowned, DI?"

"Don't mind if we do, DS." Bridge tilted his head. "You should probably lose the coffin nail, though. Representing your force and all that malarkey."

"Prick."

But Dev ground the shrinking butt under her thick-soled boot and treated Bridge to another smile, this one a little more tight-lipped.

"You ready, boss?"

"I've asked you not to call me boss, Dev."

"And I've called you everything under the sun, but that's the only word that makes you flinch. No chance of me retiring that one from my arsenal."

"Could you save it for special occasions at least?"

"Anything you say, boss."

The horns blasted a final warning as both water cannon pumps tapped into a 9,000 litre tank. Dev edged a little closer to Bridge. She stood on her tiptoes and widened her eyes. Bridge looked up at her before setting his sights on the slow progress of the massive white vehicles. Two of them had been deployed. The gleaming trucks bore PSNI insignias and three-digit serial numbers, each one prefixed by a double zero. It was as if somebody had decided that the country might need hundreds of these Lego brick monstrosities at some point in the future, but for now, single-digits were adequate. The water guns perched atop the front corners of the vehicles' roofs moved independently; sought prey like chameleon eyes. Precision engineering. They thrummed with the threat of deadly power.

"Them big yokes sound a bit like bin lorries, don't they?" Dev said.

Bridge leaned into her to knock her slightly off balance. It was a playful gesture, and Dev's punch to Bridge's shoulder, though more violent in execution, shared the intent.

They were a little giddy.

The first water cannon unleashed a burst of water into the air. A fine spray rained down on the riot. The water cannons held the attention of the entire assembly; cops, protesters and media alike.

"Just watching this, Dev, I'm thinking that somebody missed a trick back when the Ice Bucket Challenge was doing the rounds."

Battle weary riot cops retreated from the fray and a fresh wave flanked the water cannons. They clumped along in step with each gear-crunched lurch of the heavy duty cavalry. Another burst of white mist exploded from the guns of the lead cannon. This time it was more sustained. The majority of the rioters scattered. Only a hardcore remained. They postured and peacocked within easy reach of the water cannons. The next burst of water was aimed lower. Trainers and trouser cuffs were saturated. One man, likely unsteady from too much booze, fell forward onto the drenched tarmac. A couple of companions hauled him to his feet and away from the threat.

"I'd say we'll be on our way home soon enough, Bridge. You still off the booze?"

"Still off it. But even if I wasn't, I probably shouldn't."

Dev looked down at him. Bridge ran a hand through his hair, from crown to nape. His hand came back red.

"Where are you bleeding from?" Dev gasped. "Why didn't you say anything?"

"Cracked the back of my head when Clark knocked me over. Thought it was just a wee gash."

"Holy shite. The grey on the back of your head's gone pink. And your neck." Dev grabbed the back of Bridge's black shirt collar. "This is soaked. You need to go to the hospital, Bridge."

"I'll be fine. Nothing a good night's sleep won't fix."

"You're probably concussed." Dev patted the lapels of Bridge's jacket, looked around her. "I'll take you now."

"We haven't been dismissed yet, Dev."

"I'm dismissing us. Who the fuck's going to notice?"

"Breaking the rules? That's not like you."

"Must be your influence. Just hope I have the same luck as you when it comes to sleekit manoeuvres."

"Is that a joke with a jag?"

"It's nothing. The head injury's messing with you. Come on. This could be serious, dickhead."

"Maybe you could call me Tommy for a while, Dev?"

"Okay, Tommy. But don't get too used to it. And don't you dare call me Patricia."

Dev led Bridge away from the Land Rover.

Behind them, both water cannons released twin jets of so-called non-lethal force. The targets flapped and flailed and skidded along the ground. Robbed of breath, sight and dignity, they might have all lived to fight another day, but any vestige of fight left within them at the point of impact was sent screaming to the abyss.

PATIENTS ARE NOT A VIRTUE

Cops, in standard PSNI uniform, patrolled the accident and emergency waiting room at The Royal Victoria Hospital. They'd been put in place to protect their injured brethren from potential threat. This threat may have been overestimated since the injured riot cops outnumbered the injured civilians. Amidst the uneasy gathering of fallen warriors, DI Tommy Bridge and Jimmy McAuley sat close to each other, one empty seat creating a little space between the two.

"Why the hell would you go to the riot, Jimmy?"

"I don't remember telling you my name, sir."

"You can call me Tommy for now, sure."

"How do you know my name, Tommy?"

"I heard you up at the reception desk there. You wanted to know why you kept getting bumped down the waiting list. The receptionist used your first name a lot."

"Yeah. Pretending her hands were tied and all that. Like calling me Jimmy made me feel any better."

"Would you have been more comfortable if she called you sir?"

"I'd probably think she was patronising me." Jimmy paused. A finger strayed to his paper stitches. "The paramedic said they'd do a better job of reducing the scarring if I got to somebody with steady hands and a bit of time."

"He was probably right."

"I know. But if he'd let me bleed, I'd have probably been seen by now."

"Not necessarily." Bridge patted the back of his head with the clean side of a bundle of blood-stained, white tissues. He showed Jimmy the fresh blood he'd gathered from his head wound. "I'm waiting for staples. But I haven't passed out from blood loss yet, so I'll have to wait."

"Shit. Are you concussed?"

Bridge shrugged. "Wouldn't be the first time."

Jimmy looked at Bridge. Really looked, his eyes narrowed and his pinched lips shoved to one side of his face. "Didn't even realise you were bleeding there, man. Should you not take your jacket off? You'll get it wrecked."

"I have other suits."

"Still, that looks expensive."

"Bought it in a sale."

"Were you at the riot?"

Bridge nodded.

"And you're giving me crap?"

"I didn't have a choice. You did."

"No choice? Everybody has a choice."

"Choices get limited as time goes by, kid. And if I were you, I'd count my lucky stars that you haven't been arrested today."

"Arrested? I was a victim."

"You think those fine young citizens over there feel like anything other than victims right now?"

Bridge nodded to a pocket of teenagers, faces painted with Union Jack colours, Rangers FC jerseys ripped and bloodied. They puppy-eyed the standing cops; kowtowed by bigger, scarier men with handguns on their hips.

"Maybe you feel outnumbered here, wee lad," Bridge said. "But you never had to grow up as quickly as those kids. You'll get out of this with a clean record because somehow, somebody will charm a judge for you and point out how you being a student lends you the potential to become an upstanding member of the community."

"You can't know that I'm a student."

"Please. That quiff? The general air of entitlement about you?" Bridge sniffed. "I bet your weed dealer makes you feel a little dangerous. Like you're from the street? That soft culchie accent gives you away too. Let me guess... somewhere in South Down? From what they call a 'good' family down there?"

"You should be a cop."

"I am. Spent my uniform days in Newry. Mostly stopping boy racers. Hell of a lot of them sounded just like you."

Jimmy touched his paper stitches again. He stuttered, "Ye-you-ye-ye..." Deep breath. "You're a cop?"

"Aye."

"Am I in trouble?"

"This isn't a police interview, if that's what you're asking. Do you think you should be in trouble?"

Jimmy's face pinged redder than a light bulb from Amsterdam's seediest streets. "No."

"You don't want to confess to drug abuse or anything?"

"I don't..." Jimmy cleared his throat. Restarted. "No."

"Daddy taught you to say fuck all to the cops, then?"

The student let the question settle for a couple of seconds. "No."

"These are changed times, you know. And I'm not interested in wee stoners, just for the record. Usually..." Bridge eyeballed Jimmy's slashed face pointedly. "Usually weed calms you eejits down."

Jimmy said nothing. Bridge smirked and pulled his phone from his trouser pocket. He fired up the screen and tapped his thumb. Got sucked into a puzzle game. Jimmy glanced at Bridge from time to time, twiddled his thumbs, fidgeted.

Before too long, Jimmy was on his feet, head jerking from side to side like a sentry meerkat.

"Probably not much point asking if you'll be seen soon, kid."

"I'm looking for a water thingy."

"There's a vending machine by the entrance."

"Cheers."

Jimmy moved to the automatic door. It swished open and strands of his hair, the gel now worn in places, flapped in the oncoming breeze. He rubbed his bare arms, the thin T-shirt he wore providing little protection, and hunched his shoulders. Jimmy was busy examining his choices when Clark Wallace passed by him.

Clark made a beeline for reception. "I'm trying to find my cousin, Victor Wallace. Somebody told me they thought he might be here."

The receptionist sighed then said, "We can only give that sort of information out to immediate family."

"I told you, I'm his brother."

"You said that you're his cousin, sir."

"Did I fuck?"

"Please refrain from cursing at me. We don't tolerate staff abuse here."

Clark looked over his shoulder to cast a glance at the patrolling uniforms. "Sorry, I forgot myself. I'm worried about my brother."

"Cousin, you mean."

"My head was somewhere else, love. We're brothers from another mother, me and Vic, you know what I mean? My da was a bit of a rascal, what? Used to tell me we were cousins before I could understand all the birds and bees business. Must have been thinking about that when I was talking to you. You understand that, right?"

"It's possible, I suppose."

Clark jammed his hand into his tracksuit trouser pocket and produced a wallet. He flipped it open to show the receptionist his driver's licence. "And we share the same last name."

"Cousins often do."

"But not always, right?" He tried on a smile that eased some of the menace from his face. "Other than trying to get a hold of my aul' fellah with one of them ouija boards, I really don't know how else to prove this to you."

The receptionist nodded curtly. "Right, okay. We'll call it a slip of the tongue. Hold on, will you?" And her little fingers danced across her keyboard. *Rat-a-tat-tat*.

"It looks like your brother hasn't been admitted, Mister Wallace. I'm sure that comes as a relief."

"Like fuck it does. After what that wee bastard's put me through, I'll be putting him in hospital myself when I get hold of him."

The receptionist pushed her glasses up the bridge of her shiny nose. "Language, please."

"Ach, up your hole with a big jam roll, you uppity cunt."

Clark slapped a meaty palm on the countertop. The receptionist and a couple of her colleagues chatting in the background jumped.

"Everything all right over there?" a uniform asked.

"Sweet to the beat, cunt-stable." Clark tipped the cop a sarcastic salute. "Sweet to the beat."

"All right, Clark?"

"Bridge?" Clark shoved his hand down the front of his trousers, rummaged about. "All right, mucker?"

Bridge got off his seat and popped his phone into his hip pocket. "I've had better days."

"Aye. Heard you got a few slaps outside the City Hall today." Clark sniggered. "Wish I could have seen that."

"That right?" Bridge took a few steps towards Clark. Bent slightly at the waist and cupped one of his ears with a curved hand. "Tell me, where exactly were you today, then? Because I've had more than a few reports that you *were* there."

Clark pulled his hands out of his trousers. He sniffed his fingers. "Must have been a look-alike, Bridge. I'm still on probation, sure. Wouldn't go near one of them protests if you paid me. Have to keep the nose clean, what?"

"Probation... right enough. How could I forget?" Bridge shifted his weight from one foot to the other. "What are you doing here, then?"

"I've been looking for our Vic. Haven't seen him since... you know, earlier."

"Heard he was at the riot too."

"Aye, he said he might pop down to the *protest*, right

enough. Would he have been scooped?"

"Why don't you swing by the station and find out? I'm sure they'd be delighted to see you there."

"Nah. Don't think I will, thanks. He'll find his way home soon enough."

Jimmy returned from the vending machine, a bottle of Sprite in his hand. He sidled up to Bridge and tugged the sleeve of his blue suit jacket.

"What?"

"I think that man was at the riot earlier." Jimmy's slender fingers traced his paper stitches. "With the scumbag who bottled me."

Clark's stare drilled into Jimmy. "You're wrong, kid." He pointed a thick finger at the kid's face. "That's defamation."

Jimmy recoiled from the finger, his face snarled up. "Your fingers are stinking, boy. Where have they been?"

"Your ma's fanny."

Jimmy's face reddened. "You're still wearing the same tracksuit you had on earlier."

"This here's no original, wee lad. I bought it in Sports Direct. So did half of Belfast."

Jimmy turned to Bridge. "It's definitely him, sir... officer... constable."

"Inspector," Bridge said. "Would you be willing to come down to the station...?"

"Couldn't have been me, Bridge. I've told you. I wasn't there. This wee lad's away with the fairies."

Bridge tried to ignore the intrusion. "Jimmy. Was this man at the riot?"

"He'd a cap and a scarf on, but look at the shape of him. You couldn't forget a big ganch like that."

"Watch the lip, wee lad," Clark said. He took a step forward.

Jimmy squeaked.

Bridge shoved Clark's chest. Hard. Clark took a half-step backwards.

"No need for that, Bridge," Clark said.

"Says you." Bridge said. "You're intimidating this young man."

"Away and shite. You two jokers are fixing me up."

"Jimmy," Bridge said. "Despite the cap and scarf, could you see his face clearly?"

Jimmy edged slowly backwards; his voice shook. "Yeah, but no. The scarf covered a wee bit of his face, just. But it was definitely him. I'm positive."

"Yeah, but no?" Clark had too much gravel in his voice to make his impression of Jimmy fly. "I don't think that counts as a reliable witness, Bridge."

"Maybe he took the scarf off for a minute, Jimmy. Is that why you're positive?"

Clark took another step forward. "Hey now. You can't do that, Bridge. It's leading the witness or something."

"If we were in court, maybe so. And if there were any witnesses to this conversation..." Bridge looked around the waiting room and pitched his voice a little higher. "Jimmy, please be very careful about this accusation. Was Mister Wallace's face covered?"

Jimmy puffed his chest. He spoke as loud as Bridge. "No, it wasn't. And that's definitely the man who was with... no, not just with. He's the man who *encouraged* my attacker to hit me. With a *bottle*."

A couple of concerned uniforms closed in on the scene. "Is everything okay here, Inspector Bridge?"

Clark didn't even glance at the officers. "Everybody's so brave when they have back-up, aren't they?"

"Fuck off home, Clark. We'll give you a shout after we've gone through the CCTV, sure."

"Aye, good idea, Bridge. Let me know if our Vic pops up on the tapes."

"You better hope he doesn't, Clark. Have you seen this young fellah's face? You could argue attempted murder for an assault like that."

"That kid's doo-lally, Bridge. Looks like a druggie to me. Probably cut himself during a bad trip."

"Jesus, it was only a bit of..." Jimmy said.

Bridge shushed the student before he could finish his sentence. Then gave the uniforms a glimpse of his teeth and dismissed them with a tip of the head. They moved away from Bridge, Clark and Jimmy, but kept their eyes on the scene from across the room.

"Just go home, Clark," Bridge said. "I'll catch you later."

"In your dreams, Bridge." Then Clark lowered his voice. "Don't forget, I know where you live. Won't be tough to find out where this wee shit-head is from either."

Clark turned on his heel and stormed out. The cheeky grin he'd treated Bridge to throughout the exchange slipped away. His teeth remained on display, however. Clamped shut. A threat to all.

Bridge turned to Jimmy, his eyebrows raised. "Pity he was smart enough to drop his voice there. I'd have gotten one of my colleagues to lift him."

"In your dreams," Clark said.

"Right enough, Clark," Bridge said. "We'd need a whole unit to lift your flabby arse, wouldn't we?"

"Ah, here," Clark said. "That's below the belt, Bridge. I've been on my holidays, just. Haven't made it back to the gym yet."

Bridge nudged Jimmy. "Ach, he's all hurt. Look, Jimmy. His fat face is shaking. He's going to cry, isn't he? Isn't he, Jimmy?"

Jimmy's mouth opened and shut a few times. Then his name was called by the triage nurse.

"I... uh, I have to go, Inspector."

Bridge nodded. "Good luck, kid. Try and stay out of trouble, will you?" He patted his breast pocket. Pulled out a business card. "In fact, take this. Get in touch if you want to file charges against that big eejit. I'll take it more seriously than an average station cop, y'know?"

Jimmy eyed the card, but didn't take it.

"He said he was going to find out where I lived," Jimmy said. "Is that not a threat?"

"Was it a threat, Clark?"

"Well, you're the lawman here, but if I'd said that I was going to kill the youngster's mother and fuck his dog, that'd be a threat."

"But you didn't say that, did you, Clarky boy?"

"Exactly."

"Your mother and your dog are both safe for now, Jimmy," Bridge said. "But you can phone me if you see this man again. Even if he just bumps into you at the shop. You hear that, Clark?"

"Fuck off, Bridge."

Bridge offered the card to Jimmy again. Jimmy, tight-lipped, took the card and scampered off.

"Are we done here, Bridge?" Clark asked.

"For now. Don't book any flights or ferry, though. We might need you."

"What makes you think I need a plane or a boat to avoid you, Bridge? If I don't want to be found, I won't be found. Don't even need to leave the city to disappear."

"We'll see about that."

"Fucking count on it, Bridge."

"Catch you later, then."

"No. You won't."

KEEPING IT CLEAN

Joe Soap tapped his iPad screen. The YouTube video he'd been watching paused. Jimmy McAuley's damaged face sneered at the world, frozen in its feral fury. Soap ran his left hand through his blond hair. The silky strands stood to attention for a microsecond before falling back into a neat parting. His right hand beat a fingertip tattoo on his oversized desk, a solitary pinky ring glinting gold flashes in syncopation. He drew his lips back from whitened teeth, the gleaming effect added to by the deep tan surrounding his smile.

"Max. Have you been able to track this McAuley guy yet?" Soap's American accent was soft; devoid of obvious regional tells.

"Still looking for that one, boss." Max Mason spoke with a New York flavour, the nasal quality exaggerated by a kinked nose. His cheekbones were boxy and scarred, his dark hair shaped into a buzz-cut. Mason's entire bearing suggested a familiarity with close combat.

"No Snapchat? Instagram? Facebook? Twitter? Blogger?" Soap's gaze was fixed on McAuley's image. "Do I need to go on?"

"I'll find out if our computer guys have looked yet, Mister Soap."

Soap broke eye contact with the paused video to fix his vibrant blue eyes on Mason. "Or we could just check right now, couldn't we?"

"Maybe *you* could, boss." Mason's brown eyes lowered from Soap's stare. "*I* wouldn't know where to start."

Soap's manicured hand swept across the iPad screen. YouTube gave way to Google.

"Facebook's still popular here, isn't it?"

Mason shrugged.

"It is, Max." Soap started typing. "I'm just trying to involve you in my thought process. Pay attention."

"There's no point…" Mason chuckled. "Is that him?"

"Looks like it. See how easy it was? Type in 'Jimmy McAuley' and 'Facebook'."

"But all those results… He can't be the only Jimmy McAuley in Belfast, let alone the world."

"I've set up some Belfast Facebook accounts for myself. Logged into the student-based one before I called you in here. The logarithms do most of the work."

"Sometimes I wonder why you even need me, Mister Soap."

"You've got your uses, Max. Don't sell yourself short."

Mason shrugged. His swollen trapezius muscles popped his shirt collar. With practised dexterity, one apish hand folded the collar back into place.

"What do you want me to do next, Mister Soap?"

"I'll email you a few places to visit." He reopened the YouTube app and returned to the paused video that housed Jimmy's image. "Get out there and see if you can find this potential poster boy of ours."

"Then what?"

"Then nothing. Just make sure you know what he does and where he lives. And not just his frat house. I want to know where he came from and where he's trying to get to."

"That, I can do, Mister Soap."

ANTI-SOCIAL NETWORK

Jimmy McAuley knocked the door then stepped back off the crumbling concrete step. He half turned his head to listen for activity from within. The undamaged side of his face was reflected in the grubby half-circle window set high in the ancient wood. Jimmy's left cheek was in slightly better condition; his paper stitches replaced by tightly crisscrossed thread, the crusty blood particles washed away. The marks were still visible in the orange glow from the streetlights, but they lacked the anger that sunlight would have provoked.

The door opened, its hinges unexpectedly quiet. Quiet enough to allow the whispered curses from within the house audibility. A bare foot kicked glossy junk mail out onto the tiny patch of concrete yard. Some fliers made their way into a lidless recycling box. The rest joined rain-damaged ancestors blown into a corner of the low wall that marked out the unimpressive yard.

The bare foot's owner spoke. "All right, Jimmy?"

Steve craned his neck out into the Belfast daylight and squinted as if the street were paved in gold and reflected sunbeams borrowed from LA. He looked to his left and then his right, his eyes never widening, then beckoned Jimmy into the shadows.

Jimmy nodded to the bare-footed squinter and had a quick left-to-right glance of his own before stepping inside.

"Were you sleeping, boy?" Jimmy asked.

"No. What kind of a waster do you think I am? I've been trying out some new stock. Come on upstairs."

Steve led Jimmy to a bedroom at the front of the house. It had two beds, one of them a jumble of blankets and sheets, the other a bare mattress. The curtains were drawn, the only light in the room a blueish haze from a paused computer game on a widescreen TV.

Jimmy sat on the bare mattress. Steve stood in the middle of the room. He settled his gaze on the still image of zombie carnage on the screen. His eyes had widened slightly and the soft illumination lent Steve an undead appearance to rival the game graphics on display.

"Fucking hell, boy. Give me whatever you're having."

Steve's head turned slowly. "Cheese."

"Like skunk?"

"Yeah, like skunk. But better. It's really..." Steve rotated a wrist by the side of his head as if to crank-start his brain. "You need to try it."

"Thanks, man. My face is killing me, you know? Thought a wee bit of medicinal marijuana would sort me out."

"What happened?" Squinty took a few steps towards Jimmy, surveyed the damage. "Ah, our fellah. That's going to leave a mark."

"Yeah, I know. I'm not long out of hospital."

"Not surprised." Steve sat on the unmade bed and got to work on a joint. He used an old Beano annual as a workstation. "State of the NHS these days."

"They did the best they could, in fairness. Busy day with that riot."

"You ready to hit this?" Steve asked.

"Jesus, man. How do you do that so fast?"

"Practice, you know?"

"I can't roll at all, boy."

"You'd learn if you had to."

"Probably." Jimmy sighed. "Really I should stick to beer."

"People try to tell me I'd be better off switching from weed to booze. My balls."

"Maybe in moderation..."

"Who the fuck drinks in moderation these days?"

Jimmy opened his mouth then clammed up. He shrugged his shoulders.

"Exactly. Come on 'til we get blazed."

Steve pinched the roach-end of the joint between his lips and gave Jimmy two thumbs up. He pointed to the door.

"Ach."

"Told you earlier. I'm not smoking in this room anymore."

Jimmy flared his nostrils. "Sure the place already reeks of weed."

"And I'm trying to fix that. The landlord had a moan about it last week. Don't want him getting too curious and checking out the attic, know what I mean? There's a skylight in the bathroom. The smoke flies out of it like a chimney."

"I know, but it was a wee bit creepy last time, no?"

"It's where I smoke now, our fellah. You don't *have* to join me."

Jimmy screwed up his face, but he followed the squinty stoner without hesitation. He folded a towel into a makeshift cushion and sandwiched it between the bath and his backside. Steve closed the door before taking a seat on the toilet lid.

The squinty stoner sparked his lighter and touched the flame to the twisted end of the joint. He puffed on the roach a couple of times to get it going before he passed it on. Their smoke wreathed above their head before making its lackadaisical journey through the square hole in the ceiling.

Jimmy puffed and passed the joint. He licked his lips and watched closely as Steve sucked hard enough to burn half an inch off the end of it.

"Are you going to leave me some of that, Steve?"

"Chill. You got any good music on your phone?"

Jimmy reached out and took the joint from Steve's slack hand. "Everything's on my phone. But I lost the fucker today."

"Ah, shit one. Would love to get my toe tapping here." Steve blew a smoke ring. "Why don't you tell me about your wee scuffle down at the riot? I take it you never had time to upload any pics or videos before you lost your phone?"

"No... but I might be on TV anyway."

"Yeah?" Steve took the spliff from Jimmy. "Tell me about that, then."

"It's a pretty long story. All right if I crash here tonight?"

"Yeah, yeah… spill the beans."

"Cool." Jimmy toked hard. "So I met Grace Doran…"

YESTERDAY'S NEWS

DI Tommy Bridge sat in the A&E waiting room. Waiting. His stare flicked between his phone and the exit, his thumb tapped and swiped the brightly lit screen incessantly. Moments later the doors shushed open. Bridge tucked his phone away and stood to greet Dev. She stomped in, gave him a quick once over. A hiss escaped her clamped teeth when he bowed to show her the staples in the back of his head.

"They look that bad?"

"Not so much the staples, Bridge. Did they need to shave away so much of your hair? Looks a sight."

"Cheers."

Dev looked over Bridge's shoulder at the remains of the untreated rioters and cops. She flared her nostrils. "State of these pricks."

"Aye. It was a bit of a war, all right." Bridge folded his arms. Lowered his head a little. "I didn't get a chance to thank you yesterday... for helping me out of that spot."

"That spot? Bit of an understatement, no? Looked to me like Clark Wallace was all set to stamp you flat, Bridge."

"Well, like I said... thanks."

"All I did was fling my baton at him. Not exactly a shining example of police procedure."

"It was enough. Threw him off, like."

Dev shrugged, uncomfortable with Bridge's gratitude.

"You been chatting to any of our colleagues?" Dev asked.

"Not a soul. I'm sure they've better things to be doing, like. It was a big day for everybody."

"You'll not have heard about Vic Wallace, then?"

"Funny enough, I did bump into big Clark last night. He was in here looking for Vic."

"He'll not have to look for much longer. So far as I know, the next of kin will be informed this morning."

"Oh."

"Aye. Poor aul' Vic got fished out of the River Lagan last night. Looks like somebody tried to sink him, but did a shit job of it."

"Sink him?"

"Tied a bunch of chains around his neck and ankles. The knots slipped out."

"Fuckwits." Bridge huffed a long stream of air through his nostrils. "Could they not have used padlocks or something?"

"I know. Shoddy as hell. You just can't get the murdering scumbags for staff these days."

"Does this totally fuck our case against Clark, then?"

"Kind of." Dev crimped the right side of her face. "Well… buys him a bit of time, just. But you know what these goons are like. Before you know it he'll screw up again and then we'll have him. Maybe he'll do something stupid when he finds out about Vic."

"Like if he tries to take revenge?"

"Exactly. There'll be eyes on the lookout for him over the next wee while."

"Right. So, good news, then."

"Aye, for us. Not so much for wee Vic, like."

"Fuck him. He knew what he was signing up for. Can't feel any sympathy for that kind of scum."

Dev shrugged. "You're preaching to the converted, DI."

"So, what now?"

"We've got the day off. You fancy a pint?"

"No. I missed an appointment with the psychologist yesterday. She's offered me a slot today. Better take it before she gets huffy with me again."

"Useless fucker." Dev turned on her heel and started towards the door. "I'll take you there, then. On my day off. *Boss.*"

Bridge had to jog briefly to catch up. His lips twisted into a rictus treat. "Thanks, *Patricia*."

DIS-GRACE

"How's the arse, Grace?"

Grace Doran looked over the top of her laptop screen. "Don't you knock?"

Andy ignored the question. "Just off the phone to my insurance company. They're going to pay out on the broken camera. I was sweating a bit there. Thought they'd give me guff for dandering through a riot. My girlfriend gave me enough grief without that on top."

"Girlfriend?"

Andy rubbed his lips. His cheeks got a little rosy. "Well, it's early days, like. Not sure we're even calling each other boyfriend and girlfriend yet... Like, we haven't had the monogamy talk or anything yet."

"Fascinating."

Andy cleared his throat. "So, you didn't answer. What about the tailbone?"

"Tailbone now, is it?" Grace closed her laptop and clasped her hands, rested them on the lid. "The x-ray confirmed that my coccyx has a hairline fracture. Nothing they can do about it, though, other than throw painkillers at me."

"Shit one." Andy winked. "No pun intended."

"That was a pun?"

"Jesus, you're in great form today."

"Feel free to take yourself off, Andy."

"Are we not hitting the streets? We could get a look at the aftermath, interview the poor fuckers that got hit with the water cannons, take pot-shots at the PSNI?"

"You've no camera, sure."

"I can get a loaner."

"I'm not in the mood."

"Sore arse?"

"Yes. Are you happy now? I broke my hole and now I don't feel like traipsing about Belfast with your useless self in tow. People are bored of this shite already anyway."

"Not sure about that, Grace. Remember the student you interviewed? Jimmy McAuley? The video footage is causing a real stir. It's ended up on YouTube and about a billion Facebook pages."

"And it'll be forgotten tomorrow."

"I don't know about that. In fact, I was going to suggest we track the lad down again and do a follow-up interview. See how he feels about his newfound infamy."

"Nobody cares."

Andy sagged. "That's not like you, Grace."

"What the fuck would you know?"

"Is this because we…?"

"We what? Finish your sentence you jellyfish."

"Nah, fuck it. Give me a shout when you get off your period, yeah?"

Grace lifted her coffee cup and drew it back over her shoulder as if to throw it at Andy. Her cameraman jolted into action and left the office like a shot. The door swung shut behind him. Grace brought the cup to her lips and took a sip. She pulled open her desk drawer and rustled about in it until she put her hands on a blister-pack of little white pills. Then she popped two through the foil and necked them. Took another sip from her cup to wash them all the way down.

She lifted her phone, tapped the screen then held it to her ear. "Harry. Any interest in a follow-up interview with that Jimmy McAuley fellah?"

Grace drummed a pen off the lid of her laptop.

"The cop? No, I don't think he's the smile-for-the-camera type."

She grasped the lid of her pen between her teeth and tugged it off. Flipped open the notebook she'd been using as a mouse mat.

"Say that again."

Grace scribbled some shorthand on a clean page.

"Shouldn't be a problem."

She underlined a symbol.

"Wait. Who…? Joe Soap? Never heard of him."

More scribbles in the notebook.

"The security company? Okay, Harry. Shoot me an email when you find out where he wants to meet."

Her mouth bowed downwards.

"Yeah, hairline fracture… No, it's okay, I'm using one of those donut cushions." She shifted her weight slightly. Grimaced. "Aye, my aunt used to be murdered with chronic piles. She was able to lend me a couple."

Grace closed her eyes and rubbed her knotted brow. Her fingers failed to massage the furrows away.

"Well *you* brought it up, Harry."

PSYCHOBABBLE

Bridge leaned forward in his chair and knocked on the desk in front of him as if it was a door. A woman with short grey hair and large-framed glasses looked up from a notepad. She seemed much younger than the grey hair would suggest, despite the thickness of her lenses and the crow's feet she'd developed from narrow-eyed peering at files and computer screens.

"Just a tick, Tommy."

She scribbled for a couple of seconds then tapped her pencil to the paper with exaggerated force to punctuate the note.

"Sorry. Had to get that down before it slipped away."

"Adding to your shopping list?"

"That's very funny, Tommy."

"You forgot to tell your face."

"Apart from the urge to make me laugh, what else is on your mind?"

"This is our last session, right?"

"Yes."

"So, did I pass?"

"Pass what?"

"The psycho test or whatever it is."

"This isn't about passing or failing. It's about a duty of care to you."

"Okay."

"And you've made some big improvements in the time since we first met."

"Improvements? So I'm winning, then?"

"No." She paused. Tapped her pencil on the pad for a couple of beats. "Sorry, that was a bit negative. Winning in what sense?"

"Ach, come on, Hillary. Can we just talk like people for now?"

"How do people talk?"

"Seriously. It's my last session. It'd be great if you could stop answering my questions with questions."

Hillary didn't answer. She held out a hand, palm up, to indicate that Bridge should steer the conversation.

"I want to know if you've recommended that I continue to work for the PSNI."

"Yes."

"So I'm not crazy."

"You've suffered a lot of emotional trauma. The death of your daughter, your wife leaving you, the suspension for misconduct…"

"I remember."

"But you've worked hard to recover. I can see that. And as long as you continue with your medication and other healthy activities – like the yoga class you found – I support the continuation of your career at the PSNI. That doesn't mean that you'll be taken off probation just yet. My report is simply one element of the process that makes up the final decision."

"And what if I'd rather leave?"

"Oh. You're having one of *those* days."

"One of those weeks."

"You do look tired. But you really should think before you speak sometimes, Tommy."

"I always do."

Hillary scribbled a note on her pad.

"Is this going to be added to the report?"

"Don't worry about it."

"I'm emotionally traumatised. You can't tell me not to worry."

"Tommy…" Her tone sweetened. "I'm not telling you to do anything. It's just a turn of phrase."

"Didn't think before you spoke, eh?"

"Please take this seriously."

"I am. And I still want to know if my thoughts on leaving the PSNI will show up on your report."

"No, Tommy. They won't. Everybody likes a good moan once in a while. I hear complaints about work all the time."

"Even so... if I could get myself a wee redundancy package, just to see me over for a few months, maybe a year, I'd walk out of here today."

"So said many a police officer before you, Tommy. Some of them even went so far as to take the redundancy cheque and ended up coming back."

"Aye. The smart ones know how to play the game, you see. I'm not that fly."

"Either way, this is all theoretical right now, Tommy. There is no money for redundancy these days. If anything, we need more bodies on the ground."

"Because of all the bodies *in* the ground?"

She blanched. "I like you, Tommy. Really I do. But your sense of humour has a tendency towards the dark."

"Aye. Humour. That's it."

"Think about it for a few weeks. If you really want to leave, then why wait around for that redundancy cheque? With your penchant for... less healthy habits—"

"Didn't you used to call that my 'self-destructive' streak."

"If I recall, I said that once." Hillary pushed her glasses further up the bridge of her nose. "But the point is, you could simply apply for another job."

"The PSNI owes me more than that."

"I disagree. They've paid you your salary, even through your suspension."

"Are you trying to talk me into quitting? I bet that'd solve a lot of problems for you and the brass."

"I'm not supposed to give you advice, Tommy. Just reminding you that nobody forced you to join the police. Nobody has the right to stop you from leaving either."

"Pfft. Tell that to Dev."

"Are you getting along better with your DS?"

"Since I started taking her forked-tongue comments

with a pinch of salt? Aye, I think we're doing okay."

"Excellent. And as for inappropriate relations…"

"If I think of anything as inappropriate, I'll go through the necessary channels."

"Fantastic, Bridge. Really fantastic. And, off the record, can I just say, you look really sharp today. Much more present than I've seen you in a long time. Keep taking your medication, and stay positive. You'll get through this."

"Thanks, Hillary. I think I needed to hear that."

"You're welcome. *Carpe diem*, Tommy."

"Should I also think outside the box, push the envelope and feel the burn?"

Hillary allowed a few seconds to pass before she answered. *Tick, tick, tick.* "I have another appointment in ten minutes. Might be a good time for you to slip out under the radar."

Bridge stood up, leaned forward slightly so he could rest his palms on the desk. Hillary edged her seat back on its castors ever-so-slightly. Her smile barely faltered. Bridge nodded slowly.

"You really do get me, Hillary."

And he left.

NEXT OF KIN

A frail woman clung to Clark Wallace's thick arm. She looked like a grey-haired child in comparison to the big man.

"I can't do it, Clark." She snuffled. "Would you?"

"Anything you need, Auntie Aggie. You know that."

Clark's eyes were red and on the brink of tearing up, but he held his head high. Jutted his chin. He hushed Aunt Aggie's occasional sobs.

The coroner, a distinguished man with silver hair and a regal bearing, dressed in fresh blue scrubs, spoke up. "Actually, neither of you really need to formally identify the deceased. The PSNI were able to confirm his identity with a fingerprint check."

"So why are we here?" Clark asked.

The coroner looked at Clark like he was some sort of wild beast. A creature to be approached with caution. He ran a spanking clean hand through his sterling locks.

"It's customary for close family to pay their respects at this point."

"I'll go in, then," Clark said. "Vic was like my wee brother."

Auntie Aggie squeezed Clark's hand and briefly rested her head on his upper arm. Her tears left little stains on the sleeve of her nephew's hoodie.

"We could do it by video link if you prefer, Mister Wallace."

"Do I look like some sort of shite-scared wee bitch to you, mate?"

"No, Mister Wallace." The coroner's face pinched up like he'd bitten into a lemon. "Not at all."

"I'll not be looking at no cousin of mine through a fucking TV screen. You got that?"

"Of course. If you could follow me, please."

Clark wrapped an arm around Aggie. "Will you be all right here for a minute, love?"

"Aye, Clark, son. Just give him a wee kiss from me, will you?"

"No sweat, Aggie. No sweat."

Clark followed the stiff-backed coroner down a short hallway.

"Stinks in here, mate." Clark said. "Suppose you're used to it, like."

"Quite." The coroner pushed open a door and stepped back to allow Clark to enter first. "He's just in here."

Clark hesitated for a second then stepped past the coroner. Fluorescent lighting glared off stainless steel surfaces. A figure on a table in the centre of the room was covered by a green blanket. Clark rubbed his hands together and blew on them. He pointed at the table.

"That's our Vic, then…? What's left of him, anyway."

The coroner took up his position at the head of the table. He scrunched a corner of the blanket up in his fist. Nodded at Clark.

"I have to warn you, Mister Wallace, his injuries are quite shocking."

"Probably seen worse, mate." Clark edged closer to the table. "At least he's not in pain."

The coroner drew back the blanket. Clark sighed and nodded. He bent at the waist and kissed an unmarked patch of skin on Vic's forehead.

"Fuck. That was weird," Clark said. He swept a hoodie sleeve across his lips. "A wee kiss from your ma, cuz. Nothing gay, you know?"

"The funeral home will make him look much better for the viewing. I think you'll be able to have an open casket."

Clark ignored him. For the time being, he only had eyes for Vic.

"Wish you could tell me who did this, Vic. It'd make my life a lot easier." Clark leaned in a little closer. Barely whispered. "Promise you, kid, I will find out who it was, and I'll make them pay."

The coroner sniffed.

Clark pointed at a huge gash on the left side of his cousin's neck.

"That's what killed him, isn't it?"

"Yes, Mister Wallace."

"It'd hardly have been a knife, would it?"

The coroner stared at Clark for a couple of seconds. Clark stared right back.

"No, it wasn't a knife. The wound had glass fragments in it. Similar to those found in the facial lacerations. It looks to me like a drunken brawl gone wrong."

Clark snickered. "Been in a lot of those, have you?"

"I don't drink. But I've seen these kinds of injuries much too often."

"Fuck me sideways. You must be tougher than you look. If I had your job, I'd be half-pissed all day long."

"That's certainly proved to be a professional hazard for some."

"And then they check into some swanky drying-out hotel, right? My heart bleeds."

"Quite. Would you like some time alone with the deceased?"

"Nah. Leave that to them Catholic ghouls and their wakes. I've said all I need to say to the lad."

The coroner replaced the blanket. "Sorry for your loss, Mister Wallace."

"Aye, dead on."

CAN'T GET THE HELP

Bridge hopped off a pink bus on Botanic Avenue and slung the holdall he carried by his side over his shoulder. He glanced briefly at a bookstore window before passing it and stopping at the café next door. A sign in the window warned that the 'card machine' was broken and that they could only accept cash. Bridge cursed and looked around. Then he unslung the holdall and rested it on the café's windowsill. Unzipped it and slipped a hand inside. He withdrew a couple of rumpled tenners and zipped up again.

The café door opened. A man in a blue Rangers FC jersey under a red hoodie stepped halfway out. He bared his teeth in a smile that revealed a lack of dental hygiene.

"You coming in or what?"

"Cool your jets, Sammy."

"I'm fucking starving Marvin. Come on."

Sammy let the door swing shut behind him. Bridge pushed it open again and followed Sammy to a booth. They slid across their respective benches, a pair of repurposed, shortened church pews. Sammy wriggled out of his hoodie and revealed his thick forearms, spattered with faded tattoos that heavily featured the Union Jack. Once settled, Bridge set his holdall beside him on the bench. He rested a hand on it.

Bridge nodded at Sammy's football jersey. "Letting your freak flag fly?"

"I don't even know what that means."

"The Rangers top. Do you have one for every day of the week, or do you just have one for when you travel outside of your estate?"

"Ach, fuck off. I'd need a calculator to count the amount of taigs I've seen swanning about in their GAA jerseys. Rubbing it in. So fuck them. I'll not hide my colours neither. And if I thought I could get away with it, I'd lamp every Catholic culchie I saw."

"They're kids."

"Aye. Best time to put them in their place."

"Right, well... good luck with that. What can we do to make this meeting as short as possible?"

"You don't want to eat?"

"Not with you."

Sammy shrugged and dropped his gaze to the laminated menu in front of him. "Suit yourself."

"I'll just leave the bag here and go, then. Aye?"

"Maybe I should count it first."

"Don't bother. I'll tell you now that it's light."

Sammy instantly forgot about the menu. His eyes latched onto Bridge's.

"Bridge... we had a deal."

"I know. And if you'd done the job right, I'd pay you the full whack. But you fucking didn't, did you?"

"He's dead, isn't he?"

"Aye, but he's far from disappeared. His body's back and now Clark knows his wee toadstool's dead. That's bad news for both of us."

"We chained him up, but."

"Well, Vic must have been briefly reincarnated as the next Houdini. He slipped them and bobbed to the surface."

"Fuck."

"I wanted it to look like he'd done a runner. So I could fuck with Clark before taking him down too."

"Aye, you said. Shite." Sammy glanced at the holdall then returned his stare to Bridge. "How much did you deduct?"

"Half."

"You what?"

"There's the waitress." Bridge pointed past Sammy to a young woman with thick dark-framed glasses and thicker, darker hair. "I'll head now and leave you to order your grub."

Sammy clamped his hand around Bridge's wrist. "Half, like?"

"You only did half the job."

"That's not on, Bridge."

"What are you going to do? Take me to small claims court?"

"Fuck you. What's stopping me going to Clark and telling him the truth?"

"Common sense. You were involved too."

"So I'll tell him half the truth."

"I'm a cop, Sammy." Bridge's voice dropped in volume to a gritty whisper. Spittle sprang from his lips, some of it landed on Sammy's face. "You don't have enough power to go against me. Settle your wee self down or you'll find out what I'm capable of. Only this time I'll hire a real professional. Not some Clampet who can't get rid of a body."

"You'll regret this, Bridge."

"I already do." Bridge flexed his wrist and rotated his hand. The movement shook loose Sammy's grip. "So don't make me kill somebody else, all right?"

Sammy reached over the table and snatched the holdall from its resting place. He unzipped it and ran his hands through the loose bundle of cash inside. Then he withdrew a mobile phone.

"What's this for?" Sammy asked.

"I'll call you in a few hours to see if you've calmed down. There's a number in the contacts list that you can use to reach me if you hear anything I need to know. It's saved under BFF."

"Fuck's that stand for?"

"Best friends forever." Bridge tipped Sammy a salute and left.

YOU TUBE, YOU

Jimmy McAuley hooked a laptop to the wall-mounted widescreen TV with a HDMI lead. He slammed his body down on an ancient sofa and raised clouds of dust. Flipped the laptop open. His long fingers tapped a few keys and his face popped up on the widescreen TV. It was a still from a YouTube video.

The YouTube video.

Jimmy's bloodied face and wild eyes dominated the screen. His mouth was frozen mid-sentence, one side turned downwards to give the impression of a stroke victim. The little cursor arrow moved towards the play button. Hovered. Then Jimmy clicked it. His voice boomed from the TV speakers.

"I am so sick of these subhuman imbeciles hogging the limelight and making our country look like some sort of red-neck, backwater, inbred dung-heap. They're a genetically inferior version of Irish Catholics..."

Jimmy hissed and hit pause. The image froze, his face set in an ugly scowl. He forwarded the video and hit play again.

"... Did you see the prams in that crowd? Babies, like. It's too late for those kids already. They can't be helped. Best they can hope for is a cot death."

The camera focussed on Grace Doran. Jimmy hit pause again. The journalist's image froze, the edge of her hand pressed against her throat, caught in mid-swipe. Cut.

The original YouTube video had amassed more than six-hundred-thousand views in just a few days. And that didn't take into account the versions uploaded to Facebook and shared around on other social media sites. Then there were the edited versions that attempted comedy voice-overs, or cut-scenes to other commentators filmed on the day of the riot.

Jimmy scrolled down the growing list of viewer comments below the video. A mixed bag of below-the-belt insults, belligerent agreement and death threats. He mumbled under his breath as he read through the most recent ones. His eyes watered.

The thud-thud-thud of heavy feet on the stairs didn't seem to register with Jimmy. His focus never wavered from the TV screen. Squinty Steve shoved the living room door open and shuffled in. He wore a pair of sand-coloured Timberland boots, the laces undone.

"All right, our fellah?"

Jimmy didn't answer.

Steve flopped down beside him on the couch and leaned forward to tie his bootlaces.

"You watching that shite again?"

"It's paused."

"How many times have you played it today?"

"This is just the first time."

Steve looked up at the screen and wolf-whistled at Grace Doran's image.

"Is she as pretty in real life?"

Jimmy nodded. "She's gorgeous."

"I love her lips. Can nearly feel them on my neck, you know?"

"As if she would."

"Ah, chill out, will you? She's not your wife."

Jimmy scrolled through another couple of seconds of the recording. Grace's hand dropped away from the image. Her mouth caught somewhere between a grin and a frown. A horizontal slash of shiny lipstick and a glimpse of white teeth.

"Did you ask her out?" Steve asked.

"She practically ran away from me after they turned off the camera, boy. Probably thinks I'm crazy."

"Could hardly blame her. The shite that came out of your mouth. Pure fascist. Do you really believe all of that, like?"

"I think I was still a bit stoned. Not sure what I believe."

"When you said you were going down to get started on your journalism career, this wasn't really what I had in mind for you."

Jimmy traced the stitches on the right side of his face with his fingertips. He snagged one with a fingernail and sucked air through his teeth.

"Would you leave your face alone, Jimmy? You'll get an infection or something."

"Itchy."

"Not surprised. But here, chicks dig scars. Another few weeks and that's going to look fucking class, like. You'll be beating them off you."

Jimmy turned to Steve, waited a few seconds for him to finish tying, untying and retying his laces.

"I'll head back to my house later," Jimmy said "Honestly didn't mean to stay here for more than one night."

"Don't worry about it." Steve squinted up at the TV then shook his head. "You've enough to think about anyway."

"This'll blow over, though, won't it?"

Steve shrugged. "Eventually, I suppose it has to. You heard from your uni yet?"

"No emails. I suppose there might be a letter at my house. I'm hoping they haven't noticed, though."

"Good luck with that. My da saw it last night. He thought you made a lot of sense."

"Yeah, right."

"Swear to fuck. Of course, my da's a complete rocket. If he thinks you're making sense, there's something wrong."

Jimmy got off the couch and went to the kitchen. He filled the kettle and called out to Steve, still on the couch.

"You want tea?"

"Yeah, mate."

"What are you at today?"

"Selling weed. Just like every other Saturday."

"Fuck, is it Saturday? Thought it was Friday."

"You need to get your head out of your hole. If the video doesn't fuck your chances at uni, all this pissing about will."

"There's another three months before the exams, like.

I'll be grand."

"If you start now, maybe. Take it from a real-life dropout, blink and it'll be Christmas and you'll not have done a thing."

"I'll get back to it on Monday."

"Up to you, our fellah. Do you want to come out and help me get through the day's deliveries? I'll cut you in."

"No, I'm okay. Just going to chill out this weekend."

"Watching your wee video over and over again? Suit yourself."

The kettle bubbled. Jimmy aimed a series of obscene gestures at the living room. He hopped from foot to foot, pumped his hips, and put his fingers to work in eerie silence. Steve appeared in the kitchen doorway just as the kettle clicked. Jimmy slipped his hands into his pockets and blushed.

"Were you dancing?" Steve asked.

"Yeah."

"You're not wise, our fellah."

Jimmy shrugged.

"I'm going to skip the tea and head on. Give me a buzz if you change your mind about helping me out. We could go see a movie after, maybe."

"Haven't got a new phone sorted yet."

"Serious? God, I'd be lost, Jimmy."

"I'm kind of enjoying the peace."

"Don't enjoy it for too long." Steve slapped his jacket, hip and back pockets. "Phone, keys, wallet and weed. All set. See you later?"

Jimmy nodded and Steve left. When the front door swung shut behind the weed dealer, Jimmy drew his hands from his pockets, Grace Doran's gold pen in his right. He sent it spinning over and under his slender fingers, his eyes dreamy.

"It'll all blow over," he told himself. "Another day or two, something else will come along. Just hold tight, boy. Hold tight. It'll all blow over."

He kissed the side of Grace Doran's pen and slipped it

back into his pocket before making a single mug of tea.

QUESTIONS & QUESTIONS

Bridge raised his hand. Dev swore under her breath. Bridge ignored her. Chief Inspector Bobby Mitchell clasped the sides of a wooden podium. His pursed lips crammed his thick Tom Selleck moustache into his nostrils. He nodded at Bridge to acknowledge his question. Bridge lowered his arm and sat forward in his plastic stackable chair. He cleared his throat before speaking.

"Any CCTV footage of Vic's final moments, Chief?"
"If there is, we haven't found it yet."
"What about witnesses?"
One of Bridge's colleagues snorted. "Aye, dead on."
Both Bridge and Mitchell ignored the comment.
"No witnesses yet, DI."
"Maybe somebody should speak to Clark," Bridge said. "They're not just brothers in crime. They're blood cousins too. He might be pissed off enough to cooperate with us."
"Good point, DI Bridge," Chief Inspector Mitchell said. "I assume you and DS Devenney were going to volunteer...?"
Dev's whisper cut through the snickering in the meeting room. "Couldn't keep it shut, could you?"
Bridge nodded. "Has he been brought in yet, Chief?"
Mitchell's thick moustache stretched over a humourless grin.
"Not yet. We believe we might have footage of him, however, at last week's disorder outside City Hall. It could well be that he'll get picked up for riotous behaviour when our tech boys have finished fiddling with their computers."
"He *was* there. He had his face covered, though."
"Not the whole time, it would seem. If we can get a clear picture of him before he covered up and another of him in action it should be enough to arrest him. It's only a matter

of time, is what I'm hearing. Of course, nobody has seen the slippery devil since then, so we may need to pour some resources into tracking him down as well. But we'll get him."

Mitchell gave Bridge a few seconds to speak again. Bridge sat back and folded his arms.

"If there are no other questions…" Mitchell paused to allow for an interruption. None came. "We'll adjourn the meeting, then. Minutes will be emailed as and when."

When Mitchell left the podium, Bridge twisted slightly in his seat to talk to Dev.

"Fancy taking a spin out?" he asked.

"You're not going to wait around until they drag Clark in?"

"Fuck, no. It could take days to find him. May as well squeeze in a yoga class or two before that shit hits the fan."

"Such a weirdo."

"Doctor's orders, like. Will you give us a lift?"

"Have I any choice?"

"Not really."

TO THE MAX

Max Mason frowned at his rear-view window.

"Who's this asshole?"

He reached forward and tilted the mirror for a better view. His grip on the plastic casing whitened the bulbous knuckles and raised the smattering of dark hair between the first and second finger joints. Then he sat back and took in the realigned view of a row of squat terraced houses. Palestine Street, smack in the middle of the Belfast student haven nicknamed The Holylands.

In the reflection, Clark Wallace battered on a front door with the side of his fist.

Mason reached out to the high-tech console embedded in the centre of his luxurious walnut dashboard. His index finger jabbed at a couple of buttons and activated his speaker phone.

"Soap here."

"Boss, some mook is banging on little Jimmy's door."

"Has Jimmy answered?"

"Doesn't look like anybody's in. Or they're hiding. Which I get. The mook looks like a mean SOB."

"Maybe he ain't looking for our guy."

"Maybe."

For ten seconds, only the sound of Soap's breathing sounded from Mason's stereo speakers. Mason held tight, his gaze never breaking contact with the mirror.

Soap clacked his tongue off the roof of his mouth. "Get a picture of the guy and send it to me. Don't bother making contact with him unless McAuley answers the door."

"Got it."

"Any other developments?"

"No, boss. I think the kid might be staying somewhere else. Clocked a few of his housemates coming and going the last few days, but there's been no sign of the boy himself."

"Right..." Soap huffed air. "Hold tight until you hear from me. I'll see if I can turn anything up on my side."

"You don't want me to follow the guy at the door?"

"No. Like I said, he might be there for somebody else. Collecting an unpaid drug tab or something, you know?"

"Up to you. I'll be here 'til you get back to me."

Mason cut the call and rooted his phone out of his hip pocket. He snapped five photos of Clark through the rear windshield and flipped through them before sending his favourite image on to his boss. He tucked the phone away and watched the mirror. Didn't blink until Clark gave up on attacking the door and stomped off.

"Man, fuck this bullshit dee-tail."

TELL YOUR FRIENDS

Bridge yanked open the Lancer's passenger door and lowered himself into the bucket seat. Dev sat behind the wheel. She handed Bridge her smartphone.

"You seen this headcase yet?"

Bridge looked at the video flickering on the phone for a few seconds.

An angry voice crackled through the little speaker: *"I am so sick of these subhuman imbeciles hogging the limelight..."*

Bridge tapped the screen to enlarge the picture. "Jesus! I met that wee lad at the hospital after the riot. Jimmy McSomething. I heard snippets from this speech on the radio earlier. First time I've seen the footage, though. Wee lad's got the crazy-eyes."

"I know. Still, even a stopped clock is right twice a day. Can't say he's wrong about the babies at the protest."

"He wished them a cot death, Dev."

"Not that bit, for fuck's sake. I'm not a monster. I just mean they shouldn't have been there."

Bridge handed the phone back. "What else are the parents going to do, though? Let the *au pair* watch them for a few hours?"

"Ha-fucking-ha."

"I'd be more worried about video-boy right now. He may keep his head down for a few weeks or the next time we see him we'll be pulling him out of the Lagan. Like Vic."

"Heard that a few times at the station. Not a lot of sympathy for the student, though."

"Do *you* feel sorry for him?"

"Should I?"

Bridge scratched his beard then tugged at his lower lip. He shook his head. "No, you're right. Fuck him. He should have known better. There's enough hatred out there without some smart-arse fanning the flames."

Dev gunned the engine. "You owe me a coffee, by the way."

"How do you work that out?"

"New rule. If you demand a lift, you owe me one."

Bridge pulled his seatbelt across his chest, clicked it into place and levered his seat backwards. He closed his bruised eyes. "Or you simply do what you're told because I'm your superior."

Dev held up her middle finger in front of his unseeing eyes. Then she fiddled with her smartphone and set it in a cradle mounted on the dashboard before pulling out into the street. A talk-radio host's voice filled the car:

"Most of our callers have condemned this video. I'm interested in hearing from those who think the young man has a point."

"Fuck," Dev said. "Even this guy's talking about it."

Bridge spoke without opening his eyes. "Sure he'd talk about anything that'd get his listeners' blood boiling. He's as full of shite as the politicians he complains about. Don't know why you bother downloading his podcast at all."

"This is a live stream. And I like him."

"That's because you're a contrary frigger as well."

"Shut your mouth."

Dev turned up the volume.

"We have Steve from Belfast on the line."

"Hiya, big lad."

"Hi back. Steve. You actually know the young man featured in the video, isn't that right?"

"That's right, aye. Jimmy's a friend of mine."

"And do you share his mindset?"

"I'm not convinced Jimmy really feels that way. He's never spoken like that to me, like. Nobody mentions the fact that he looks pretty beat up in the clip. I think it was a reaction to getting assaulted after happening upon a riot. That'd make anybody angry."

"Well, it's hard to know, Steve. We haven't been able to get a hold of this Jimmy guy to get his side of the story."

"Well, can you blame him? If he was listening to your show today he'd think that the whole country hated him."

"Could *you* convince him to come on and tell it from his perspective?"

"I suppose I can ask."

"Or you could leave his number with our producer."

"He's lost his phone." Steve's voice trailed off. "I'll ask him to call in next time I see him. Might even let him use my phone. Chat to you later, mate. Somebody's at the door."

"Is he gone?" A pause. "Sorry about the abrupt end to that exchange, listeners."

Steve squinted at his phone, tapped the screen and pushed it into his pocket. He drew the curtain back from his bedroom window, peeked at the street and shut out the light again.

"Busy, busy."

He left his dull bedroom and tramped down the stairs. The caller hammered hard at the door.

"Jesus, lad, just a second!"

Steve pulled the door open and kicked some glossy fliers out onto the front yard.

"All right, Steve?"

"Mickey Walsh? Well now. You don't normally call around without Jimmy. What's the *craic*? Looking a toke or something?"

"Can you sell it to me at cost?"

"No. We're not exactly besties."

"Only slegging. I'm here because I'm worried about Jimmy. Haven't seen him at the house in ages."

"Come in."

Mickey looked at his watch. "I have to be somewhere. Would you do me a favour and try to get in touch with him? Let me know if he's all right?"

"Last time I saw him he told me he'd lost his phone."

"When was that?"

"When did he lose it? Last week some time."

"He'll be on a computer somewhere. Wasting time on Twitter or some shite. Maybe shoot him an email or something?"

"Yeah, good thinking, our fellah. Could try Facebook or Skype, even."

"Whatever works." Mickey stepped away from the doorstep. "You're definitely going to try and get in touch?"

"Of course."

"Good, good. He's closer to you. Don't think he listens to me."

"It was good of you to call."

Mickey huffed air through his nose. "Aye, right. I'm just fed up of people asking me where he is. Everybody wants to meet the YouTube star. And I've had his ma on the blower more than once. Starting to feel sorry for the aul' doll." Mickey snorted and spat at the gathered flyers in the corner of the front yard. "Catch you later, Big Balls."

Steve waved Mickey off then closed and locked the front door. He clumped up the stairs, shoved his bedroom door open and went straight to his keyboard. The widescreen TV on the wall lit up when he hit the spacebar. Steve blinked at the glow as if he'd stepped out of a dark cave into harsh sunlight. He cracked his knuckles then worked his keyboard.

Steve opened his Facebook account and started typing a private message to Jimmy.

Hey Jimmy. They want you on the radio. Interested?

Jimmy read the message and closed the lid of Steve's laptop without replying. He unplugged his earphones and raised the computer over his head and looked set to throw it at the TV before sighing and lowering his arms. Then he laid the laptop on the floor and stood. He reached into his right hip pocket and drew out Grace Doran's gold pen. It weaved over and under his slender fingers.

Jimmy went to the living room door and dragged it open. He yelled up to Steve from the bottom of the stairs.

"You know I'm still in your house, don't you?"

A rumble and a clatter reverberated from upstairs. Steve poked his head out of his bedroom door.

"Jimmy?"

"Yeah. I slept on your couch last night. Did you not notice?"

"I was stoned to fuck, our fellah."

"You want a cuppa?"

"Yeah, why not? You want a toke?"

"Yes."

"Bring the tea up when it's ready, then. I'll start rolling."

"No worries."

Steve withdrew into the shadows then stepped back out onto the landing. He leant over the handrail to get a better look at Jimmy.

"Here, by the way, our fellah, Mickey came to see if you were here."

"Mickey Walsh? Did you tell him anything?"

"Nah. Figured you'd go see all those guys when you're ready. You might want to get in touch with your mum, though. Mickey says she's been looking you."

Jimmy slapped his forehead. "Fuck, right enough. I haven't talked to anybody from home since the video. Never even occurred to me."

"We need to release you back into the wild, Jimmy. Let's put a strategy together."

"Fine. After we get a little toasted, right?"

"Of course."

DOWNWARD FACING COP

DI Bridge was on his knees. He rolled his blue yoga mat into a tight tube and slotted it into its little canvas tote-bag. Then he pulled on the drawstring with more force than was necessary.

"You seem angry, Tommy."

"Do I? Sorry, Penny. I don't mean to be."

Penny looked down on the kneeling Bridge from a standing position. She crinkled her nose at the sight of the staples holding his head together. He loosened and readjusted the tote-bag drawstring. Penny crossed one long shin in front of the other and slowly lowered herself into a cross-legged sitting position. Her hands didn't touch the floor. She laid a palm on each of her slender thighs and straightened her lower back. Bridge looked up from his packed yoga mat and raised his eyebrows. He rested his backside on his heels and sacrificed good posture to accommodate eye contact.

"I thought you would understand," Penny said.

"You told me this was a unisex class."

"It was. But there doesn't seem to be that much male interest around here. I have to listen to the majority."

"I get it. It's a business."

"Business?" A mild tic tugged at one corner of Penny's mouth. "I barely cover my petrol with these morning classes."

"Aye, you've said before."

"I don't see yoga as a commercial enterprise."

"Is that so you don't have to fill out a tax form?"

"You see, Tommy. That's the kind of remark that makes the ladies uncomfortable."

"That seems personal."

"Excuse me?"

"You started this little chat with the old 'It's nothing personal' line."

"You're right, Tommy."

"Am I?"

"Yes. I definitely said that."

"And is it personal?"

"No. Not really."

"That's not really a no, is it?"

"I feel like you're attacking me here."

Bridge took a deep breath. His chest expanded and his spine straightened. The change in posture raised his battered head higher than Penny's. He slumped again as he exhaled.

"Do you want to chat about this over a coffee or something, Penny?"

"I have a boyfriend."

"I'm not asking you on a date. Just thought that if you felt threatened you'd rather be in a more public situation."

"I'm not worried about you *physically* attacking me, Tommy."

"Glad to hear that."

Penny pointed to a glass bubble fixed to a ceiling tile above the door. "The CCTV in here actually works."

"I doubt there's anybody watching it, though."

"I'd have thought a policeman would have more faith in security."

"I knew telling you lot about my job was a mistake."

"It's nothing to do with you being a policeman. You do ask an awful lot of questions, though."

"That's a pretty important part of my job."

Bridge looked over Penny's head, at the camera and then the door. He rocked backwards from a kneeling position into a crouch and straightened his legs slowly, rising to his full height. Penny's movement to a standing position was smoother and faster than Bridge's. Thanks to her long limbs and poker-straight back, she stood almost as tall as Bridge, but being so slender she looked like a sprouting sapling in a motion capture video. In comparison, Bridge looked as wide as a sheltering tree trunk, and almost as solid.

Penny took a step towards Bridge. He backed up then rounded her and headed to the door.

"You don't have to skip today's class, Tommy. Since you're already here."

"That's okay, Penny. I don't want to make your other customers feel uncomfortable again."

"I prefer to call them clients."

Bridge's grip tightened on the door handle. Veins rose on his forearm. Orange koi scales and blue water rippled as muscles contracted under the Japanese sleeve tattoo that flowed from underneath the sleeve of his cotton T-shirt.

"Aren't clients and customers the same thing? The meaning of the words, I mean? Like... synonymous?"

"More questions, Tommy?"

Bridge opened the door slowly and looked into the hallway. The rest of the yoga class were lined against the wall. None of them looked at Bridge.

"Penny's ready for you now," he said.

Bridge kept his head down as he strode through the leisure centre cafeteria area. He passed some junk food vending machines where kids in tracksuits argued over how they should spend their money. Barely spared them a sneering glance. Then he was in the car park. He made a beeline for Dev's Lancer. The driver's door was opened. Dev sat side-saddle, her feet on the white stripe marking out the parking space. On her knees a sandwich nestled in sheets of white takeaway paper. She scowled at Bridge.

"Thought you said you could get a decent sandwich in Andytown these days."

"You can."

"This one's stinking. Can you not go to a class in South Belfast?" She checked her watch. "Your instructor phone in sick?"

"It's not a unisex class anymore."

"Fuck's sake. She could have texted you or something."

"She seemed to be treating it like a break-up."

"Stupid bitch. What now, then?"

"May as well go back to the station. See if Wallace got scooped yet."

"Here was me thinking you might suggest a wee booze bender. You never want to do anything fun anymore."

Bridge grunted and fastened his seat belt. "Fuck off."

Dev extended the index and middle finger of her left hand and pressed it against Bridge's right temple. She blew a puff of air through her lips, just noisy enough to be heard over the Lancer's engine, and mimed the kickback of a fired pistol.

Bridge nodded; welcomed the sentiment.

MISTER SLIPPY

"Are you trying to tell me that I'm a slippery character, Grace?"

Joe Soap smiled for Andy's borrowed camera. Grace smiled too, but her polished teeth looked a little off-white compared to Soap's.

"I'd do no such thing, *Joe*."

"Oh, come now, Grace. Just because I'm American, doesn't mean I'll sue you."

"To be honest, I think we might have overtaken the old US of A on that front. This shithole of a country loves a good claim."

Soap's smile wavered. "Can you say that?"

Grace licked her lips, eyed the lens and turned back. "We can say anything we want. This isn't live."

"But, Grace... the camera is rolling. You must really trust this guy."

"Oh, I don't edit the recordings," Andy said. "We have a whole bunch of *guys*."

"And gals," Grace said.

"I think you two might be having a little fun with me," Soap said. "But that's cool. I understand that I look like the typical moneyed Yank trying to fix everything with buzzwords and old dollar bills." He raised his hand and rubbed his fingers against his thumb to signify cash. His pinky ring glinted in the camera lighting. "Hell, I even sound like that. But here's the thing... I. Actually. Care."

"What do you care about?" Grace asked.

Her eyes were glued to Soap now.

Andy, giving the impression that the whole world had just leaned in for this moment with the faint whirring of his camera's mechanisms, zoomed in.

Soap let both the interviewer and the world dangle for microseconds. This pause wouldn't hit the cutting room floor. It was a moment. Soap opened with the slightest of head flicks. His hair got the message. Settled into place, ready for inspection. And sure enough, those manicured nails grazed his scalp. Again his hair unsettled and resettled. Soap talked around his grin.

"I care about the little guy." And then he dealt out his headline. "And I'm not talking about leprechauns here."

Grace allowed herself a chuckle and a pantomime-prissy swat at the air. She allowed a few seconds to pass before saying, "Now who's having fun?"

Soap waited for a real question.

"You believe you can make a difference here in Northern Ireland, Joe. Can you tell me a little bit about that?"

Soap nodded slowly, as if the question had been fed via a satellite hook-up that suffered a slight time lag. He sipped some water and set the glass back down on a small table; out of shot. Andy held the frame steady.

"Grace, as you know, I run a security firm. The Agency. We do great work around the city, not just at nightclubs but also for celebrity events. We've taken care of glamour models, celebrity chefs, visiting investors… you name it, we've handled it and never once have we messed up. Our business here has grown over the last few years. With times as tough as they are right now, crime can only increase. Security is not a luxury, it's a human right."

"Some would argue that it's up to the Police Service of Northern Ireland to provide this security."

"If that's the case, then why are bars and nightclubs expected to provide their own security? Unless you're royalty or some sort of politician," at this, Soap's smile morphed into a cruel twist of the lips, "well, you just don't get the special kind of treatment that those who are more equal than others are afforded."

"Do you blame the PSNI for that?"

"I blame the whole system, but that's a debate for

another day. I want to look to what we can do, rather than complain about the places where the government is failing. I want to work *with* the police. Form a partnership that'll allow my security employees to help with the donkey work and allow the police to do what they should be doing."

"Can you clarify that? What should the police be doing?"

"The police, in my mind, are expected to arrest criminals through intelligent investigation and attention to due process. They should not be distracted by babysitting duties. Every year, in certain areas of Northern Ireland, pockets of troublemakers try to throw a wrench in the system. And the police suffer terrible publicity as a result. They're too heavy-handed or not heavy-handed enough. They react too slowly or too swiftly. They hurt people who look at them sideways; according to some of those bleeding heart journalists… present company excluded."

Grace didn't quite smile, but her slight nod encouraged Soap to continue.

"We need to be able to trust the police, but they've been beaten down constantly, even after the grand attempt at rebranding."

"I think the transition from Royal Ulster Constabulary to Police Service of Northern Ireland was seen as more than a rebranding exercise, Joe."

"Tomayto, tomahto…"

"The people you need to convince would most likely expect you to respect the hard work that has gone into community policing."

"Believe me, after countless meetings with senior officers, I know how precious they can be. But it has to go both ways. They have to listen to constructive criticism too."

"So this is a serious endeavour."

"I'm done with pointing out problems without suggesting solutions. Respectfully, that's what the media is for. I, through my security company, want to go further than that."

"So, your company would enforce the law in some way, even at riots?"

"Hopefully. Eventually. For now, we're happy to work with the PSNI in any capacity we can. You'll soon see our agents on the streets of Belfast, though. That's a fact."

"One of the things that the RUC had been heavily criticised for was exclusivity. Especially on the grounds of religion. It's being addressed now, but the majority of RUC officers were of the Protestant faith. Interestingly, your own company has been accused of something similar."

"I haven't checked the equality statistics in a while."

"But just last year, according to my research, a story ran that claimed your company hired more Catholic than Protestant people. And that the gender balance also leaned heavily towards men. Has that been addressed since?"

"We hire on merit. It seems as if Catholic men are better suited as security agents in my firm."

"Is that based on evidence?"

"Anecdotal, mostly."

"And what does your anecdotal evidence suggest?"

"That ex-IRA men are much more professional than their Loyalist counterparts, whatever the three-letter abbreviation may be."

Andy moved his head so that Grace could get a look at his facial expression. Both of his eyes had widened and his lips were pursed. Grace circled a finger and Andy let the camera roll on.

"You could get into a lot of trouble with that one, Joe."

"I stand by my words."

Grace gave Andy the signal to cut and stood up to stretch the small of her back.

"I should probably ask you to sign a waiver for that last statement."

"Why? I said it, it's on tape. What more could you need?"

"Trust me. This is Northern Ireland. Paperwork is nonnegotiable."

Soap shrugged. "How are you guys for time, Grace?"

"What do you have in mind?"

"I'd like to go to a riot, try to engage with some of those who seek to be heard."

Andy lowered his camera. "Russell Brand tried that a few years ago. It didn't really go anywhere."

"His people wouldn't let anybody take pictures," Grace said. "Seemed like a wasted moment to me."

"The guy's a comic, right?" Soap said. "Like stand up and all that bullshit? Were you guys expecting him to come up with a solution to the situation or were you hoping for more sound bites from a left-wing whiner with nothing to offer the world but weird hair and God knows how many STDs?"

"You didn't get any of that, did you Andy?"

"Give the kid a break, Grace. You know I would have toned it down a little for the camera. The STD bit was too far for you guys, right?"

"Unless you were a stand up comedian with weird hair," Andy said. He looked to Grace for approval. That didn't happen. Grace death-stared him into silence.

Soap laughed, though. "I could grow this mop out a bit, Andy. See how it goes." And Soap flicked his head again to display his fearless dominance over his 'do. "This isn't my first dance, Grace. You don't get to where I am without learning from the best. And the best know when to talk to the camera and when to talk about it."

"I've never heard it put that way before," Grace said.

Soap didn't bite.

"Media manipulation, I mean."

Not even a nibble.

She looked to Andy for something. Nobody could know what she wanted from him, and Andy played it safe. He said nothing.

"So, what do you say, Grace. Is there a riot on today?"

"I honestly don't even know how to answer that, Mister

Soap."

"What happened to calling me Joe?"

It was Grace's turn to hold her tongue.

Andy attempted to skim over the brief bumpy patch. "I actually lost the use of the best cameras I ever owned at the last riot, Mister Soap. And Grace got injured. I doubt either of us would be in a rush to cover another, even if they were timetabled in advance." Andy paused for a second to power down his camera. He fiddled with the lens cap, missed the shared look between Grace and Soap. "They're not timetabled, by the way. Kind of goes against the spirit of civil disorder, don't you think?"

"You were injured, Grace?"

"I fractured my tailbone."

"I don't mean to make light, but I'll get on board with anybody who busts their ass to make an honest living."

"Wish I'd got that on camera," Andy said.

Neither Grace nor Soap reacted to Andy's jibe.

"I'm not sure how honest it is," Grace said. "It's the news."

"There's still a little more focus on the facts than on the finance on this side of the pond. That's the impression I get anyway, Grace."

"Not everybody would agree with you, Mister Soap."

"I don't need everybody to agree with me. Just the ones who are smart enough to listen."

Joe Soap stood up and held out a hand for Grace. A cloud of confusion passed over her face. Soap dispersed it with a brief wiggle of his extended fingers. Grace took the offered support and allowed him to gently pull her out of her seat. She rose, like the belle of the ball, composed, confident, but coy. If they'd only had music, their brief union might have been beautiful camera fodder.

But Andy had capped the lens too soon, and the only sound, apart from breathing and beating hearts, swelled and faded in the form of a passing siren. There was an emergency somewhere in Belfast. There always would be.

Soap stepped away from Grace, is search of a window that would provide access to the right street. "Is that a cop car?"

Seasoned veterans of Belfast both, Grace and Andy shook their heads. Without the aid of a visual, and in perfect harmony, they said; "Ambulance."

Then Andy blessed himself and Grace left his side.

"That's a shame," Soap said. "But, hey. Are you guys absolutely sure riots can't be timetabled here?"

A young uniform stopped Bridge outside the station canteen. "Clark Wallace is waiting for you up in Interview Room 4, sir."

Bridge unbuttoned his suit jacket. "What was he arrested for?"

"Nothing. He came voluntarily."

"Aye, dead on."

"Seriously. Said he had information for you on Vic Wallace's murder."

"It's a murder now? Since when?"

"His throat was cut."

"By who? Under what circumstances? Was it premeditated?"

"I don't know."

"And yet your mind is made up. Murder."

The uniform shrugged. "Alleged murder?"

"There's a good boy. I'll be there in a minute. Don't let anybody arrest the big ganch until I get speaking to him."

"Why?" The uniform hunched his shoulders and lowered his voice. "Is Clark the alleged murderer?"

Bridge didn't offer a response. He pushed through the canteen door, sniffed the air and frowned. Bypassing the dried bacon, cremated sausage and congealed baked beans on display behind a sneeze-guard, he went straight to an upright fridge and picked a bottle of mineral water and a tin of Fanta. He eased the glass door shut and left a couple of pound coins on top of the unmanned till.

"Two quid there for you, Liz."

A middle-aged lady wearing a white cap over a blue hairnet sat at a table closest the door, a steaming cup and a copy of The Sun on the table in front of her. She looked up from the newspaper's front page headline.

"Dead on, Tommy. Will you be up for some grub later?"

"I don't think so."

"You're losing weight."

"It's all right, it's on purpose."

"You need a good sausage and bacon soda, son. Used to love those, so you did."

Bridge patted his belly. "Getting too old to eat like that now."

"Load of shite. You need to eat or you'll fall through one of the cracks in the street."

"See you later, Liz."

"All right, son."

Bridge glanced down at the article Liz was reading. The headline blared: PROTESTERS RUN RIOT IN BELFAST. Underneath it, a picture of the protest was set beside an image of the water cannons, their jets in full stream. The first and last frames of a storyboard. Beginning and end. No middle.

He shook his head. Liz didn't notice.

"Any spare papers on the go, Liz?"

"Thought you stopped buying them. All you youngsters get your news from your phones now."

Bridge raised a hand to his grey-streaked hair. "That Dev one doesn't like me picking up The Sun. Says the page 3 girls are disgraceful."

Liz took a sip from her cup. Sighed. "Now, why doesn't that surprise me? They're just diddies."

Bridge nodded. "Sure you know what she's like. I saw her spit on a stack of them in the newsagents once."

"You did not!"

Bridge laughed like he meant it. "But she's not the worst. Gives me a lift in for every shift, so... you know."

"Say no more. Take mine, but don't tell the big bitch where you got it. Don't want her blackening up my eyes. We'd be like a pair of pandas."

Bridge took the paper, tucked it under his arm and treated Liz to a smile. "These shiners didn't come from Dev. Not this time."

"Well I hope you got a few digs in."

"Long runs the fox, Liz. Long runs the fox."

Bridge let the door slam on the way out of the canteen. Liz's shoulders jerked. She drained her cuppa, stood up and swept scone crumbs from her apron. Eyed the closed door.

"Fucking nutter."

Then she went back to work.

INTERVIEW ROOM 4

Bridge took the stairs up to Interview Room 4, two at a time. He rapped his knuckles on the door twice before he opened it. Clark Wallace switched his gaze from a smartphone to the DI. His face was scratched and bruised. Minor damage and fading; nothing too dramatic. Clark looked like a scrapper. Bridge looked like he'd taken a beating that cost him his belt.

"Where've you been?" Bridge asked. "Nobody's seen you since the riot."

Clark laid the phone facedown on the tabletop then stood to shake Bridge's hand. Bridge passed him the tin of Fanta instead. He sat down opposite Clark. Placed Liz's copy of The Sun on the table, sports-side up.

"You drink fizzy juice, don't you, Wallace?"

"When I'm hungover, just."

"So? You stay dry last night?"

Clark gave him a sarcastic smile and cracked open the tin.

"Why are you here?"

"Is this being recorded, Bridge?"

Bridge shook his head, pointed over his own shoulder with his thumb. "All picture and no sound. You've not been arrested, surprisingly. I'd have thought my colleagues would've rugby tackled you at the door."

"Sure I haven't done nothing."

"Aye, I know. You *haven't* done nothing." Bridge flipped over the paper. "And that's not you on the front cover of this rag either, is it?" Bridge jabbed a finger at a figure standing head and shoulders above a young couple who had their hands in each others' back pockets. The print version was grainy, but the photographer had made Clark the central subject. "Wearing the same clothes as the man who tried to take my head off on the same day. Right down to the scarf and cap. I could probably double-check that with Billy Andrews there. I *know* he'd recognise you. And it just so happens he couldn't make bail. Isn't that terrible? But I bet he takes comfort in the fact that you're out there... looking after Caroline."

Clark pushed his baseball cap back and scratched his stubbly widow's peak. Dried skin appeared on the front of his black hoodie. He stared at Bridge in silence. The clock behind him ticked, ticked, ticked. Bridge tapped his wrist.

"What do you want, Wallace?"

"I'm here about Vic."

"You want to confess?"

"Quit acting like Billy Big Ballix. This is serious."

Bridge twisted open the cap on his bottle of mineral water. He took a couple of chugs and sighed. "What's the *craic*, then?"

"He's dead."

Bridge took a pen and notebook from the inside pocket of his jacket. He flipped the book open to a fresh page and licked the pen's tip, scribbled in the margin.

"Aye, we know. It's part of the reason my colleagues are keen to speak to you. When did you last see Vic?"

"At the protest at City Hall the other week."

"Most people are calling it a riot."

"That's just propaganda. Fucking Taig journalists, know what I mean?"

"I really don't, Clark. I'm sure there are as many Protestant journalists as there are Catholic."

"Aye, but only the fucking Taigs cover *our* protests, don't they?"

"You might be surprised."

"Nothing about this country surprises me. Did you ever pick a side, by the way?"

"Maybe we should get back to your cousin, Wallace." Bridge jotted a note down that looked like an uneven zigzag. "So you didn't kill him, then? Are you sure?"

"That's not funny."

"Who's laughing?"

"Probably our Vic." Clark swept his wrist across his nose. "Bet he's looking down at this mess and pointing at the pair of us. The idea of me asking you for help. Aye, he's pissing himself."

"What do you think happened to him, Wallace?"

"You're the cop. Can you not figure it out?"

"Evidently not."

"Evidently? Is that what Sherlock's doctor used to say?"

"No."

"Somebody else must have got to Vic. Somebody who'd leave him face down in the River Lagan."

"No disrespect, but Vic wasn't the most popular lad I ever met. What with the paedophilia rumours and all that. Any chance you could narrow your suspicions down a bit?"

"No disrespect? Suck my dick." He flipped the smartphone over to reveal a cracked touchscreen. "Look at this."

"Somebody should have taken that off you before they left you unattended. Where'd you hide it? Up your hole?"

"Fuck up and look."

Clark's fingers swiped and tapped the screen until a photo of a group of young men dressed in green popped up. They sat on a sofa that had been dragged out onto a residential street, drinking Buckfast tonic wine from the bottle.

"Look at the waster in the middle." Clark double-tapped the waster's image and magnified the picture. "Recognise him?"

Bridge leaned over the desk for a closer look. "It's our friend from the hospital, isn't it? The one that was willing to put you at the scene of the crimes. And I see he's a YouTube star now, whatever that's worth."

"He's called Jimmy McAuley. Student at Queen's."

"I know that. How do you, though?"

"Vic spotted him trying to film the riot. They had a disagreement about it."

"Then Vic bottled him. I know. Looks like he'll be

scarred for life."

"A lot happened that day."

"Have you approached Jimmy McAuley since?"

"Arrest the prick and you can ask him for yourself."

"I can't arrest someone for being the victim of an assault." Bridge reached out for the phone. "I could maybe return his mobile and ask a few questions, though."

Clark slid the phone across the table towards Bridge. "*Now* you're thinking like a peeler should. All that shite with your daughter might have worked out better if you'd have... you know." Clark covered his mouth with a big hand, his eyes on the camera behind Bridge while he spat words through the tiny gaps between his fingers. "You'd have found a reason to put me *and* Vic away back then if you'd done it the right way. The sneaky way. But instead you got suspended for beating up my wee cousin. Was it worth it?"

Bridge paused for a few seconds. He studied Clark's face then said: "You know what? I gave the kid my card after you stormed out of the hospital. Maybe he got distracted by his newfound fame, but he was certain that it was you who encouraged Vic to glass him. Wonder if I could swing that as accessory to attempted murder? Ask the respectable young student if he'd like to press charges."

Clark waved away the weak threat. "Nothing respectable about that cunt. See this picture? It was taken last St Paddy's Day outside his house in the Holylands. Remember when they had their own wee riot there? Fucking Taigs. They're always messing that place up."

Bridge sat back in his seat. "Jerusalem Street?"

"Palestine."

"How do you know?"

"He dropped the phone at the protest. I tried to track him down. To give the phone back, like."

"Very cross-community minded of you, Clark. Did you get his address from the phone?"

"No, he's not *that* stupid. But I figured he had to be

from somewhere studenty. They'd hardly drag that big sofa any further up the street, like. Lazy bastards would have dropped it right on their own doorstep. You can make out the house number right here, see?" Clark tapped the cracked corner of the screen.

"Well spotted. I'm a wee bit surprised that you didn't... pay him a visit."

"I'm no vigilante."

"You're not exactly the type to run to the cops either."

"I don't really think of you as a cop, *mate*. Not anymore."

Bridge stood up quick enough to knock his chair over. Clark followed his example, though he moved a little slower and his chair remained upright. Bridge looked up at Clark.

"You watch your fucking mouth, Wallace."

"Hah. There's the old dirty peeler I used to know."

"I was never dirty."

"Aye? Keep telling yourself that."

"Get the fuck out of here."

"Are you not going to look for Vic's murderer?"

"No."

"That's it?"

"That's it. His case has been assigned to DC Prescott. One of our sharpest minds. They've pulled out all the stops to solve this one, Wallace. Just let the system take care of it."

"Who are you trying to impress? Me?"

"One more word out of you and you're fucked."

Clark heehawed like a mule. "You wish you could fuck me. Dirty bastard."

"Maybe I can't, but there's something you don't know about our little student friend. He comes from an IRA family. One close to the border; my old stomping ground. And I reckon you'd be safer dealing with me rather than the kid's da. Rumour has it that McAuley senior is a dissident. You know what kind of an operation them Newry Comanches are running, right? Bomb first, ask questions later."

"You're full of shite, Bridge."

"Whatever helps you sleep tonight, Clarky boy. I reckon you fucked up bigtime, though."

"It's your job to help me."

"No, Clark. It's my job to arrest you, but we haven't got the evidence for it yet. Vic's case is going to slip through the cracks. I'll make sure of it. And with any luck, you'll be killed before anybody here uncovers enough evidence to scoop you." Bridge moved to the door and pulled it open. He called out into the hallway. "Could somebody escort Mister Wallace out of the station, please?"

"I won't forget this, Bridge."

"Don't let the door hit your big hole on the way out, Clarky boy. Wouldn't want you claiming police brutality, like. Not again."

Clark didn't wait for an escort to show up. He jerked a shoulder as if to hit Bridge on the way out the door. A dummy move, intended to put a fright in the inspector.

Bridge didn't flinch.

But when he went to the table to retrieve the bottle of water he'd left there, next to Jimmy's phone and Liz's paper, his shaking hand almost knocked it over. Bridge slipped his unsteady fingers into the inside pocket of his suit jacket. He pulled a cheap phone from there. One with buttons rather than a touchscreen. And he jabbed at those buttons hurriedly with his thumb.

"Sammy? Clark's been in. It looks like we might have caught a break." He paused for a couple of seconds. "Shush. It doesn't matter. Let him waste time figuring out he's wrong. Oh… and by the way, I saw you drop your kids off at school this morning. You should work on your punctuality. Set them a good example. It's not good for a child to have to hurry into the classroom like that."

Bridge held the phone away from his ear. Sammy's voice crackled through the little speaker. The words were impossible to make out. They melded into a guttural roar. Bridge waited for it to pass then placed the phone against his ear again.

"Aye. I'm threatening your kids now. Tell Clark nothing

or I'll take everything away from you."

Bridge hung up and tucked away the phone. He held his hands up in front of his face and examined them. They'd stopped shaking.

"What about the lease, Jimmy?"

"Ah, Steve. If you don't want me to be your business partner, just say so."

"I never said anything about a partnership either. You'll get fucked if I don't show you the ropes. It's a favour, just."

"He's a friend of the family anyway."

"Who?"

"The landlord."

"So?"

"You were asking about the lease."

"Oh, yeah." Steve giggled.

"Shush."

"You shush."

"Here it is. Palestine Street. Shithole that it is."

"Looks the same as my street, Jimmy."

"It's not the same. Way more students here."

"You're a student."

"So's your ma."

"Did I tell you about my idea for a reality show?"

"Hash in the Attic?"

"Ach."

"Tell me about it again if you want."

"Nah, fuck it. Let's just get the money and run."

"Can't wait to double this shit."

"And your housemates definitely won't be in?"

"They're all homebirds. It's the weekend. You do the math."

"Geography, surely?"

"Biology."

"Just get in."

Max Mason waited for the pair of stoners to step inside

the house on Palestine Street then got out of his car. He eased the driver's door shut and moved with stealth to the front of the mid-terrace hovel. His overcoat whipped at his thighs, enlivened by a gust of wind. One of his gnarled fists unclasped and he laid his palm on the wood just below the night latch keyhole. He applied pressure and was rewarded by a little movement, but not much. Max looked up and down the street, shifted his stance and shoved his shoulder into the spot his hand had just tested. The door popped open with a sound no more noteworthy than if it had been slammed shut.

Mason swept imaginary dust from the shoulder of his black overcoat and entered Jimmy's house. The front room on the ground floor had been set up as a bedroom. Mason sat on the unmade bed and looked out into the hallway. He waited.

Steve was in the kitchen. He turned away from the open fridge-freezer for a moment, like he'd been disturbed but wasn't sure by what exactly, then shrugged.

Upstairs, Jimmy called down to his friend.

"You okay down there, Steve?

"There's no ice cream, our fellah."

"No way. Bet Mickey stole it." Then he muttered to himself. "But I know where you keep your money, Walsh. Teach you to respect boundaries."

"I'm away to the shop before it closes."

"Get some juice as well. I'll throw you a few quid when you get back, boy."

"Yeah, sure you will."

Steve swung the front door shut. It rebounded off the frame. The squinty stoner slipped his hand into the letterbox and pulled it against the frame a few more times. It didn't catch.

Upstairs, Jimmy closed a wardrobe. He had a fistful of cash.

"What are you doing to the fucking door, Steve?"

The banging had stopped, but his friend didn't answer. Jimmy cocked his ear to the creaks of loose boards on the stairs.

"Steve? What's up?"

Max Mason announced himself with a sound that came all the way from the Bronx; "Yo." He stepped into the bedroom.

"Jesus Christ!" Jimmy dropped the fistful of cash.

"You're Jimmy, right?"

"Where's Steve?"

"Your buddy? I watched him leave. Don't think he saw me. His eyes were practically shut."

Jimmy called out, "Steve?"

"He's gone."

Jimmy backed away from Mason. "What do you want? Money?" Jimmy kicked at some of the dropped notes. Wrinkled tens and twenties, mostly. "Take it."

"No. We need to talk."

"But Steve... he's just getting ice cream."

"It'll be okay, little Jimmy."

Clark stood by the side of the bed and buckled his belt. A small amount of soft flesh jiggled on his hips, but for the most part, he had a solid torso.

"You look good in jeans, Clark," Caroline said. "Nice change from the trackies."

"Right."

"What's the rush, anyway?"

Caroline sat up, to a chorus of pinging bedsprings, and pressed a rumpled duvet against her chest. Aiming to tease, she lowered the puffy fabric a little.

"Stay a wee while longer, Clark. I was just getting warmed up."

"No wonder Billy's as skinny as he is. You must wear him out, love."

"Don't, Clark."

"Don't what? Don't mention your husband?"

"He left me."

"He got arrested."

"Same thing to me."

"Not to him."

"Well, it's not like he's going to catch us."

"The way people talk around here? I've already heard a wee remark or two. No, I have to go. It's all well and good me checking in on you, but sure as God, if I stayed the night it wouldn't be long getting back to Billy."

"People are always going to talk."

"Not if I can help it." Clark scooped his T-shirt off the floor and pulled it on. "Speaking of which, I don't want you to talk to the peelers at all when they come sniffing around. You weren't at the riot and you've no idea where Billy was that day."

"How does that help Billy?"

"Fuck Billy. I want you to be my alibi."

"But what if I was seen?"

"Sure you had that dopey cop helmet on for most of the ruck. There's little chance anybody could have… what-do-ye-call-it…? *Identified* you."

"So you're worried about the neighbours talking, but you don't care if I tell the peelers that you've been riding me?"

"What of it?"

"They'll use that to mess with Billy."

"Better hope he doesn't drop either of us in it, then, Sweet Caroline." Clark looked around the room. "Pass me my hoodie."

Caroline leaned out of the far side of the bed. The movement bared her back and the top half of her bum.

"Stop flashing your arse at me. I haven't time to fire another one into you."

Caroline threw the duvet aside, pushed herself up onto her hands and knees and wiggled for him. "A real man would just show up late." She looked over her shoulder and winked.

Clark reached out to a dressing table and lifted a tube of lipstick from a scattering of cosmetic products. Then he moved over to the bed and slapped Caroline's round buttock. The one with Billy's name tattooed to it. He uncapped the lipstick and drew a red line through the Indian ink.

"You're a wee hoor, aren't you?" Clark slipped the lipstick into his pocket and slapped Caroline's other bare arse-cheek.

"Only for you." She worked here hips a little harder. "Come on. Just a quick one."

Clark's hand closed around his belt buckle. He watched her work it for a few seconds then reached for the Duvet. Threw it over the top of her so it settled like a table cloth.

"Fuck yourself, Caroline. Fuck yourself all night long. I've work to do."

Caroline rolled onto her back, wrapping her body in the duvet, and poked her head out from the edge of the material.

Her features twisted. She bared her teeth.

"Faggot."

"Call me that again, Caroline, and I'll be looking for two new alibis. One to replace you, and another to protect me from being arrested for your murder."

"Stop slabbering, will you?"

"Who's slabbering? Watch your mouth, or I *will* kill you."

"What is it, Clark? Am I getting a wee bit old for your taste? Thought you'd finally figured out that women were better than wee girls."

Clark grabbed the duvet and pulled it towards himself. Caroline went with it, too surprised to scream. Clark yanked again and she spilled off the bed. She didn't have time to find her voice before Clark kicked the air out of her lungs. Winded, she wheezed.

"You have to learn to control that forked tongue of yours, Caroline. You're good for the odd shag, but that's about it. Don't mistake me getting my dick wet for anything more than it is. Nothing else about you interests me, and if I'm honest, I'm already getting bored of your loose cunt. It's like driving a minibus up the M2."

He kicked her again. She wheezed faster.

"So stop getting ideas above your station, get a story ready and make sure I know my part. Don't phone me, I've changed my number again. I'll be back here later."

He stepped over the fallen woman onto her bed, trampled across the mattress, retrieved his hoodie and left Billy's wife to struggle for breath.

SMOKE 'EM WHEN YOU GOT 'EM

DI Tommy Bridge sprinkled ground herbal cannabis on top of tobacco. He scooped the combo up in a king-size cigarette paper and got to work shaping it into a spliff. His phone rang just as he was about to lick the thin strip of gum. He cursed, laid the unfinished joint on top of his coffee table near a cluster of empty prescription pill containers, and rooted his phone out of his hip pocket. Bridge swiped the touchsceen to answer the call and pressed the mobile to his ear.

"Just a second, Dev."

He set the handset down on the table, selected the speaker phone option and got back to work on rolling his spliff.

"Sorry, go ahead, Dev. What's the *craic*?"

"Just checking in on you, Bridge. You seemed a bit upset earlier."

"Upset? Yeah, that's one way of putting it." He licked the gum and sealed up his joint. "Fucking furious would be another."

"If we'd lifted Wallace prematurely, it might have jeopardised a conviction. We have to play the long game with this one. He's too seasoned and too well connected to do anything half-assed."

"He swam right into our net and backstroked straight out again. Laughing all the way."

"You're taking it too personally."

"How the fuck could I not?" The volume of Bridge's voice didn't rise much, but there was a turbo injection of venom in those words.

For a few seconds, the only sound on Dev's side was the sniff and blow of a breathing exercise.

"I know there's history there, Bridge, but you have to work through it. We got over our history, right?"

"The Wallace boys took more from me than you ever could, Dev."

"So it'll take longer to get over it. Maybe you came back too soon, though?"

"The psychologist signed off on my return. Let's not talk about that again."

"Do you not think that's weird, though, Bridge? We should be able to talk about this shit."

"As much as they took from me, Dev, my balls are still intact. Save the chit-chat for your gal-pals, eh?"

"Well fuck you, then. I thought you were better than that, Bridge. I get enough of the sexist shit from the Old Boys' Club... Or did they take on a new member?"

"Just speaking from the heart, Dev."

"It'd make a change. You've not had an honest conversation with me since you got back. We used to be close."

"And that was the start of our problems." Bridge put the spliff between his lips, sparked it with a blue Bic lighter, and sat back on his sofa. He inhaled and exhaled. A nimbus of blue and grey smoke floated above his head. "We got too close."

"Are you smoking?"

"What? No?"

"I heard the lighter."

"It's..." Bridge looked at the joint and shrugged. "It's not a cigarette."

"Ach, Bridge."

"Chill out."

"Like you? No thanks. Could you not just have a beer or something?"

"How could you ask *me* that, Dev? I'm never drinking again."

"So ask your doctor for something legal, then! You're meant to put weed dealers away, not finance the fuckers. Unless... you didn't skim evidence or anything, did you?"

"The way they're watching me? Fuck, no." Emboldened by his confession, Bridge sucked down another hit and chased it with a blast of oxygen sucked through his teeth. After three long seconds, he exhaled with a sigh.

"Does your dealer know you're a cop?"

"He barely knows what day it is."

"You're an eejit."

"An eejit who's low on weed. Would you give me a lift to the Holylands so I can see my guy?"

"Get a taxi. I *have* been drinking."

"Big surprise."

"I'd be offended if that wasn't coming from Puff the Magic Dragon."

Bridge giggled.

"Something funny or are you just high?"

He wrestled his stoner chuckle into submission. "I've had a wee thought, Dev."

"Is it a sensible one?"

"You tell me. You see... weed makes me a bit horny."

"Good night, Bridge."

Dev ended the call. Bridge raised the joint to his lips again. He sucked on it three times, sending smoke through his nose every time he kissed the roach. Then he stubbed it out. He looked at his phone and then at the empty baggie beside it. Reached into his left hip pocket and drew out a second phone. This one had a cracked screen. Bridge picked a name from his list of contacts. When it started ringing, he selected the speaker phone option again.

"You well?" The voice was friendly but half-buried in sounds from a busy road and a footpath full of revellers.

"All right, man?" Bridge's voice raised a little in pitch and his twang had softened. "Jimmy here. Steve gave me your number for when he's out of the good gear. You about tonight?"

"Hiya, Jimmy. Didn't know Steve had run out. He usually gives me a shout about it, like."

"Maybe he hasn't, but he didn't answer my texts earlier. Could be off the grid for a bit, just."

"Sounds like him, all right. The only dealer I know

who'd let good money go if he was into a computer game or a movie."

"That's the boy. And I've a bit of partying to do tonight. So, can you meet me? I'm looking a good quarter at least, like. Skunk, if you have it."

The dealer whistled through the speaker. "That's a big order for a student."

"I'm not a student anymore. Not quite the oldest swinger in town, but getting there."

He laughed politely. "I'll have to pick some up from my grower's pad, but that's cool. Give me half an hour, maybe forty-five minutes?"

"I've to wait for a taxi anyway. I'll be in your end of the town in less than an hour, then." Bridge paused for a second. "By the way, I got a new phone today. I'll send you the number. Text me on that when you're set."

Bridge ended the call before the dealer could respond. He crossed the living room to get to the mantelpiece, lifted his small bottle of eye-drops and washed away some of the bloodshot from his whites. When he'd blinked away the synthetic tears, he placed Jimmy's cracked phone on the mantelpiece. The picture of a teenage girl with brown eyes stared at him. He stared back. Winked at it and spoke:

"Fuck does Dev know anyway? Weed's barely a drug at all. It's a fucking plant, like. Been around longer than her whiskey." He kissed a fingertip and placed it on the photographed child's forehead. "Sorry for cursing, love."

ON THE JOB

Grace Doran had dressed to impress; a black shirt and skirt ensemble that concealed much of her skin, but clung to the contours of her body. The effect was that of a sensual silhouette. She ran her finger along the rim of her wine glass and the deep red contents rippled.

"I'm not going to quit a steady gig to work on something that could amount to a stack of empty promises," she said.

Joe Soap halted his forkful of steak within licking distance of his mouth. "Empty promises? What do you mean, Grace?"

"You run a security business, Mister Soap—"

"For the last time, I want you to call me *Joe*."

"Joe... you could employ anybody to market your company. I'm a journalist, not a PR guru."

"My security company is just the start. I plan to build media outlet based here that'll deliver news in a way that'll get the younger intellectuals involved. Internet based at first, but you know how these things grow."

"And until this is up and running you'll make use of my media contacts to promote the expansion of your security business, right?"

"A rising tide lifts all the boats."

"And on which of these boats will I find my salary?"

"We'll talk about that."

"Talking is free. I'd like to know if you're going to make me rich."

"And Maslow reckons money isn't a motivator."

"That's the guy with the triangle thing, right?"

"The hierarchy of needs, yeah."

"Always thought that was a load of shite, to be honest. You can't eat self esteem."

"That's the kind of honesty that would make any sensible businessman want to woo you."

"And that's what the fancy dinner is about, is it?"

"If you think this is fancy, you're easily pleased." Soap snatched the chunk of steak from his fork with a practiced snap of his pearly whites. "I've had better steak at a corporate barbecue for Christ's sake."

"This place has a Michelin star."

"Must be the kind of thing you can buy these days."

"That's a bit unfair."

"It was unfair to serve me this lump of leather."

Joe Soap's mobile phone, or cell phone in his parlance, cut through the string quartet's atmospheric melody. A fair few patrons screwed up their faces at the brash intrusion. Grace lowered her head and raised her hand to form a peak across her eyebrows as if to deflect the stares. Soap wasn't the least bit concerned. He snatched the bleating handset from the tablecloth; spoke loud and proud.

"Soap here. Just give me a second, Max." Soap smiled across the table at Grace. "Sorry. I wouldn't normally take a call during a meal, especially not when in such esteemed company, but I'm expecting some good news. I'll be quick."

He said all of this in a voice that was pitched to fill the room. The string quartet got a little more aggressive with their bows. A few knives and forks clanked off the gleaming crockery. Soap addressed the caller.

"Tell me what I want to hear, okay? And be brief."

Soap nodded along with whatever was said. He took a tiny sip from his wine before cutting in with his own two cents.

"This may not be the best place to take him, then, Max. Bring him to the hotel. Book him a room and allow him a little time. I'll meet with him after I've finished my meal. Grace Doran will be with me."

Grace widened her eyes slightly but didn't protest.

Soap continued after a short pause. "No, that won't be necessary. Allow the guy something to take the edge off, though. Borrow from my own supply if you have to."

The American ended the call and focussed his laser-sharp attention on Grace.

"I'm not expecting anything that might go against your morals, Grace, but you'll accompany me back to my hotel, right? We can continue our discussion in the car."

Grace didn't hesitate. "Okay."

"Great. Let's go, then."

Joe Soap stood up and rounded the table. He pulled back Grace's chair as she rose. Her eyes twinkled in the candlelight. The music swelled like a cresting wave. Threatened to sweep through the restaurant's clientele, tsunami-style. Soap clicked his fingers and called for the coats, his voice somehow able to compete with the string quartet's crescendo. The maître d' approached tentatively, against the tide. His voice, when he was within earshot of Joe Soap and Grace Doran, was honey; too sweet to be wholesome.

"And how would sir wish to settle the bill tonight?"

"He wouldn't," Soap said.

"I don't quite follow. Is it the lady's treat, perhaps?"

"No." Soap puffed his chest. "The food was atrocious and the wine was mediocre. You phoney bastards don't deserve a dime."

"Sir, if there's been—"

"This isn't a negotiation, pal. Chalk it up to customer dissatisfaction and step aside. Wouldn't want to have to steamroll you."

"Surely there is some way we can settle this amicably."

"Indeed there is, Frenchy."

The maître d' didn't have a French accent, he was English, but he didn't correct Soap. "That is a relief, sir."

"Yeah, you can get the fuck out of my way, and put a little more effort in next time."

A pair of waiters appeared with the coats. The bigger of the two held Soap's up so he could don it more easily. Soap punched his fists through the sleeves of his long overcoat as if he was expecting major resistance. The aggression was not lost on the maître d'. He nodded at both Soap and Grace then moved off to polish egos at another table.

"You're diddling them out of quite a bit of money, Joe."

"Fuck them."

"Seriously. I'll not be able to show my face in here again. Was it really that bad? The meal, I mean."

"No, it wasn't bad, but it was a long-ass way from being worth the money they were charging. Your people need lessons in class."

WHAT WOULD JESUS DO?

Clark Wallace sat in the passenger seat of a Bedford Rascal van with a KFC bargain bucket between his legs. It was difficult to make out the colour since he was parked between two streetlights, one of them dead and the other flickering. The van had been parked with the driver side adjacent to a concrete wall to hide the broken window. An oversized Christian fish decal, jazzed up to contain the word 'Jesus', on the passenger side window obscured Clark's view slightly. But when Bridge left his apartment building to jump into a taxi, Clark saw him.

Clark dropped a half-mauled chicken drumstick into the cardboard bucket of gristle and bones. He spat a lump of chicken skin out of the driver side window. The gob splattered against the concrete wall then fell to the pavement, to be nabbed by the first rat or seagull to spot it. Clark took the bargain bucket with him when he left the van through the passenger door. He didn't lock it.

With little concern for the possibility of a witness or three, Clark strutted across the street and shoved open the front door of the apartment building. Either Bridge hadn't closed it properly, or the electronic keypad lock was busted. Clark moved with the confidence of a lifelong resident. He bypassed the broken lift, skipped up the communal staircase, and made it to Bridge's first floor apartment without doubling back or making one wrong turn.

Clark tested the door handle. He wasn't as lucky as he could have been. The door held its own. He grinned, glanced over his shoulder, and then went to his knees. Placed the bargain bucket on the floor. From the back pocket of his jeans he pulled a small, black leather case. It unzipped to reveal a row of thin metal strips. Clark selected two and got to work. Less than half a minute later, Bridge's apartment door swung open on well-oiled hinges.

"Old school, motherfucker," Clark said, under his breath.

He picked up his KFC, went inside and eased the door shut.

In the living room, Clark sniffed the air on his way to the sofa. He picked up the little empty baggie Bridge had left on the coffee table and pressed it to his nose. Then he sat on the same patch of sofa Bridge had occupied less than half an hour previously and set the bargain bucket on the cushion to his left. Clark reached for the cigarette papers and the tin of tobacco that Bridge had left behind. He helped himself to a non-psychedelic rollie. Sparked up and French-inhaled a dense cloud of smoke from his open lips, up through his nostrils. He rummaged in the bucket for the half-eaten drumstick with his free hand and nibbled on it between draws.

Eventually, he was satisfied and he dumped the end of his rollie into the remains of the KFC. Grease popped and sizzled on contact with the lit end of the butt. Clark spat on it and the little red cherry faded to ash.

"Right, no rest for the devil," he said.

Clark stood up and went to the mantelpiece. He picked up the picture of the teenage girl with brown eyes. Stared at it for a few seconds before he caressed the frame then rubbed away a greasy streak he'd left behind with the hem of his hoodie. The little bottle of eye-drops toppled and rolled off the wooden ledge. It hit the granite hearth and the cap popped off. Clark watched the contents drip out for a few seconds then looked away. He didn't bother to pick it up.

With the photograph back in its place, Clark picked up Jimmy's damaged phone, still in the spot Bridge had left it. He sighed at his own reflection in the mirror above the mantelpiece and tucked the phone into his pocket.

Clark reached back into his pocket, as if he'd had second thoughts about taking it. But he shoved his hand a little deeper. Scratched at his crotch for a few seconds then plucked Caroline's tube of red lipstick from underneath Jimmy's phone. He opened it and wrote on the surface of Bridge's mirror. The lettering was large and childish:

Guess who
CA luvs BA 4eva
XXX

He stepped back to admire his handiwork and nodded. After a quick stop-off at Bridge's kitchen sink, where he gulped water directly from the tap, he left the apartment; turned off the lights on the way out, but didn't relock the door.

Outside, the Bedford van had attracted the attention of a gaggle of teenagers. They surrounded it, the densest cluster concentrated at the broken window. Mutters and nudges. Clark walked away and left them to dare each other to take it for a joyride.

HOTEL CALIFORNIA

Soap handed Jimmy a dram of Scotch in a crystal tumbler. No ice. The amber liquid sloshed against the sides of the glass. Jimmy couldn't hold it still. They faced each other, planted in the middle of a matching pair of luxurious sofas, a glass and chrome coffee table between them. On the table, a crystal decanter on a tray. Soap reached out and refilled his own tumbler with a generous splash. Behind Soap a huge window provided a view of Belfast's streetlight constellations. The big wee city from a presidential suite perspective.

"You look a little shaken, Jimmy. Is everything all right?"

"No."

"What's wrong?"

"I've been fucking kidnapped."

"Jeez, Jimmy. Overreact much?" Soap swept his hair backwards with a deft hand. "You haven't been kidnapped. You're free to leave at any point. Totally up to you."

"Is that right?" Jimmy pointed to Max Mason, stationed by the suite's entrance. "Because the man you sent to pick me up didn't make that very clear."

"Max?"

Mason blinked slowly. He spoke in a measured, calm cadence. "He was pretty high, boss. Didn't think he would, you know... *retain* much information."

"He just told me to get in his car. Who'd say no to that guy? I never even got to tell my friend I was going somewhere. He'll be worried. And I've no phone to text him and let him know where I am."

"Max. Get Jimmy a phone, will you? Use the business account."

"Sure, boss. I'll pick it up tomorrow."

"Tomorrow's Sunday," Jimmy said.

"I've been here a few times, Jimmy," Soap said. "I don't think they keep holy the Sabbath these days. Getting a phone won't be our greatest challenge."

Max Mason reached into the inner breast pocket of his black suit and withdrew a Moleskin notebook and a stubby pencil. He licked the nib and scrawled a quick note, then tucked the Moleskin away again.

Soap leaned forward in his seat. "Are you still flying high, Jimmy?"

"Are you a cop or something?"

"Oh, hell no, Jimmy. And I ain't no stuffy anti-drugs Yank either. I have a medical marijuana licence, in fact. State of California approved."

"Really?"

"Can't beat that Cali weed, my friend."

Jimmy took a sip of Scotch. Winced.

"You're not a whisky man, then, Jimmy?"

"I usually drink beer, just. Vodka and Coke sometimes."

"That's a crying shame, kid. You have access to the finest whiskies known to humanity. Between here, the Republic and Scotland, you Celts have it nailed. And yet, I haven't met a soul with a real taste for it since I got here."

Jimmy sniffed his drink and set it down on the coffee table. "It's just not my thing."

"What is your thing, Jimmy?"

"I told you, beer and vodka."

"Those aren't *things*. They're just easy ways to get fucked up. What I mean is, what do you do, besides crash riots?"

"Like a hobby?"

"Hobby, interest, passion... whatever. What floats your boat?"

"I haven't really thought about it."

"Maybe you should." Soap reached for his own glass of Scotch, sniffed, sipped and sighed. "When I saw you on that YouTube video, I thought to myself, this is the kind of kid who takes life by the balls."

"I'm really not."

"Well, you definitely have the potential to be that kid. Now's the time to change."

"How?"

Soap took another tiny sip of scotch, then looked over Jimmy's head to address Max Mason. "Now would be a good time to get Grace in on this."

Max nodded and left the room.

"You've met Grace Doran before, right?"

Jimmy's hand slipped into his pocket for a few seconds. His long fingers flexed under the denim. "Yeah. Just that one time. Is she coming here?"

"She sure is. Grace has a part to play in my plan too."

"I need to use the bathroom."

"Feel free."

Soap pointed towards a door, Jimmy followed his direction.

The bathroom was bigger than an average living room in a Holylands student house. Jimmy took Grace's pen from his pocket and sent it spinning under and over his knuckles. He spent a little time checking out the shower, the bath and the complimentary toiletries before he slipped the pen back in his pocket and took a minute to fuss over his quiff. A little water to reinvigorate the hair products and some expert teasing with his dextrous fingers, and Jimmy was ready. He winked at himself in the mirror before he left.

"Hi, Jimmy."

Grace Doran had taken a seat beside Joe Soap at the coffee table. She had a glass of red wine in front of her. Jimmy's scotch had been taken away and replaced by a fat, brown bottle of craft beer. Condensation bubbled on the neck like gooseflesh.

"Uh... all right, G-Grace?"

Jimmy walked slowly to his sofa. He looked towards the door before he sat down.

"Max has gone out for a bit, Jimmy," Soap said.

"Nothing to be alarmed about."

"Okay."

Grace shone that heart-stopping smile on Jimmy. "Joe says you'll make a great addition to the team."

"I don't even know what that means."

"Well, let's get everything cleared up now, Jimmy," Soap said. "You're passionate about peace, right? That's what fuelled your righteous indignation in the riot video, isn't it?"

"I suppose, Mister Soap. I, em… I had smoked quite a strong joint as well. And I'd just been beaten up. In hindsight, I probably should have kept my mouth shut."

"Not at all, Jimmy, not at all. If you'd kept your mouth shut we wouldn't be having this little meeting tonight. And I just know that what I'm about to propose will be right up your street."

"Mister Soap—"

Soap held up his hand to cut Jimmy off. "Call me Joe, Jimmy. Call me Joe."

"Joe… I'm not sure where this is going to go, but I don't think you can really judge me by the video. I wasn't myself that day, you know?"

"You were a better version of yourself, I bet. An honest version. Am I right?"

Jimmy opened his mouth to answer Soap's question. The American didn't wait to listen.

"Jimmy. I want you to embrace that version of yourself. It's the angry voice of *your* generation that I want to tap into. A good college kid from a middle class family, finally getting his say on the mess that is Northern Ireland right now."

"Like a politician or something?"

"Fuck the politicians, Jimmy. They get in the way. This is something else. Think of it as a corporate takeover of your government."

Jimmy looked to Grace, doubt writ large on his face.

"It's actually a good plan, Jimmy," Grace said. She withdrew a thin document from a laptop case that had been propped against her end of the sofa. "I was in the lobby, reading Joe's mission statement before Max called me up. Hear the man out, at least."

Jimmy didn't waste any more time on thought. "Okay."

"I just knew you two would work well together. When I'm right, I'm right. Right?"

Jimmy's spine straightened. He cocked his head. "I'll be working with Grace?"

"And that's only the start of your good fortune, Jimmy my boy."

FIRST ON THE SCENE

Mickey Walsh, backpack slung across one shoulder, raised his key to the night latch. The door moved on contact with the lock. It didn't swing all the way open, but with a slight shove and a grunt, Mickey was able to push through the folded fliers and envelopes that had been used to wedge the door temporarily shut.

"Is somebody in here?"

There was no answer.

Mickey made a little more noise before he crossed the threshold. "Hello?" His voice deepened slightly. "Who's there?"

Absolute silence.

Mickey took a step backwards, breathed deep, and then shoved the door open hard enough to wallop the internal wall. He left the door ajar when he stepped into the hallway. Dropped his backpack so that it walloped off the floor tiles.

"Hello? Anybody there?"

He went to the living room, looked at the TV that showed little sign of life, except for the red standby light in the bottom right corner. Mickey tutted and reached behind the cabinet to switch the electric supply off. He straightened up, looked around and half-smirked.

"Jimmy?" Mickey's voice echoed in the low maintenance living room. Without curtains, cushions or indeed any sort of fabric aside from the faded couch and armchair upholstery, there was little to absorb his now-guttural yells. "Did you come back?"

No answer.

Mickey retraced his steps to the abandoned backpack. Then he noticed the open door leading to the ground floor bedroom. And that the bed had an occupant.

"Jimmy? For fuck's sake, is that you?"

He stepped into the room.

"Did you not hear me guldering from the front door, you weirdo? My heart's going like a dinger and you're lying in bed, smelling up the place with your rotten feet."

Mickey yanked the blanket from the bed and exposed what lay beneath.

"Squinty? What the fuck…?"

It took a few seconds for realisation to hit.

Bulging eyes, bruised neck, no sign of life.

"Steve. Where's Jimmy?"

Then Mickey ran out, bumped into the doorway on the way into the living room and clattered through the kitchen door. He heaved and retched. Made it to the kitchen sink and let go of the last thing he'd eaten.

BAG AND TAG

Dev sat on the bonnet of her Mitsubishi Lancer and sucked on a cigarette. Bridge stood in front of her. His eyes went from the burning end of her cigarette to the front door of nine Palestine Street. The doorway was crisscrossed with white and blue PSNI crime scene ribbons. The blue of the ribbon almost matched the blue of Bridge's fresh suit.

"Do you want a smoke, Bridge?"

"No."

"Well could you stop staring at mine with your panda eyes? I feel like I'm eating a fish supper in front of Bobby Sands on his last Friday."

"Dev!"

"What? I'm a Catholic. I can say it. And so are you. Sort of."

"I'm a Buddhist."

"Since when?"

"It doesn't matter. I am what I am right now."

"So you'll be reincarnated, will you? What are you going to come back as?"

"We don't choose, Dev."

"Fuck that, then. I'll be looking forward to my cloud and my harp. Except I want my Harp in a pint glass, you know?"

"Aye, Harp Lager. Very good."

"Fuck's sake. Tell your face we're having a laugh, will you?"

"Are we?"

"What else is there to do until the SOCO boys finish up?"

"Same thing we always do. Wait."

"Sometimes I miss the Bridge who'd have suggested a sneaky pint at the nearest pub."

"I'll not say nothing if you want to slope off."

"Forget it. Wouldn't be the same."

"Oh, here. Looks like we're set."

Bridge pointed to the men and women in white jumpsuits who'd spilled out of the front door, their heads bowed under a cloud of respectful silence.

"Will we go in, then?" Bridge asked.

Dev took a final pull from her cigarette before she dropped the butt and crushed it under her shoe. "Nah. We'll hang about here and scratch our balls some more."

Bridge followed Dev's lead. He stopped short only when Dev's charge to the front door almost knocked one of the SOCO jumpsuits inside out.

"Excuse me," Bridge said.

"Why?" He drew back his white hood. "It wasn't you who almost went through me."

"Take it as an apology on my colleague's behalf."

"That apology isn't worth the steam off my piss, Rocky."

"Fair enough."

Bridge bumped into him on his way past.

"Fuck's sake, like."

The DI ignored the SOCO's rage. He met Dev at the crime scene, a downstairs bedroom.

Dev trampled from one end of the bed to the other. She didn't touch anything, but her movements were less than reverential.

"You want to take it easy there, Dev?"

"Do you? It fucking stinks in here."

Bridge sniffed the air. "It could be worse."

"I know. *Your* flat might edge it."

"My apartment smells of artificial roses. I'm not talking about the hum of dirty socks in here. I mean that he must be a fresh enough... you know." Bridge indicated the bed with the flick of a wrist. "The..."

"The victim?"

"Aye. *If* it's a murder, like."

"Look at the bruising, Bridge. Do you really need to wait for a report?"

Dev pointed at the body's neck. Bridge glanced at it and looked away again.

"This can't be your first stiff since you got back, can it? It's been months."

"Almost a year, Dev. And no, it's not my first, and it won't be the last. That doesn't make it easier or harder or anything. I just don't like looking at dead people in their beds, okay? Especially the ones that didn't pass quietly in their sleep."

"Untwist your knickers, Bridge. I was only fucking asking. You're acting like I forgot our anniversary."

"You nearly did, in a way."

"Are you trying to be funny?"

Bridge left the bedroom.

"Where are you going, *boss*?"

"To see if Goldilocks is in one of the other beds." Bridge stopped at the foot of the stairs and returned to the bedroom doorway. "Or should I wait for the report on *that* as well?"

"Now I know you're trying." Dev let that hang for a few seconds. "In more ways than one, what?"

Bridge tutted and turned away.

"I'll check out the ground floor, then, will I?"

He didn't answer her. His dress boots clumped down on every second step until he got to the top. The upper floor was deprived of natural light. Bridge used his elbow to flick a light switch. An energy-saver light bulb went from zero to sixty watts in thirty seconds. It had little effect on the shady ambience.

Bridge drew a pen from his inner breast pocket and used it to prod open a bedroom door. A little extra light spilled onto the landing. He stepped inside. There were numbered cards on the floor. Bridge reached back into his breast pocket again and came back with a little black notebook. He flipped it open and scrawled across a fresh page.

Jimmy scritch-scratched the crook of his elbow, subconsciously jonesing for God knew what. His head swept from side to side, his widened lamps like searchlights. Grace, beside him, seemed much more comfortable in the shiny office-block reception; her right hand rested on a cocked hip while she thumbed her iPhone screen. The receptionist's desk, her uniform, and indeed the entire room, lacked any sort of organisational branding.

The lift pinged and Joe Soap stepped out with Mason in tow.

"You're early!" Soap's voice was unnecessarily loud.

Grace's lips slid across her polished teeth to frame that TV smile of hers. "Just by five minutes."

"The perfect amount of early."

"Hi... um, Joe."

"Jimmy, my boy. You're looking good, kid. Working on a beard?"

Jimmy's slender fingers rasped across his jawline. "Can't really shave around the stitches yet. The scar's still too tender."

"But you look like a badass. All good, right?" He looked beyond Jimmy, towards the reception desk. "Jenny, I'll be unavailable for an hour or so. Transfer my calls to Rick."

Jenny pulled a pen from her hair, knotted up in a loose bun. "Do you mean Richard? What's his number?"

"Richard, Rick, Dick, whatever. You can figure out a way to find his number, can't you?"

Jenny didn't answer. She attacked her keyboard with stiff, clawed hands instead.

Soap had crossed the space between the lift and his visitors. He grabbed hold of Jimmy's limp hand and pumped his floppy arm with too much enthusiasm. Then, after a quick flick of his well-tended mane, the American moved onto Grace. He wrapped his arms around her slender shoulders and kissed the air at either side of her face; waist bent to keep his crotch a respectable distance from hers. Jimmy cleared his throat a few seconds before Soap released Grace.

Mason was content to greet Jimmy and Grace with a single nod directed at the space between them.

"Let's get this show on the road, people." Soap clapped his hands and turned back towards the lift. "We'll take the elevator."

Mason trudged behind his boss. Grace tapped Jimmy's elbow to get him moving. He shuffled along a few steps behind the group. The lift doors clamped shut just as he made it into the unit.

Soap hummed on the way to the top floor. He stood closest to Grace. Jimmy had trouble occupying his hands until they found a resting place on a waist-height chrome bar just beneath the mirror. Mason stood still, his battle-scarred face neutral. Grace made a little noise of approval when the doors opened.

"Welcome to my office," Soap said. He stepped out of the lift and moved to the middle of the room.

There were a dozen desks scattered about in a poorly thought-out open-plan style. Little cubicle walls that were too low to serve any purpose other than prevent pencils from rolling off one side of the desks had been placed between some of the desks in closest proximity to each other. The desk Soap stopped at was the biggest in the room but nothing particularly fancy. It could have been picked out of an Ikea showroom.

Grace turned full circle to catch a glimpse of every corner. She'd learned how to move without giving away the fact that she'd fractured her tailbone already. "You're taking the whole floor as your office?"

"Sure, why not?"

"Seems a bit wasteful."

"You would think, wouldn't you? But I'm not selfish. As the organisation grows, those smaller desks will become occupied."

Jimmy snickered. "Like the occupy movement? All hashtags and tents and dogs on strings? You could fit a lot of hippies in here, right enough."

"What the fuck's that supposed to mean, Jimmy?"

"Um, nothing. Sorry, Joe?"

"What are you apologising for?"

"I really don't know."

Soap looked to Mason. "Did you give little Jimmy a druggie doggy bag or something?"

Mason shook his head.

"I'm not high, Joe. Just tired."

"Don't worry, kid. Nobody could stay mad at you. You're too cute." Soap stared at Jimmy until the blushing student broke eye contact to stare at his Converse. "Can you organise some coffee, Max?"

The security man didn't flinch or grumble about his job description. He trundled over to the nearest desk and picked up a phone. It looked like a cheap plastic toy in his massive mitt.

"Will Jimmy and I *occupy* one of these desks?" Grace asked.

Soap tipped her a wink. "Straight to the point as always."

"So...?"

"What I have in mind for you doesn't really require a desk. There'll be space here for you if you want it; somewhere to store files and check your emails, but for the most part, you guys need to be out on the streets. If anything, you should think of this place less as an office and more like a station."

Jimmy moved away from Grace and Soap. He seemed to be headed towards the desk Mason had stationed himself at after ordering the coffee, but then he stopped. The student looked around then headed towards the nearest window. It was tinted to reduce screen-glare. There were no curtains. The view of the Dublin Road had a tinge of sepia to it. On the road, cars taxis and buses weaved in and out of their lanes. Pedestrians gathered at a set of crossing lights.

A young Roma woman sat close to a cash machine across the street from Soap's building. She had one copy of The Big Issue in her lap and a crumpled cardboard cup in front of her. Most pedestrians walked by her without a glance. Jimmy watched one old man stop his mobility scooter to chat to the woman. She smiled at him and nodded.

Soap called Jimmy's name. He didn't look away from the window. Instead, very quietly, he said, "Just checking out the street, Joe. Plenty going on out there."

Soap chuckled and indicated to Grace with a quick tilt of his head that they should go stand with Jimmy. They crossed the room and took up positions on either side of the student; Grace on Jimmy's right, Soap on his left.

"Tell us what you're looking at," Soap said.

"See the guy on the scooter? Talking to the wee Romanian beggar?"

"She's a Roma traveller, Jimmy," Grace said.

"Yeah, her."

Soap glanced at Jimmy. "So what?"

"I'm just wondering if the aul' lad's going to give her money."

"He won't," Soap said.

"I think he will," Grace said. "She's still smiling at him."

"Look," Jimmy said. "He's reaching into the wee shopping bag in his basket."

"If he gives her food, I bet she throws it back," Soap said. "Anybody want to bet against me?"

Neither Grace nor Jimmy answered.

Below them, playing out like a silent movie, the old man pulled out a tin of Coke. The woman cocked her head, let her fixed smile slip. The man shook the tin for a few seconds and cracked the tab. A burst of beige spray shot out of the can and he directed it at the woman. She was on her feet fast enough to avoid getting her face covered in the sugary jet. The Coke soaked into her layered clothing, barely visible against the dark, dull colours of the fabrics. She skipped away when he tried to throw the can at her. He scooted off.

A cluster of student-types had stopped a short distance away from the scene. They watched as the woman took a few seconds to mumble to herself before she sat back down on the little box that served as her seat. She wiped the front cover of her copy of The Big Issue after she retrieved it from the footpath and rested it on her lap. None of the students approached her. After a little jostling between them they passed her by, heads down, shoulders bouncing.

Jimmy looked to Soap. "This is the kind of street you want us to work on? How much do you know about Belfast, Joe?"

"I know plenty, Jimmy. And that old fart isn't part of our demographic. Nor the travelling beggar. Maybe those pansy-ass kids that let it happen…" Soap backed away from the window. "Max, get the car and wait for us out front. We're going on a little school trip."

"Straight into the hard stuff, Bridge?" Dev pointed at the beer taps on the other side of the bar. "How about a pint to warm up?"

The stocky barman popped one of his eyebrows so it chased his receding hairline. Bridge answered the unspoken question with a slow shake of his head. "Two Bush, mate. The single malt. Neat."

"Ten or sixteen year old?"

"Ten. I'm not made of money."

The barman snorted and turned to the clutter of bottles on the top shelf.

"There's nothing wrong with a bit of Black Bush, Bridge," Dev said.

"It's innuendo like that that gives you your reputation, Dev."

"That wasn't… ugh, you fucking pig. I meant there's no need to go for the fancy schmancy shite with me. I was reared near the distillery. I know the stock that's put in the blends by the locals. You know… *real* whiskey drinkers."

"Trying to emasculate me only further serves the rumour that you are, in fact, a flaming lesbian."

"Do lesbians flame, Bridge?"

"I don't know. Maybe they rage instead. Point is, you're not doing yourself any favours."

The barman plonked two thick-bottomed glasses in front of Bridge and waited for payment. Bridge shoved a note at him and muttered about change. The barman shrugged like he'd thought the tip was coming his way anyway. He didn't thank Bridge. Didn't add his two cents to the discussion on Dev's sexuality either. Some other business took him away from the pumps. He headed out the front door with his mobile phone and a pack of cigarettes clutched in one hand.

Bridge passed Dev one of the glasses. They clinked

rims and took their first reserved sip. Dev set her glass down immediately. Bridge had a quick sniff of his and another sip before he laid his to rest on a soggy beer mat.

"Do you really think I'm gay now?"

"Ask me later, Dev." Bridge jabbed a thumb at the front door. "Do you think humpy-hole will be back this day? I'd like to order another drink here."

Dev broke eye contact with Bridge. She rubbed the knuckles on her right hand. "The cauld weather's coming in quick this year. My skin's as dry as your so-called sense of humour already."

"I tipped the fucker well enough. Ungrateful shite should be hanging around to make sure he gets another one."

"Do you think I'd look weird if I started wearing gloves at this time of year?"

"No weirder than usual. Should I go out and tell your man to flick his fag?"

"Cut the man's smoke break short? Weren't you a union rep for years?"

"All the good it did me."

"For fuck's sake, Bridge. How long's it been since your last drink?"

"I'm not one of those AA coin-collecting, day-counting, never-anonymous wankers. The fuck should I know how long it's been?"

"More than a year anyway, right?"

"You don't know. I could have had a beer here, a glass of wine there. It's not like I've *asked* you to keep tabs on me, Dev."

"I don't think you did, though."

"Aren't you the one who bitches at me every other day about how it used to be?" Bridge hiked his voice up a couple of octaves, gave it a lisp. "'You used to be fun, Bridge. We never go for pints anymore. Why are you so boring now?'"

"Is that how I sound to you?"

"Drink your fucking whiskey."

Dev raised her glass. She tipped the rim in Bridge's direction. Acted like she was about to splash him with what was left. Then she raised the single malt to her mouth and downed it. Bridge watched her, his lips slightly parted.

"You happy now? I've just thrown your top shelf gesture down my big gob. May as well have been fucking vodka, right? Or even better, one of those fucking green, minty nightclub shots. That's what women drink, right? Real women who like their skirts small and their hair big?"

"Right, point made. I'll go with the standard blend for the next one, will I? White label? Because if you drink it like that, even your precious Black Bush would be too good for you."

"Or we could take it all down a notch and have a pint."

"I want whiskey."

"You have whiskey." Dev pointed at Bridge's half-empty glass. "Appreciate it."

"Like you did?"

"I was making a point. You were the one throwing money away."

"So the next round's on you then."

"Gladly. Black Bush?"

"That piss gives me heartburn."

"Aw, poor little boy blue. You can have a Captain Morgan instead."

"You're the queer, Dev. Not me."

Dev punched Bridge's upper arm. He shifted on his stool, went to rub his assaulted bicep then redirected his reach to his own whiskey.

"I've actually missed this, Bridge, believe it or not."

"It's not like you to miss anything."

"You know what I mean."

Bridge shrugged. Downed his whiskey.

"I miss the banter, Bridge. We used to be mates first, colleagues second."

"My psychologist said that it's better to keep some relationships professional."

"What we've had this last year couldn't be mistaken for a relationship by any shrink. But you go ahead and take the advice of some bitch that never had to depend on a professional relationship over a friend to back them up."

"And I suppose that's my fault as well, is it?"

Bridge stood up. Dev reached out and caught hold of his elbow. He pulled away from her.

"Where are you going, *boss*?"

"To call that lazy cunt in here."

The front door opened. A flash of daylight snuck in behind the barman. "The cunt's here. Did you two decide on your next drink yet? I lost track out there."

"You heard her, then?" Bridge said.

"You might be a wee bit quieter than your girlfriend, mate, but your voice travels too."

"Black Bush?" Bridge asked Dev.

Dev smirked at him. "Aye. But I'm paying."

The barman returned to his post and scooped the black-labelled bottle off the lower shelf. "A man should appreciate any woman who's willing to put her hand in her purse at the bar."

"I've been telling him that for years, barkeep."

Bridge drummed his fingers off the bar and waited for his whiskey.

Soap was in the back seat, Grace to his left, Jimmy to his right. The clean cut American leaned forward to address the other, less clean cut, American in the driver's seat.

"Pull in just up ahead here, Max. Find a spot in front of the gates."

Mason did as he was told. Grace and Jimmy exchanged a glance behind Soap's back just before he settled back in his seat and obscured their view of each other.

"Do you know where we are, Jimmy?" Soap stretched his arm out and indicated the view from Grace's window. He didn't acknowledge Grace's slight squirm when his arm invaded her space.

"Don't you?" Jimmy's scarred cheek twitched. "The driver followed your directions, boy."

"Are you saying boy or bye?"

"B. O. Y."

"That's cute, and so's your little attitude. Just tell me what I want to hear for now, Jimmy."

"That's Stormont. The building our politicians work out of."

"Well, the MLA's, anyway," Grace said.

"Yeah, I know," Jimmy tried to soften his voice. "Those are politicians."

Soap saved his scrutiny for Jimmy. "What does MLA stand for, Jimmy?"

"Minister of something and something."

"It actually stands for Member of—"

"That's okay, Grace." Soap treated her to a quick flash of his mighty white teeth. "I'm interested in what Jimmy knows right now. I'm sure you'll supply me with a wealth of knowledge when I need it. Just wait for me to ask, will you?"

"Oh… yeah, okay."

"So, Jimmy." Soap tilted his head to the side. "It's fair to say that you don't know what MLA stands for, right?"

"If you want to know something like that, you'd be better off Googling it." Jimmy twisted his waist to get better access to his hip pocket in the limited space. He drew a new iPhone and hit the home button to awaken the screen. "You can get the app for your phone and everything now."

"I've been using the internet since before you were born, kiddo."

"I was born in the nineties, Joe."

"And I don't have to check my phone to know that the World Wide Web became available to the public before you did."

Jimmy looked at his phone screen, his finger poised to swipe it, until it faded to black again.

"So do you want me to look MLA up or not, Joe?"

"No, Jimmy. I want you to talk from experience, not from your handheld teleprompter."

"Right, well... I don't know what MLA stands for."

"Thank you, kiddo. Now, tell me this: Do you know what happens in that building?"

"It's where politicians make decisions, I suppose."

"What kind of decisions?"

"Political ones."

"Come on, Jimmy. Try harder."

"I don't know. They decide how much nurses get paid, what school gets more money than the other, which signs should be translated into Irish or Ulster Scots or both or neither. All that stuff."

"Really? Isn't there a health board? An education board? Some other group that argues about languages?"

"I don't know." Jimmy looked out his own window, away from the Stormont building. "Who cares?"

Soap clapped his hands so loud that Jimmy and Grace jerked in their seats. Mason didn't.

"That's the answer I was waiting for," Soap said. "And I knew it was in there."

"Most governments depend on apathy—"

"Thanks, Grace. It's still Jimmy's turn, though. I'll tag you in when I need you."

"Sorry." It didn't sound like she meant it.

"So, Jimmy... back to Stormont. You ever been in the building?"

"My mum took me to the play park up the road once. It was shite."

"Never went on a field trip?"

"You what?"

Grace huffed air through her nose.

"Say what you want to say," Soap said.

"It's nothing. Just, we call them school trips here."

"Yeah," Jimmy said. "Field trips usually happen in October, when the magic mushrooms can be harvested."

"You guys." Soap forced a chuckle to show he was a good sport. "I didn't think 'shrooms were big over here. I have a theory about psychedelics and conflict, you see..."

"It's really just the hippy-types and students that mess about with those things," Grace said.

Jimmy nodded along.

"We're getting off the point."

Grace sniffed. "I'll just be nice and quiet again, will I? Like an obedient geisha?"

"That'd be swell, dollface." Then Soap cackled at his own exaggerated accent. He toned it down again. "I'm really not trying to be sexist or anything here."

"It just happens naturally, does it?"

"Jesus, Grace. I just don't like distractions. When you talk out of turn, you derail my thoughts. Let me stay on point for now, and then we'll all go for coffee or something. Shoot the shit."

Grace looked towards the Stormont building. Away from Soap.

Jimmy fiddled with the leather pocket on the back of Mason's seat. "What's the point of all this, Joe?"

"You ask the best questions when you're not trying too hard, Jimmy. What *is* the point?" Soap waited a couple of seconds to allow for another interruption. None came and Soap ploughed on. "My point is, politicians are supposed to represent people. Hey, aren't you a person, Jimmy?"

"Yeah."

"That's right. And yet, you don't know what's going on at the end of this long-ass driveway, do you?"

"No."

"Doesn't that seem odd to you? I mean, have you ever had a conversation with a politician?"

"My dad knows this guy from Newry who's in Sinn Féin."

"Your dad's buddy, huh? What's he done for you?"

"He gave me money when I made my confirmation."

"Funny, I figured you for a Catholic. It's the way you look guilty all the time." Soap slapped his own thigh. "I'm kidding. Your YouTube video was the first hint. But back to the point. Other than the kind of thing any other friend of your dad's might do, has this friend of the family done anything that affected you directly?"

"I don't think so."

"And that's my point."

"Politicians don't do anything?"

"They don't do shit, Jimmy. Jack shit." Soap invaded Grace's space again to point out the window. He butted the tip of his index finger against the glass to punctuate each sentence. "Fuck the politicians. Fuck the government teat. They don't own the power. The people own it. We have to play to our strengths. We have to create."

"That's a bit aggressive, Joe," Jimmy said.

Grace nodded in agreement until Soap lowered his arm again.

"That's not aggression, Jimmy. It's a fucking mission statement. We're at the beginning of a new dawn here, kiddo. Like I said the other night, we're planning a corporate takeover.

With enough private investment we can bypass your rinky-dink politicians and start making a difference where it matters. Grace, you tell him."

"Em... yeah, Jimmy. What Joe just said pretty much encapsulates the mission statement I read, though it's a little... saltier when Joe says it like that."

"But what's it all got to do with me? I don't have a clue about out government."

"Believe it or not, Jimmy," Soap said. "But that's a good thing."

A horn blasted through the profound silence that followed Soap's words. Mason turned, his first movement since the car had stopped at the gates of Stormont, and squinted at something through the rear window.

"Looks like a garbage truck, boss. You want me to let him through?"

The bin lorry's horn sounded again, this time a little longer than last.

"Nobody should get in the way of trash removal from that pile of stone and bullshit. Am I right? Move on, Mason."

BACK IN THE SADDLE

A near-empty bottle of Bushmills – the standard white-labelled blend – stood sentry on Bridge's nightstand, right next to his Glock and his phone. The screen lit up as the handset juddered to life. Vibration mode. Bridge's tattooed arm snaked out from under the covers. He missed the phone on first, second and third grab.

"Fuck's sake." The voice was whiskey-blasted but feminine. "Answer your fucking phone, Bridge."

"All right."

"It's so loud."

"It's on silent."

"Fucking answer it."

The vibrations stopped before Bridge could get it to his ear.

"Probably for the best," Bridge said.

"Who was it?"

"Don't know." Bridge, head still covered by his blankets, set the phone back on the nightstand. "They'll call back if it's important."

The phone started to buzz again.

"For the love of fuck." Dev sat up in the bed. She clutched the blankets to her bare chest and reached over Bridge's body to snatch his mobile off the cabinet. "Unknown number."

"Good. Cut it off."

Dev killed the call and dropped the phone on the bed between them. She slumped back, closed her eyes for a few seconds then opened them again.

"I can't believe we did that," she said.

Bridge muttered through the blankets. "Believe it."

"It's not like it was even worth it."

"Cheers."

"You know what I mean. We were that pissed. I think I might have blacked out before we finished."

"I stopped when I realised you'd fallen asleep."

"Gentleman."

"Not really. I had a good aul' gawk at you while I finished myself off."

Dev pulled the blankets away from him and slapped his chest. Left a red blossom on his left pec, an almost match for the pink flowers running through his tattoo sleeve.

"You're a dirty bastard."

"Take it as a compliment, sure."

"Probably the closest I'll ever get from you, right enough."

Smiling, Bridge reached for the whiskey bottle.

"Really, Bridge?"

He twisted the cap off. "Need a cure." His grin wilted.

"We'll get a fry, then."

"Like a breakfast date?"

"Don't make it weird."

"*You're* making it weird. Trying to tell me what to do already." Bridge took a sip from the bottle. "This is what I really need."

"It's the morning after your first night before in a long time. You might be running before you learned how to walk again."

"Just taking the edge off the hangover, Dev."

"And the next one?"

Bridge shrugged and drank from the bottle again. "Let me work on this headache first, will you?"

"We've a shift later."

"Fuck off." Bridge opened his mouth, closed it, opened it again. "It was just a shag, Bridge. We're not married. You don't get to tell me what to do."

Dev rolled out of the bed. She trailed the blankets behind her and swaddled herself. Went about the bedroom and gathered her abandoned garments.

"You haven't changed a bit, Bridge."

"Is that a bad thing?"

"Fucking tragic."

Dev sat at the foot of the bed and pulled her knickers up under the blanket. She let it fall from her chest before she put on her bra. Bridge watched her broad back while she worked the straps and catches.

"Ach, don't huff, Dev."

"I'm beyond huffing, dickhead. This is the part when I realise I've been a mug again. It was a bad idea back then, and it's an even worse one now."

"At least I'm not married this time."

"Is that why you haven't phoned a taxi for me yet? Or have you it booked already?"

"We had some good times."

Dev was almost fully dressed. She turned to face Bridge while she closed her buttons. "Aye. The day your wife found out has a special place in my heart. Remember how she phoned the station about it? We almost lost our jobs."

"God, you always focus on the worst bits. Maybe if you weren't so negative all the time you'd have found somebody by now."

Dev winced. "Thanks for the advice." She spotted her jacket and snatched it from the floor in front of the wardrobe. "Do me a favour and phone in sick later, will you? I'd rather not catch sight of you for a few days."

She threw the blankets at him and left.

Bridge raised the whiskey to his mouth one more time, but stopped short. He saved the last few mouthfuls in the bottle and replaced the cap. Sat up and swung his legs over the side of the bed. He opened the drawer in his cabinet and found a crooked pre-rolled joint amongst a collection of empty pharmaceutical blister-packs. Sighed and almost smiled. Bridge sparked it up and drew deep. Then he scooped his Glock from atop the cabinet. He pushed the muzzle into the soft flesh behind his chin.

Pulled the trigger.

Click.
Empty.

Bridge put the gun back in its spot and hit his joint again. Blew a series of smoke rings and giggled. His phone buzzed again. He ignored it.

PIPE DOWN

Caroline Andrews flicked through the channels. Settled on a reality TV show for a few seconds, tutted and moved on. A few more channels attempted to woo her with their wares before she hit the red button at the top of the remote control. The radiant widescreen picture collapsed into black.

"Ugh." Caroline dropped the clicker on top of the cushion beside her. "Billy?"

Then she shook her head, smiled for a second before frowning. There was a cluster of empty cider cans by her feet. When she shifted her weight her foot toppled them like skittles.

She took a few seconds to brace herself before she got off the couch.

"Fuck's sake."

Her hand scattered the cans further away from her when she tried to pick a couple up. She swayed on unsteady legs, bent at the waist. When her knees buckled like rotted stilts, Caroline ended up on her backside.

She giggled, cried and giggle-cried.

The doorbell sounded.

Caroline stiffened. "Clark?"

She scrabbled at the couch with clawed hands until she found purchase between two seams. The doorbell clanged again.

"Hold on!" Her volume rose in direct correlation with her thickening slur. "Fuckin' wanker Wallaaath!"

Caroline bumped her backside off the laminate flooring twice more before she got her legs under her. She straightened the best she could. Wavered like a Jenga tower near the end of the game. And by some miracle, she remained upright. Her next challenge was to stay upright on her way to the door. The visitor had given up on using the doorbell and was banging with heavy fists or feet.

Caroline bumped her thigh off the arm of the sofa. She'd have gone over if the door to the hallway had been left open. As it was, her head butted the panelled wood. She performed an upright press-up against the door and fumbled with the handle.

"I'm coming." She giggled. Pulled the handle and stumbled into the short hallway. "Who's gonna come first, though, Clark?"

The doorbell started up again.

"Relax, for fugs hake."

The letterbox flap clattered against its frame.

"I'm here. Wake a dead, big bazza."

Something fell through the letterbox slot. The flap clattered once more. Caroline hunched over to get a closer look at what had just landed on her door mat.

A short, thick cylinder spat orange sparks against the wall. A fine plume of smoke snaked upwards.

"Fireworse?"

Caroline had bent too far. She toppled. Landed on her splayed hands. Crawled a little closer to the hissing length of pipe.

"Oh, shit."

Her slur had disappeared. She popped her eyes wide open.

"No, no, no."

But her sudden return to sobriety hadn't reached her legs.

The pipebomb exploded before she could gain even an inch of distance from it.

CLARK'S MARK

Dev pushed open the door to Bridge's apartment. She sniffed the air and cursed.

"Bridge? You in?"

No reply.

She stepped inside and swung the door behind her. Let it bang in the frame.

"Bridge."

Still silence.

Dev poked her head in through the doorway leading to the living room. Both it and the open-plan kitchen were in need of a good clean, especially the mirror above the mantelpiece. The glass surface had red lipstick smears and streaks all across it. But there was no sign of Bridge. She moved on down the hallway and pushed open the bedroom door. Bridge was in bed. Dev picked the bottle of Bushmills up from the bedside cabinet and knocked back the couple of mouthfuls that remained.

Bridge stirred when she clunked the thick glass base back down on the cabinet, beside an ashtray full of roaches. He opened one eye, looked at Dev and turned away from her.

"Bridge."

"Leave me alone."

"No, get up."

"I phoned in. Super was fine about it. Said I had plenty of leave carried over from last year and I could use that if I wanted to avoid adding to my sick record. Surprisingly understanding of him, like."

"You left the door unlocked again."

"No, *you* did. You were the last one to use it."

"I don't have a key."

Dev rounded the bed to get to the small window across from the door. She yanked open the curtains and blinds. Bridge pulled the pillow out from under his head and laid it across his face.

"You know where I hang the key." The pillow muffled Bridge's voice slightly. "Did you not think of slipping it back in through the letterbox after you locked up? I mean, how hungover were you earlier?"

"Don't talk about letterboxes. And how long ago do you think I left? It's tomorrow already. Today. You know what I mean."

"Nobody knows what you mean. Leave me alone. You can handle one shift without me."

"I know. Already did yesterday's, didn't I?"

Bridge sat up. The pillow landed on his lap. "It's tomorrow?"

"Aye, like the day after yesterday, which is the last time I saw you."

"Wait." Bridge whipped back the blankets.

"Fuck's sake, Bridge. Put on your boxers or something."

Bridge waved her away, but he reached for the blankets and draped a corner of cotton sheet over his crotch. Then he grabbed his phone and checked the date.

"I lost a day."

"That's not all you'll lose if you don't catch yourself on."

"Told you. The boss was sweet."

"Aye, I bet he was. And then he was probably straight onto human resources to see how he could use this against you. You're still on probation, aren't you?"

"Psychologist won't let him fire me."

"That doesn't rule out transfer, demotion, suspension… but that's not even what I'm talking about. What if someone else came to see you? Clark Wallace maybe? He already had a go at you during the riot."

"Locks don't stop Wallace. I know. When he gets around to it, he won't need to huff and puff."

"You heard, then? Why didn't you call me? The only

reason I'm here is to update you."

"Heard what?"

"How Wallace blew Billy Andrews' place down. With Caroline in it."

Bridge lifted the whiskey bottle; only noticed it was empty after he spun the lid off.

"I finished it for you." Dev said.

"I've been saving that." He reached for the ashtray and pulled out one of the roaches.

"Put it back, you dirty blurt." Bridge rested her hands on her hips. "It looks like you've sucked the life out of it anyway. Get in the shower."

"Why?"

"You smell like my wee dog before a grooming. I'm not letting you into my car 'til you wash your hole."

"I'm on leave."

"There's nothing wrong with you that a coffee and a fry wouldn't fix."

"It's not that simple."

"It's always that simple. If you want to feel better, you can." Dev pointed at the window. "All you need is out there."

"What would you know about it?"

"More than you, by the looks."

Bridge rested his head in his hands, his elbows propped up by his bare thighs. Dev shook her head, then sat down on the bed beside him. She draped an arm over his shoulders. He shrugged her half-a-hug away. Dev took a deep breath and eyed her boss for a few seconds. She wriggled out of her jacket and rolled up her shirt cuffs. Then she slipped her hand under the sheet protecting Bridge's modesty.

"You're not done, are you, Bridge? There's life in you yet."

Her hand moved under the sheet.

"Aye, there you are. Plenty of lead in the pencil."

Bridge slid his hands over his ears and interlaced them behind his neck. He straightened his spine and filled his lungs with a long inhalation. Dev's hand worked a little faster under the sheet.

"You coming, *boss*?"

"Keep this up and it won't be long." His breathing had sped up; hitched his voice.

"That's good." Dev stood up slowly, her hand still pumping under the sheet. She turned so that her backside was pointed at the doorway.

"Dev... Dev. That's a bit tight now."

"Just follow my lead. It's all good."

Dev took a step backwards. Bridge rose a few inches from the bed. His pecs and abs jerked under his tight skin. Dev moved back another step and Bridge was upright on his feet.

"That's right. Let your dick lead you, *boss*."

He didn't resist when Dev walked him into the hall. Before he really understood what was going on, Dev had taken him to the bathroom. She let go of him and nodded towards the showerhead.

"If you want me to go any further, you'll have to get washed."

"Are you serious?"

"I don't put unwashed dicks in my mouth."

Bridge was under the spray of water before it could heat up. Dev sat down on the toilet lid.

"Maybe I could have a little privacy, Dev?"

"So you can play with yourself? No way. Just hurry up."

"You're not going to suck it, are you?"

"Probably not today. We've work to do first."

"Dyke."

"Don't start that again."

"Tease, then. Whatever happened to getting to man's heart through his stomach?"

"For one, I already offered you a fry and you knocked me back. Secondly, I'm not sure you actually have a heart."

"Pass me a towel, you bitch."

She took an off-white bath sheet from the radiator and tossed it to him after he twisted the taps shut. He moved it briskly over his skin.

"Listen," Dev said. "Once we step out of this bathroom, the name-calling has to stop. And no witty banter about handjobs or blowjobs either. We've another job that's more important."

"Says you. Don't forget who's got superiority here, though."

"You're off duty." Dev pointed at the empty whiskey bottle. "And you're not to tell anybody about the boozing or the riding from the other night, got it?"

"It might be better for your reputation than you know."

"I'm not thinking about that, dopey hole. But if they find out *you're* boozing and whoring again, your headshrinker won't be long withdrawing her support."

"Lovely opinion of yourself."

"I'm just honest. You should try it some time." Dev got off the toilet lid and strode down the apartment hall towards the front door. "Get dressed and get out. I'll be in the car. No weed and no wanking. I want you clear-headed and edgy."

"Where are you taking me?"

"To find Clark Wallace. The pipebomb that ripped Caroline Andrews to shreds? The nails and the casing were speckled with melted plastic, and I don't mean Semtex. Understand? The nails weren't bundled together with tape or string. They'd been slotted into corrugated plastic grooves. Corriflute. Our Clark's signature."

THE FIRST EPISODE

Jimmy and Grace trudged down the Falls Road, heads bowed as if they were checking the pavement for hazards. They wore long overcoats that flapped around the backs of their legs like black flags.

"Okay, guys." The voice broke like it wasn't quite done with puberty. "Stop there for me, please."

Jimmy and Grace turned to look at their crew; three teenagers, armed with a notebook, a boom mic and a small video camera.

The kid with the crackly voice and the notebook shouted to them again. "We're going to take a side profile shot to get the murals in the background. We'll have to do it from the other side of the road. Can you go back ten steps and start walking when I say action?"

Grace turned 180 degrees and started walking backwards immediately.

"No, sorry, Grace. I meant for you to go back the way you came."

She gave the teenager the thumbs-up then leaned towards Jimmy and pitched her voice for his ears only. "Jesus, it's so easy to wind these eejits up."

"I know. Very funny." Jimmy licked his lips. "Could you stop, though? It's just making everything take longer and I'm wild bored here."

"How can you be bored when you're with me?"

"I... uh."

Grace swatted his shoulder. "I'm only messing. Come on. Let's get back to our marks before the *director* loses his shit."

"Is this a bit of a step down for you, then?"

"Ach, not really. It's just different. And I think I'm still a bit pissed that Soap wouldn't take Andy on. I mean, he was crap at his job and all, but we had a good dynamic."

"What was that all about anyway?"

"Soap said he didn't have room in his budget for a pro, so we get these fucking schoolboys instead."

"They're not being paid?"

"Only in exposure." Grace said. "Like a plumber fixing toilets for free to further their career, you know?"

"So they get nothing for this?"

"Well, they're going to use the documentary as a project for their media studies class or something. They seem happy enough to be telling me what to do as well."

"Still, seems a wee bit unfair."

"You could always throw them a few quid, Jimmy."

"Fuck that. Soap hasn't paid me yet."

"Aye, thought so."

The director's voice managed to overcome the revving engine of a black taxi. "Action, guys!"

Grace sucked in her cheeks and nudged Jimmy. "Ask him what we're supposed to do."

"He just wants us to walk down the road, like."

"Go on. Just for the *craic*."

Jimmy's overcoat couldn't hide the exaggerated hunch of his shoulders. He wasn't into it, but he played Grace's game. "What do you want us to do?"

The director's first response was spat through his upper teeth but a passing bus carried it away. He tried again.

"Cut!"

The cameraman lowered his lens. Temporarily off duty, the soundman leaned into the boom mic pole to prop himself up from the footpath. Exhaustion or boredom; could have been either.

The director crossed the road, jogging to avoid death by angry driver.

"Guys, I thought I explained it to you?"

Grace nibbled on her index finger and gave him the Disney Princess eyes. "We weren't sure if we were meant to act like we were talking or just keep looking at the ground."

"Just walk past the murals."

"Shouldn't we look at them at least? Or stop in front of one of them? Maybe the George Bush one would be good. A little hat-tip to our American leader."

"Please, just walk past the murals."

"Are you sure?"

"Jimmy?" The director pleaded silently, his countenance puppy-like. "You get it, don't you?"

Grace took a very short sidestep towards Jimmy. Her intent wasn't lost on him. They were on the same team. Jimmy played.

"It just seems a bit weird, two people walking along the Falls, not talking to each other. Look at these guys, like."

Jimmy pointed to a cluster of prepubescent boys in a black school uniform. The majority of them wore hoodies under their blazers. They all ate out of white paper bags. Sausage rolls, bacon and cheese jambons, other stodgy pastry delights. Fat wrapped in fat. One of them took their face out of their feedbag long enough to spot the camera. Like a good meerkat, he informed the others immediately.

The teen director had enough experience under his belt to react appropriately.

"Ah, fuck. Hold on." He cupped his hands at either side of his mouth, megaphone-style. "Lads, come over here. Quick."

Cameraman and soundman weren't quick enough to react. The school kids upped their pace and a sudden burst of traffic prevented the crew from crossing the wide lanes. They weren't going to make it.

"This place is a fucking nightmare," the director said.

"It's a bit rough, all right," Jimmy said.

Grace nudged Jimmy again. "Bet you prefer the south, eh?"

"South Belfast or South Down?" Jimmy asked.

"Either would suit me right now." The director's uneven voice carried a little extra world-weariness. "I better go help these two. Just wait here."

The director's seeming lack of disregard for his own mortality helped him across the busy road in seconds. He joined the soundman in a tug-o-war for the boom mic against a trio of schoolboys who seemed to be auditioning for a TV talent show into the black furry end. Three more of the high-energy tortures were clowning about for the camera. The cameraman smiled as if he enjoyed it.

"We've been waiting all day," Jimmy said. "TV's definitely not what it's cracked up to be."

"This is pretty good, though." Grace aimed her phone at the impish chaos across the road from them. Their mischief played out in duplicate on the screen.

"It'll pass some time, I suppose."

"Helps us to test our crew's mettle as well."

"Yeah, I suppose."

"We need to be able to rely on them for the more challenging shoots."

"Yeah."

"Because we've that riot scheduled later in the week as well."

"Yeah." Jimmy pulled his attention from across the street and laid it on Grace. "Wait. What?"

"Well, not so much a riot as a skirmish. One of those organised fights that are so hot at the moment."

"I'm still not with you."

Grace tutted and turned off the camera on her phone. "Do you never watch the news, Jimmy? Or read a newspaper."

"No. Never. I get my news off Facebook, mostly."

"Oh, sweet Jesus. The future's bright."

"The future's Orange."

"That's actually quite clever, considering."

"Considering what?"

"That your head's up your hole."

Jimmy looked at his Converse. "Bit harsh."

"Don't be a baby."

Grace gave Jimmy an awkward, one-armed hug. His spine straightened and his mouth twitched.

"We friends?" Grace asked.

Jimmy tried to make eye contact with the journalist. Failed. "I hope so."

"Good. Friends give each other a hard time. Don't be so sensitive."

"Okay."

"And pay attention when Soap's chatting to us. I know you were there when he came up with the plans for the big set-piece."

"But he never stops talking."

Grace laughed so hard and loud that even the torturers and the tortured from across the street stopped to watch her. She touched Jimmy's elbow. The schoolboys cheered and pointed. One of them yelled:

"He's getting the ride the night."

"Sorry about that," Jimmy said.

Grace breathed through her final chuckle. "You didn't say it. And I've heard a hell of a lot worse."

"How does Soap know where and when these kids are going to fight during the week?"

"He helped orchestrate it. On WhatsApp or something like that."

"And you're okay with that?"

Grace shrugged. "I don't know yet. But I want to see what happens. Don't you?"

"Not really. Somebody could get hurt."

"Hopefully."

Jimmy opened his mouth to say something else. Grace held up her hand. "Hold on. Looks like the wee messers are heading on."

Across the street, the school boys had moved a little up the road. The crew busied themselves checking that their equipment still worked.

Grace waved to catch the director's attention then

cupped her hands around her mouth before she called out to him. "What do you want us to do now?"

"Hold on, I'm coming over."

"Right, we better stop messing," Grace said to Jimmy. "We'll talk more later on."

"About Soap's mini riot?"

"Don't call it that, but yeah."

"Can't wait."

"Sarky wee shite."

"All right, you two?" The director huffed and puffed to recover from his sprint across the road. "Sorry about that. I hope it doesn't affect your chemistry. You guys look great together."

Jimmy rubbed the back of his neck. "Do you think so?"

"Ach, wise up, Jimmy," Grace said. "That's just director speak. He's good at it, though."

"Oh." Jimmy kicked a Red Bull tin onto the road. "Okay."

"He fucked my wife, and he killed her."

Billy Andrews thumped the tabletop. The portable voice recorder bounced. Bridge and Dev sat opposite the angry widower. Dev turned to her superior. She wanted direction. He shook his head and she relaxed her own clenched fists. They let Billy take his emotions out on the table for a little longer.

Each word came with a hammer blow to the table's wood veneer. "Fucker. Bastard. Cunt. Ballbag. Fucking, bastarding, cunting, ballbag!"

"Okay, Billy," Bridge said, his voice stern and loud. "You're going to have to take a few breaths for us."

"That's right." Dev's voice was softer. Kinder. "We're going nowhere fast here and we should be out trying to catch whoever did this to Caroline."

Billy's eyes blazed through held-back tears. "Then get out. Go. It was Clark. Clark Wallace. What else do you need to know? If I could find out where he was, I'd draw you a map."

"How can you know for sure that it was Clark?" Bridge asked. "You've been in custody since the riot."

"Fuck's sake. There's nothing but time in here. You hear things."

Bridge opened his hands to invite more detail. "So what's the gossip?"

"Women gossip." Billy eyeballed Dev. "Men share information."

"Maybe you can tell me and DS Devenney about the information you've gathered on Clark Wallace and his alleged affair with your wife?"

"Nothing alleged about it. Soon as I got scooped he was sniffing around my Caroline like a dog with two stiffies. He was seen going into *my* house more than once."

"Did he stay overnight?" Dev asked.

"No, but he was always there long enough to get what he wanted."

Bridge scratched his beard. "If he was having an affair with your wife, why would he decide to kill her?"

"Because I was stupid enough to send word out that I was after him."

"You threatened big Clark Wallace?" Bridge didn't laugh, or even smile, but he couldn't keep the twinkle out of his eye. "Was that wise?"

"Doesn't matter what size you are. Nothing you can do about a bullet in the back of the head." Billy finally caught himself on. "Not that I have access to a gun or anything. It was just words said in anger. And they got back to him. So, no. It wasn't wise. Not one bit."

Somebody knocked the interview room door. Dev got up and answered it. A uniform leaned in, his voice low but still easily heard in the silence he'd caused.

"Mister Andrews' lawyer is here."

"Dead on," Dev said.

"He wants some time alone with his client."

"No problem. Will you grab the recorder, Bridge?"

Bridge got up and did as Dev asked. Then, with his back positioned to obscure his colleagues' view, he slid a thin envelope towards Billy. Bridge met Dev and the uniform by the door after Billy tucked the envelope down the front of his trousers.

"When did we start calling them lawyers instead of solicitors?" Bridge asked. "Bit American, isn't it?"

He didn't get an answer.

"We'll be in the canteen," Dev said to the uniform. "Come and get us when the solicitor is ready."

"Yes, ma'am."

"Thank you," Bridge said when the uniform was out of earshot.

Dev scowled. "For what?"

"No, not thank *you*. I mean, you didn't say thanks to that officer. It's that sort of attitude that makes people think you're hard to work with."

"You've been very generous with your career advice lately. Are you grooming me for anything in particular?"

"Nevermind. Canteen time. You're buying."

They took the stairs two at a time. Dev was a little out of breath when they got to the landing.

"You skipping your cardio workouts again, Dev?"

"What's cardio?"

Dev shoved the canteen door opened. It narrowly missed Liz, who stood about an inch outside of the arc with a copy of The Sun tucked under her arm.

"Sorry, Liz. Didn't see you there. You all right?"

"Fuck's sake. You scared the heart out of me."

"Sorry. This one was winding me up."

"Well wait 'til his eyes are back to normal and blacken them again. Leave me out of it."

Dev looked from Bridge to Lizzie. "Again?"

"We were just going to get a coffee, Liz," Bridge said.

"Machine's broke. Waiting for the man to come out for it. Youse can have a Coke out of the fridge or make yourselves some instant. Leave the money by the till. I'm away out for a smoke."

"You throwing that paper away?"

"Aye, I've it read. Thought I'd get rid of it before I offended anybody."

Liz looked Dev up and down, creased her face into a sarcastic smile for an instant, and left them to look after themselves.

Dev watched the door swing shut before she spoke. "What was that all about?"

"She must be having a bad day. Don't worry about it."

"Think I'll start taking a packed lunch and a thermos in. That wee woman's a witch."

"Forget about it. We've more important stuff to talk

about. Like Clark Wallace."

Dev took a Diet Coke from the glass-door refrigerator. Bridge picked a bottle of water. They took a seat at the table farthest from the door.

"Wallace'll be lifted before the day's out," Dev said.

"Confident. What if he did a runner after he took out Caroline?"

"We'll still get him. It's just a waiting game now. Any word on the Holylands murder?"

"No. They're still looking for Jimmy McAuley. He seems to have done a midnight flit."

"He's a student, right? Maybe he's gone back to his ma's."

"Funny you should say that. I've been on the phone to her. She said she hadn't heard from him in a few weeks and she's not one bit surprised after the embarrassment he caused the family with that video."

"Is she not worried about him?"

"Apparently he has a habit of losing touch for a few weeks." Bridge said. "It's been a regular thing since he started uni. He likes to party, I suppose."

"Why am I only hearing about this now?"

"We've been busy."

"Busy... Right."

"It's been a while since I checked in with Missus McAuley, though. Might be worth another try. See if he's checked in or anything."

"You don't fancy him for it, do you? He doesn't look like much in the video. Not sure he'd have the strength to strangle somebody barehanded."

"No. When I saw him in the hospital I noticed he had these long, skinny fingers, like a piano player or a magician or something. And the way he lost the bap at the riot...? Spouting all that fascist nonsense that would embarrass a typical idealist student. No idea how to handle his adrenalin. I'd say it was the first time he'd ever been in a fight. It scared the shite out of him."

"Have you got a theory, then?"

"Clark Wallace had it in for him. Blamed the kid for Vic's messy end. Even knew his address."

"Again, how long have you known this?"

"Since the day Clark Wallace walked away from the station without being arrested. If we'd lifted him then we wouldn't be dealing with two more murders on top of Vic's. And now he's off the grid. A ghost."

"Fucking bogeyman, more like." Dev twisted the cap off her Diet Coke. "Maybe if you let me in on some of this stuff, I could have backed you up on that call. Just because you've thought of it, doesn't mean we all know it to be true. You have to talk us through these things, Bridge. Or start small and share the odd thought with *me* at the very least."

"Right."

"That's it?"

"I don't know what else you want."

"Don't know or don't care?"

"Could we stay on point, DS?"

Dev took a long glug from her Diet Coke bottle. She burped quietly and set the fizzy drink down. Stared at Bridge for a ten-count. Breathed.

"What next, then, DI?"

"I think I might go back on the sick."

"Aye, your ma."

"I'm serious."

Dev picked up the Diet Coke, sipped at it in an almost ladylike manner then replaced the twist-off cap. She took a deep breath before she spoke.

"Fuck you, Tommy Bridge."

Bridge watched the canteen door close behind her. He folded his arms and sat back. Allowed his head to tilt so that he looked up at the ceiling. When the door reopened he jerked to stiff-backed attention. It was Liz.

"What's going on with you two now?" Liz asked. "The mad bitch near knocked me down again. I was on the stairs, like."

"When did you stop taking the lift?"

"We're waiting on a man to fix that too."

"Fuck's sake. It's just falling down around our ears, isn't it?"

"The station?"

"Aye. And everything else."

"Oh." Liz smirked. "That's what's wrong with her, then. Lover's tiff? She's not a lesbo at all, is she?"

Bridge got up and tucked his chair back under the table. He picked up his water bottle, closed it and tucked it under his arm before he answered the canteen lady.

"She's gayer that a rainbow, Liz. Hopeless cause. Wouldn't even consider praying away the gay."

"You can't fool me, Tommy. You're just saying that because she knocked you back. Amn't I right?"

Bridge tipped her a wink that wouldn't have looked out of place in a *Carry On* movie. "No fooling you, is there?"

"You want a fry on?"

"No thanks, Liz. I'm away on out. No rest for the wicked, what?"

"Isn't that the sad truth? Take care of yourself."

"Nobody else will."

Bridge whistled an off-key tune on his way out the door.

CUT THE SHIT

Grace and Jimmy sat with their young director. The three of them faced a pair of computer monitors on a long desk that supported a bank of computers. Jimmy and the director stared hard at the flickering of a video in play. Grace leaned back a little and rolled her green eyes. They were slick with tears following a long yawn, and the shiny film highlighted the vibrant colour of her irises in contrast to her dark hair and swarthy Black Irish skin.

"Grace, you look terrific in this," Jimmy said.

"You sound surprised."

"No, Jesus, not at all." He averted his attention from the monitor to face the journalist. His gaze landed on hers a little longer than it should have. "It's just that you're taking the bad look off me, you know? Appreciate it." He nudged the director. "And thank you for making the best of my good side." He stroked the stitches on the left side of his face.

"Are you happy with it, Grace?" the director asked.

"You're the director, Ronan. Just do what you think is right and I'm sure it'll all turn out great."

Young Ronan's face flooded with blood and his usually pale skin burned bright. "You've no idea how much that means."

"Aye, yeah," Grace said. "Excuse me a wee minute. I've a call to make."

The lads got back to discussing the footage on the screens. A scene featuring a talking head shot with Jimmy doing his best to look serious made them both laugh. Grace let the classroom/studio door swing shut behind her. She was alone in the corridor. Drifted towards a dirty window while she worked her phone. Her call connected.

"Harry, it's me." A beat. "Yeah, Grace."

She used her finger to draw a line through the grimy

glass in front of her.

"This Soap guy is some *craic*."

The line became a V.

"Did you read through the copy of the mission statement I sent you?"

She closed off the top of the V with a pair of bumps to form a cartoon heart.

"That's what I thought. He'll be one to watch all right. And he's got himself a wee grasshopper in the shape of Jimmy 'the YouTube star' McAuley. Poor kid. Soap's setting him up as the subject of a short documentary. Only it's not a short documentary at all. Judging by the script, it's a long commercial for Soap's security company." A pause. "The Agency. Registered in the British Virgin Islands."

An arrow head was added to one side of the heart.

"Ach, I'll pull Jimmy to one side if I think he's getting in too deep. He's not a bad wee lad. Just gormless. But sure we all were at that age, right?"

She aligned the feathered end of the arrow on the other side of the heart.

"Well, you must have been special then, Harry. Do me a favour and let me know what gets dug up on his background, ASAP. He's telling me as little as he can get away with about his previous 'projects' and I don't mind telling you, that makes me a bit nervous. I can't even get his real name out of him."

Grace swiped the edge of her hand through the schoolgirl doodle on the window pane.

"No, it didn't work. I'm not a hundred percent sure if it's just me or the whole gender, but my powers of flirtation seem to have no effect on the man."

She peered through the window.

"Not all gay men are flamboyant, like."

Grace faked a laugh.

"Fuck you, Harry."

She turned her back on the streaky glass.

"No, I'll leave you alone until you come back to me

with something on Soap. He could be for real or he could be a global snake oil salesman. Either way, his ideas are definitely going to make for quite a story." She paused. "Of course, if he's on the level and he actually pays me what he claims he can, you might get my letter of resignation before you get my copy."

Grace grinned.

"No, I'm not joking. Unless you want to talk about a pay rise, like. It's been a while."

She jerked the phone from her ear. Eyeballed the screen. "Fuck you, then."

Two swipes of her thumb later, she was on a second call. This one shorter, if no sweeter.

"Andy. I know you've gotten my texts. And I know you'll get this message too. Just know that I know that. Get out of bed and get your arse down here. I promised these wee fellahs you'd be down to check out their camera work today. It's terrible, but don't be a prick. We need them. And the director's cut we talked about doesn't need to look pro. Might even work better if it isn't. So, yeah. Hurry up or I'll find out who your new girlfriend is and tell her that we're having our fourth abortion this week. See what that does to your honeymoon period."

She hung up.

Jimmy opened the studio/classroom door as Grace tucked her phone back into her handbag.

"You sorted, Grace?"

She nodded. Zipped her bag.

"Ronan wants you to take a look at your talking head bit now that he's trimmed it."

"Ach, Jimmy. My tailbone's killing me. Sitting on that plastic chair isn't helping." She pushed out her lower lip and shifted a strand of black hair from her face with a quick puff. "I told him I'd sign off on whatever. Does he need me to tell him again?"

Jimmy lowered his voice. "I think he's just proud of himself, Grace. Throw the wee guy a bone, will you? He's not the worst."

"Fine, I'll scratch the puppy's tummy and tell him he's a good boy."

"It'd mean the world to him. He's a fan."

"He wants to shag me, you mean."

"Probably that too, like. He's only human."

That got her a little choked up with laughter. Jimmy looked like he'd been chosen by the winning team in the midst of the Rapture. Their moment was interrupted by the sound of Grace's phone.

"Your handbag's ringing," Jimmy said.

"Aye. It's probably my baby-dada."

"You have kids?"

Grace grinned and shook her head. "No, I'm only kidding. It'll be Andy looking to apologise for keeping Ronan and his mates waiting. I'd just texted him a wee reminder."

The phone rang off.

"That makes more sense. Couldn't imagine you two together."

"No way. I wouldn't touch that dirty stop-out with yours."

"With mine? Do you know what that means, Grace?"

"Of course I do. Don't be a *craic* vacuum."

"Are you going to phone him back?"

"Andy? No, I'd say I gave him a wee jolt with my message. He'll move faster if he thinks I was serious."

"You're kind of mean sometimes, Grace."

"Just sometimes? I thought you knew me better than that, Jimmy."

She stood on her toes and kissed his cheek before her cracked coccyx waddled ever-so-slightly back into the studio/classroom. Jimmy rubbed his cheek.

"I wish you'd let me get to know you better," he said.

SCOOPED

Clark Wallace reached across the bar and placed an empty pint glass under a Harp pump. He pushed on the handle and poured a pint that was fifty percent head. The barman looked on as Clark took his first sip. He didn't complain. Clark licked froth off his upper lip then turned – pint glass in hand – so that he could lean back and prop his elbows on the bartop. All that he surveyed was a clutter of unoccupied table and chairs.

"Quiet here today, Freddie."

"It's quiet here most days, Clark. That's why I struggle to pay you at the end of the month."

"Aye, I'm hearing that from a lot of the landlords in the area. But they all find the cash somewhere in the end."

"Except for Max Jenkins."

"And may the useless cunt rest in pieces." Clark looked over his shoulder to wink at the twitchy barman. "Pour me a big brandy there, will you? Don't bother measuring it. Just be generous."

"I've to go get a fresh bottle, then."

"Work away, Freddie. I'll look after the place. Isn't that what you pay me for?"

"Aye, good one, Clark." Freddie didn't look all that amused, though.

While Freddie was away, Clark took a heroic gulp of his frothy lager and refilled the glass as he had before. This time the head grew to two thirds of the pint. He set the glass on a soggy beermat and flipped the counter flap open. On the other side of the bar he punched a button on the till and the drawer sprang open. He dipped in and withdrew a thin wedge of notes. Tucked them into the pocket of his trackie bottoms and returned to his spot on the patron side of the bar. He left the drawer and the flap open.

When Freddie returned with the Brandy he quietly put to rights the signs of intrusion. Again, he didn't dare complain.

"Needed to make a quick transaction there, Freddie. Hope you don't mind."

"Not at all. Just tell us how much and I'll take it off the total for the end of the month."

"Aye, good one, mate. You pouring that fucking drink or what?"

"Might have one myself, if you don't mind?"

"Fire away there, Freddie. Sure there's nobody else here to drink with. Could use the company."

Freddie free poured into two cloudy snifters and slid the larger one towards Clark.

"Will we take a seat?" Freddie asked.

"Aye. Bring the bottle."

Clark re-foamed his beer then carried it and the brandy to the little round table closest to the door. He plonked the glasses down on the tabletop and moved a stool so that he could sit facing the entrance. His knees didn't fit under the table so he scooted back a couple of inches. The drinks were still within easy reach. He downed the brandy and licked a little foam from the top of his pint.

"I should probably teach you how to do that right." Freddie nodded at Clark's Harp just before he sat down opposite the big fellah. He refilled the empty brandy balloon.

"I like it like this. It's the way they do it in Germany, and they know a thing or two about beer, them fuckers."

"That right?" Freddie took a sip of brandy, held it in his mouth for a few seconds and swallowed. "Each to their own, then."

"Fucking right. Met this Nazi one time and asked him why they did it like that. He said it released the smell of the hops and helped keep it fizzy."

"Was he really a Nazi?"

"Yeah. Shaved head, swastika tattoos, eighties fashion sense. The works. He was over to visit Johnny Adair. Hadn't heard the Mad Dog had scooted across the water with his tail between his legs."

"Was he raging?" Freddie glanced over his shoulder at the door.

"You expecting somebody?"

"Em… Not really. Hoping for some customers, just."

"Stop trying to make me feel sorry for you."

"I'm not, Clark. It's just… you know. You asked me, like."

"Don't mention business one more time." Clark downed his brandy again. "And fill 'er up."

Freddie did as he was bid.

"What happened then?" Freddie asked. "With the Nazi, I mean."

Clark tapped his empty brandy glass. "*Fill* that up."

Freddie added enough brandy to take the contents to the rim. Clark bent forward and sucked a half inch from the balloon before he raised it from the table.

"The Nazi…" Clark sniffed the snifter. "Do you know, I've dealt with a Jew or three in my time."

"That right?"

"Aye. And I never had one of them annoy me. For all the jokes about them being as stingy as the Scotch, they never held back from me. Jews with businesses understand economics. They know that some expenses are unavoidable. Unaccountable one of them called me once. My favourite one. He had this big grey beard like a dirty, fenian blanketman. Never a good word to say about anybody. But he paid his bills and he called me unaccountable. Like he couldn't put me on his books, do you get it?"

"Very good, Clark."

"I know it is. So fucking tell your face, Freddie." Clark slurped on the Brandy, chugged a few inches of lager and got up for another trip to the bar. He topped up the pint glass from the same awkward position as before. Spoke to Freddie over his shoulder. "So, anyway. Never had a Jew annoy me. That there

Nazi, though. Fuck me, he was a pest."

"What did he do?"

"It's not important, Freddie. A fly comes buzzing in your ear, do you consider its actions, or do you swat it?"

"I hit it with a newspaper or something. Hate touching those dirty things."

"There you go, then."

"So you killed him."

"Jesus, Freddie. Do I need to spell everything out?"

The front door swung open and daylight invaded. Hot on its heels came Dev, her sturdy frame stuffed into a new pinstripe suit, and a uniformed officer who stood a little taller than the DS. Both of them had to tilt their heads back to pass a dirty look to Clark. He was still at the bar, his lager glass somehow surviving his white-knuckled grip.

Dev nodded at the pint. "You want a flake in that, Clarky?"

"Fuck you, big tits."

"Aw, now. If you think my tits are big, you should see my balls." Dev turned to her accompanying officer. "Constable Prescott, could you do the needful, please?"

"Can't wait, DS." Prescott moved towards Clark, a pair of handcuffs in hand. His bushy moustache twitched.

Clark shook his head. "You'll need more than those bracelets, cunt-stable."

"You're grand, Reggie." Dev snaked a hand under a lapel and produced her Glock. "Give me a reason, Clark."

"You'd have his blood on your hands?"

"No, Clark. Just yours."

"Put down the glass, please." Prescott had stopped just outside of long-legged kicking distance. "You're under arrest."

"Full blown arrest, is it?"

"Clark, put down the beer." Dev's voice was firm, though a touch higher in pitch. "Right now."

"Down the beer?" Clark raised his foamy lager to his lips. "Don't mind if I do."

"DS?" DC Reggie Prescott looked away from Clark for a second.

Clark made his move.

Prescott howled. His upper body jerked away from Clark. He dropped the cuffs and raised a hand to the side of his face. It came back wet. With lager. Clark giggled. He placed his empty glass on the bar, base up.

"You tipped them off, didn't you, Freddie?"

Freddie snatched his hand back from the neck of the brandy bottle. His cheeks filled up; puffed out like a greedy squirrel's. He turned his head to the side and let a stream of vomit fall to the dirty floor. Dev sidestepped away from the barman. Her bead on Clark barely wavered.

Wide-eyed, Freddie wiped puke from his lips with his bare forearm. "Swear to god, Clark. I did not."

Clark held his wrists out to Prescott. The uniformed cop's hand went to his belt automatically and found the empty pouch where his handcuffs should have been. Clark looked beyond Prescott when he squatted to retrieve his cuffs from the lager-spattered patch of worn tiles.

"You had me on your side, wee man." He let Prescott cuff him but kept his stare focussed on the landlord. "Like the Jews tell the Nazis, Freddie, never again."

HOTEL PARANOIA

"Can I pay for this with a credit card?"

The hotel employee looked down on Bridge, slouched on a lobby sofa. She placed the cup on the table in front of him, bending low to prevent the steaming contents from splashing over the rim. Bridge averted his gaze from her impressive cleavage.

"You want to put your coffee on a card, sir?"

"It's Inspector Bridge, not sir. And yes. The coffee… if you could charge it to my Visa, that'd be lovely. I'd like a receipt too."

"No problem at all, Inspector."

"If there's any extra charge, make sure it shows up on the receipt."

"I'll be back with the chip and pin machine, Inspector."

"Cheers. No rush."

She turned her back on him and Bridge watched her metronomic swish. Her journey back to the bar was far from rushed. Bridge plucked a foil-wrapped treat from the edge of the saucer and left it on the low table. He shuffled through three newspapers, neatly arranged on the tabletop. Found nothing of interest and laid them in a fan with their headers on clear display. He blew on the surface of his coffee and sipped.

"Are you here to see me?" Jimmy McAuley flopped onto the sofa opposite Bridge's.

Bridge barely reacted. "They actually *did* phone your room, then?"

"Yeah."

"Half an hour ago?"

"I was in the shower." Jimmy patted his shiny quiff then stoked the sprouting hairs on his undamaged cheek. "Only got the call after I got out. They didn't tell me if they'd tried more than once."

"Do you know why I'm here?"

"I think so." Jimmy yawned. "No idea how you found me, though."

"Your mother told me."

The younger man sat up straight. "You've been talking to Mum?"

"We'll get back to that. You really should phone her more often, though."

Jimmy attempted to chuckle. "You sound like my aul' fellah."

"Aye? Never got talking to him now. Maybe we'd get on well."

Jimmy prodded his stitches. "Probably. He's a solicitor, so, you know, same sort of job, like." He looked to the bar. It was unmanned. "I could use a pint."

"It's only lunch time. On a Tuesday. Your mother told me you'd started a new job."

"Day off."

"Already?"

"It's kind of like shift work."

"We'll get back to that too." Bridge took his little black notebook from his breast pocket. He licked the nib of his pencil before scrawling across a page.

"Why are you writing that down?"

"Desperate memory, just. Nothing to worry about."

"Said the undercover cop."

"I'm plain clothes."

Jimmy looked to the bar again. "Still a cop."

"You're acting guilty and I haven't even accused you of anything."

"Not guilty. Just confused."

"We'll start again, then." Bridge scribbled in the notebook again. The sketchy results bore no relation to any kind of handwriting. "Do you know why I'm here?"

"Because I forgot to call you about this." Jimmy pointed

to the stitches on the left side of his face.

"You're healing nicely, lad. But are you serious?"

"Why else would you be here?"

"Did you know Stephen Swain?"

"Em."

"A lot of people called him Squinty Steve."

"Steve?" He lowered his voice, leant forward. "You said you weren't interested in the weed thing."

"It's not about the weed."

"Because I never sold any. I never would."

"Nobody said anything about weed except for you."

"But *you* mentioned Steve."

"When was the last time you saw Stephen Swain?"

"Steve."

Bridge tapped his notebook with the point of his pencil.

"Aye."

"I've lost count of the days, to be honest. But it was before... you know."

"I don't know. Before Christ?"

"Before I got my new job."

Bridge made an X in the corner of the page he'd been working on. Jimmy watched as he flipped the half-blank sheet over and started on a fresh one. Bridge noted the date and time. Jimmy's leg started bouncing.

"Jimmy?"

"Yeah?"

Bridge softened his voice. "Have you phoned Steve lately?"

"No, man." Jimmy shifted his weight to his left buttock and straightened his right leg. He struggled to drag his phone from the pocket of his skinny jeans. "I got a new one but I couldn't get my contacts off the old one."

"Because you lost it at the riot."

"Jesus, did I tell you that at the hospital? I thought you said your memory was crap."

Bridge tapped the side of his head with the end of his

pencil. "It's a short term memory thing."

"Hah. Like a stoner?"

Bridge's face didn't even twitch.

"Sorry. Just a joke, like. I'm not obsessed with cannabis or anything."

"And yet, you keep talking about it." Bridge closed his notebook. He nodded towards the empty bar. "Maybe if we sit up there you can get your pint quicker."

"I don't mind waiting."

"I do."

Service

Joe Soap adjusted Max Mason's crooked tie. After a couple of tweaks it was less crooked. He patted Mason's pecs and stepped back. Tilted his head to the side.

"Who taught you to knot a tie, Mason?"

"Mutha."

"Your mom?"

"That's what I said."

"If I may be so bold, perhaps you should ask a man to teach you."

Mason's boxy cheeks reddened. "I prefer a woman's touch, Mister Soap."

"Relax big guy. You're not my type. I like 'em young and pretty." Soap's own tie hung across his neck, open. He swept back his platinum hair before he got to work on the red silk strip. "Watch me."

Mason obeyed and Soap manipulated his tie like a talented magician with an elusive handkerchief. He knotted it into a Windsor without hesitation. After a quick hair and collar check in a large wall-mounted mirror, he was ready for the suit jacket. Mason held it up for him.

"You see that?"

"I saw it," Mason said. "Sure. Now, do you want to see Jimmy?"

"He's here?" Soap adjusted the hang of his jacket with a series of shrugs and shoulder rolls. He blew into the cupped palm of his hand and sniffed the collected breath.

"Yeah. Downstairs."

"Drinking?"

"Worse. He's talking to a cop."

"How do you know?"

"It's my job to know."

"Touché." Soap spent a little longer at the mirror. Checked his teeth. "What's the cop's name?"

"DI Tommy Bridge. I called HQ to see if they knew anything about him. He applied for a security position at The Agency a few times over the last year. His less than exemplary record with the PSNI put off the recruiters."

"Let's join them."

Mason followed Soap at his customary distance, just short of kicking Soap's Achilles tendons. Soap stepped to the side and waited for his man to push the 'elevator' call button. They descended in silence and Soap led the way when the doors pinged open. He spotted Jimmy and his companion at the end of the bar, both of them standing. Jimmy red-eyed and solemn.

"Jimmy?"

The student jerked to attention. He forced a smile after a guilty sideward glance at his bottle of Corona. There was a wedge of lime beside it on the bar.

"Mister Soap. I mean, Joe. How are you?"

"You seem surprised to see me, Jimmy. Who's your friend?"

The cop turned to face Soap. He raised his whiskey glass. "Detective Inspector Tommy Bridge."

"A detective *and* an inspector? Fancy. Are you on duty?" Soap indicated the whiskey with a nod.

Bridge made a show of checking the time on his chunky wristwatch. "Not right now."

"Nice timepiece," Soap said.

"It's a fake."

"A passable one. And at least you're not reading the time off your goddamn phone like the rest of the world."

Bridge eyed Soap's wrist. "That'll be the real thing weighing your left side down, then?"

"Yes. I collect them."

"A slave to time, Mister Soap?"

"I'm a slave to nothing. And since you're off the clock…" Soap slapped the bar. "Can we get some service here?"

"You have a two o'clock, Mister Soap," Mason said.

"You go ahead of me, Max. I'll get a taxi. Might be half an hour late. Tell them I'm with someone who thinks they're important. One of those terrorist-politicians."

Bridge made a noise that could have developed into laughter. He opted to drown it in whiskey instead.

Mason didn't question his boss any further. He looked at each of the other three men in turn, not so much acknowledging them, but rather studying their faces as if committing their features to memory. His attention was held by Bridge's hound dog eyes for an extra beat.

"Detective." Mason's parting word was accompanied by a slight pursing of the lips.

"Inspector, actually." Bridge tilted his glass towards Mason. "See you later."

Mason didn't commit either way. He left.

"Your bodyguard is some *craic*, what?"

"He's more than a bodyguard."

"Secretary as well?"

"Sort of."

"Talented big bastard, then."

"You have no idea, Inspector."

"Hah. You have to love that accent, right Jimmy? 'You have no idea.' Say that like one of us and it sounds like an insult."

Jimmy sniffed. It sounded watery. "I suppose."

"What's wrong, Jimmy?" Soap moved a little closer, edged Bridge away. He clapped a hand on Jimmy's shoulder. "You look upset."

"My... my friend died."

"Oh my God," Soap said.

Jimmy glanced at Bridge. "*Gawd.*"

It sounded nothing like Soap, but Bridge gave the student an actual smile. Soap missed the moment. He'd spotted a hotel employee. The same one who'd served Bridge his coffee. Soap tried to catch her attention with a wave. She raised a finger to let him know he was on her to-do list.

"Jesus, service sucks in this country."

"Aye," Bridge said. "It'd be different if they worked for tips."

Soap pushed a hand through his blond hair. "They'd be skinnier for a start."

"I like a bit of meat on a woman," Bridge said.

"We could get a drink quicker in my room," Soap said.

"Do you think…?" Jimmy checked the time on his phone. "Ah, here. I told my parents I'd be home today. And I should go see Steve. Or, you know… his grave." He dry retched. "Excuse me."

Jimmy hurried away from the bar, moved towards the lifts with his hand pressed against his lips, paused, turned 180 degrees and spotted a subtle clear-plastic sign with the universal symbols for toilets – the man, the woman and the wheelchair – imprinted in burnished gold. He jogged in that direction, his shoulders hunched.

"Poor kid," Soap said.

"Aye. Hurts to lose somebody. Even your weed dealer."

"You just threw that out there, huh?" Soap waved at the distant hotel employee again, his movements jerkier than last time. "Trying to shock me?"

"Maybe so."

"It'd take more than that. I have a medical marijuana licence back home. My views on drugs are pretty liberal."

"Lucky for Jimmy."

"Since you tried to throw him under the bus?"

The hotel employee bounced by Soap and Bridge. "Are you looking for a drink, sir?" The question was asked before she got to the other side of the bar.

"No, I'm waving at you because I want your number."

"Sir?"

"Sarcasm, in case you need a clue."

"I'm sorry, sir. We're a little understaffed today. One of my colleagues called in sick."

"I'll file that under I don't give a fuck."

"Please don't curse."

"Please be better at your job."

Bridge laid a hand on Soap's forearm. "There's no need."

"Yes there is. Do you know how much they charge for a suite in this shithole?"

"I live in Belfast, mate."

"Which suite are you in, sir?" The employee dragged an ID card through a slot on the cash register. Her fingers jabbed at the touch screen. No small feat, since her hands shook.

"Presidential."

Her eyes had the glossy sheen that threatened to spill over. "I can offer you a free drink for the inconvenience."

"Is that all?"

"I can refund your friend's drinks too."

"How many have you had, Inspector?"

"Just one!" Bridge thought for a second. "And three coffees before that."

"Jesus, Inspector. Do you hate your stomach?" Soap turned to the panicked employee. "Make that happen and give me something Irish from the top shelf."

"We don't have much of a range at this bar."

"And why the fuck would you?"

Bridge dug into his pocket and produced a couple of business cards. "Will you ask Jimmy to get in touch with me when he feels a little better?"

"You done drinking?" Soap prodded the cards with his index finger. "Because I've been told that you cops sometimes have trouble putting the brakes on your boozing."

Bridge barely reacted. Barely. His eyebrows twitched. "For now."

"Can I have your credit card, sir?" The employee was barely audible. "For the refund?"

"Forget it. Just give the young fellah something when he gets back from the bogs."

Soap snorted. "How quaint."

"I can put the credit against his room bill. Is that okay, sir?"

"Whatever."

"You're only lining *my* wallet, Inspector Bridge." Soap said. "I'm paying for Jimmy's room too."

"I'm sure your OBE is in the post, Mister Soap." Bridge patted his pockets before moving away from the bar. He pointed at the employee. "Take it easier on her, will you? She's just trying to earn a crust."

"Only if you let me take you out for a drink some time. I'm working on something you might be interested in. Your past applications for a job at The Agency would suggest you might be open to this offer."

"Have your people call my people, Hollywood."

"I'm a Santa Monica boy, but that's not bad."

Bridge nodded to the little rectangles of card on the bar top. "You have my details. One for you and one for Jimmy, okay?"

Soap watched Bridge leave then picked up the PSNI business cards. He slid both into a black wallet. Tucked the neat leather rectangle back into his right hip pocket. The well tailored material concealed what could have been a bulge. He hooked his phone from the left pocket. Used it to make a call.

"Max. You far away…? Good. Come back for me. Change of plans." He hung up and clicked his fingers at the employee. "Tell my young friend, Mister McAuley, I'm sorry for his loss and I'll call him later."

She nodded. "And I'm really sorry you were dissatisfied with the service earlier, sir."

"I'll forgive you this time. Make sure you pass my message on. Word for word."

He turned his back on her and she shook her middle fingers at him until he made it to the front door.

"It's not an excuse, Mum! My friend died." Jimmy flushed the toilet. "I wasn't peeing. I threw up after the policeman told me about Steve."

He slipped out of the cubicle and stood in front of the sinks. "I can't wash my hands until I get off the phone... Inspector Bridge? Yeah. Same cop." Jimmy leaned over the sinks to get a better view of his damaged side. "The stitches are starting to dissolve already, but it still stings."

Jimmy tried to press the phone against his ear with his shoulder. The handset slipped and he snatched his hands away from the taps to catch it.

"It *was* an assault." He stuck his tongue out at his own reflection. "Yeah, Steve. I've mentioned him before. He's from Newry."

Jimmy tested out a wide smile. The left side of his mouth twitched and he let it drop so that he was smiling on the right side only.

"How am I all over the place, Mum? You're the one asking all the questions." He breathed deep and paced the tiles from the sink to the hand dryer and back. "Can I call you tonight or tomorrow or something? I kind of left my new boss talking to the cop."

He removed the phone from his ear and gave the screen a silent-scream face.

"I know! That's why I'm trying to get you off the bloody phone. Stop making this all about *you*. I'm the one that has to be reminded about it every time I look in the mirror."

The phone went back to his ear. Two more breaths.

"I'm sorry, Mum. I'll be down on my next day off. Promise."

Jimmy ended the call and shuddered. He gave his hands

a quick wash and bypassed the dryer. Made do with a quick back and forth swipe across the arse of his jeans.

Back at the bar he looked at his unfinished bottle of beer, Bridge's empty glass and then the hotel employee. She was engaged with an elderly couple who looked to be dressed for a golfing holiday, though they were miles from the nearest course. They shared an insulted facial expression when the employee cut the man off in mid-sentence to address Jimmy.

"Mister McAuley? Could you wait there for a second? I have a message for you."

"Finish what you're doing."

The employee turned to the couple. "Could you bear with me just one minute? I have to wait on word back from house-cleaning before I can give you your keycards anyway."

The man shifted his angry face from the employee to Jimmy.

"Sorry, man," Jimmy said.

The elderly lady fired Jimmy a nervous smile. It flew under her husband's radar. The aging golfer had managed to puff his chest enough to compete with the round tummy beneath. His shoulders were squared. The employee missed her customer's pugilistic pose. She had a receipt clutched in her left hand, something scrawled in blue ink on what would have been the blank side.

"Who's the message from?" Jimmy asked.

"Mister Soap."

"Shit. Was he raging at me?"

"You?"

"Yeah."

The employee let a little West Belfast into her twang. "I thought it was just me."

"I had to run to the toilet in the middle of talking to him."

"So what? Are you not allowed to... you know."

"Oh here." Jimmy held his hands up. "I wasn't, like, *using* the toilet. Well I was, but it was for a boke. Not, *you know,* like."

The tip of her tongue slipped out from between her red lips. Levered her lips into a cheeky little grin. "A number two?"

Jimmy leaned his elbows on the bar. "There's no way I can answer that without asking for a number off you."

Her grin widened. "You're not wise."

"Sure I know." He pointed at the receipt still clutched in her left hand. "So what'd the boss say?"

"He said he was sorry for your loss and he'd see you later."

Jimmy sagged. His face drooped like a worn-out rubber mask. "Fuck's sake. Talk about a *craic* vacuum."

The employee leaned a little closer to Jimmy. "The policeman that was with your boss wanted me to get you a drink. Can you wait here for a second or two until I deal with these 'uns?"

"Yeah." His spine straightened. Chin up. "Yeah. Lovely. Thanks."

"Good. And I'll think about giving you my number."

Jimmy's phone rang.

"Unless that's your girl, like," the employee said.

Jimmy shook his head. "Couldn't be." He checked his phone. The screen informed him Grace was calling. "It's my sister. Just a minute."

The employee moved back to the dissatisfied elderly couple. Jimmy answered his phone.

"Yeah?" He backed away from the bar and scanned the tables and chairs around the reception area. "Outside? Ah right. Here, do you have any cigarettes?" A pause. "Can I bum one? My baccy's upstairs."

JOKER, SMOKER, MIDNIGHT TOKER

Jimmy met Grace at the back of the hotel. There was a bench tucked into a little patch of city shrubbery. Next to the bench, a shiny stainless steel bin for butts caught stray sunbeams and gleamed orange. Grace lit a cigarette for Jimmy. He nodded his thanks.

"Did you give that cop my phone number?"

"Which one?"

"How many do you know?"

"Well... I don't *know* him, like. But I was talking to one called Bridge a wee while ago. Inspector Bridge. Met him after the riot." He pointed at his scar. "At the hospital."

"Yeah, I met him at the actual riot. He was actually pretty useful. But I didn't stay in touch with him after he helped me out. I certainly didn't give him my number."

"Maybe Joe did. He was talking to him too."

"What about?"

"What did Bridge help you with at the riot?"

"I asked first." She lit her own cigarette and blew smoke at Jimmy. It was a playful gesture, followed by a smile, but she let a silence build between them.

"Somebody I know died. Bridge was telling me about it."

"Sorry for your loss."

Jimmy dimpled his good cheek. "Thanks."

"The student who got killed at the Holylands?"

"He wasn't a student, but yeah, he died in my old house. How'd you hear about it?"

"It was on the news. In the papers and online too." She sucked on the filter-tip. "And Bridge mentioned it earlier. Just before he asked me if I knew anything about Joe."

"Did he know you're working for him now?"

"He didn't ask and I didn't mention it."

"Weird."

"That doesn't mean he doesn't know somehow."

"Are you worried about it, like?" Jimmy traced his slender fingers along his scar.

"I'm more worried about the fact that your friend died in your house days ago and you're only hearing about it now. But really I just want to know who gave Bridge my number."

Jimmy flicked his butt into the shrubs. Grace looked at the bush it landed in, the stainless steel bin, and then Jimmy. He exhaled his last puff and shrugged.

"I didn't give him your number, Grace." He shrugged; devil may care. "But here, you know the girl that works at the bar in there?"

"The one missing buttons from her blouse?"

Jimmy tilted his head to one side. Grace held her hands a couple of inches away from her breasts. Jiggled an imaginary enhancement.

He pointed at her and tapped his nose. Let a little chuckle escape. "That's the one."

"What about her?"

"I think she's going to give me her number."

Grace smiled around her cigarette then drew deep. She exhaled. "Filling the contact list on that new phone up rightly, huh?"

"Well, I only had yours and Joe's this morning. Oh. And Mum's landline. But that's one of the few numbers I know off by heart anyway."

"You've only got my work number so far." She arched an eyebrow. "Not my personal one."

"Oh."

"You don't have Bridge's?"

"He gave me a card at the hospital." He placed a hand on his right buttock. "Never got around to calling him, but I think it's still in my back pocket."

"Ugh. How long have you been wearing those jeans?"

Jimmy blushed. His hand fell to his side without checking his back pocket. "I haven't had time to pick up my gear from Palestine Street yet."

"You called it your old house a wee minute ago. Have you moved out or not?"

"Max didn't give me time to pack. Sure I thought I was being kidnapped."

"That was ages ago, Jimmy!" A thought occurred. "Were you the last person to see this friend of yours alive?"

"Apart from the murderer, like? Maybe. Bridge didn't say."

Grace grabbed her phone from her handbag. Called up the Google app.

"What date did Max pick you up?"

"Same night I met you at Soap's suite. The fifteenth, wasn't it?"

She showed him a BBC news article she'd called up on her phone that confirmed the date. "Days ago."

"Yeah."

"And Inspector Bridge is only talking to you about it now? Why didn't he get in touch sooner?"

"He wouldn't have known I was there that night. I'd been staying at Steve's house since the riot. My housemates probably assumed I'd gone back home for a while."

"So, how did Bridge figure out you were there?"

"I don't know. Didn't think to ask."

"What did *he* ask *you*?"

"Not a lot. It was more of a courtesy call, I think."

"This is too weird. Cops don't track down a dead guy's friends. They inform the next of kin and look for suspects."

"Maybe he'd have asked more if Joe hadn't interrupted us."

"Maybe."

Grace offered Jimmy another cigarette. He waved it away.

"No thanks. I don't normally smoke them. Sort of

fancied a joint and coffin nails are the closest substitute, you know?"

"Not really. I don't smoke weed."

"Way better for you than tobacco, even if it's not socially acceptable."

"Says everybody who smokes weed. My wine-snob friends say the vino is better for you than vodka. And my friends who eat clean say it's better a better diet choice than Paleo."

"It's true when it comes to weed, though."

"Do you have any?"

"Joe gave me a baggie of the stuff Max got for him. It's upstairs. Some of the best I've ever had. He told me I should try it without tobacco, but I can't really take a hit from a pipe in broad daylight. Looks way more sus than a sneaky joint, you know?"

"Maybe I should see what the fuss is about."

Grace closed the distance between them with one smooth step. Jimmy twitched a little.

"I don't sting," Grace said.

She reached into her handbag and took a credit card-sized piece of plain white plastic from it. Pressed it into Jimmy's hand. Jimmy held it at arm's length and squinted at it.

"It's my spare keycard. Why don't you roll a doobie, or whatever you call it, and drop it into my room? I'll try it out tonight. See what all the fuss is about."

Jimmy hesitated.

"Is that okay, like?" Grace asked. "I mean, you have enough to share, don't you?"

"Yeah, yeah. No sweat. I'll just need to get more papers. I'm a bit low on baccy too." He shrugged. "It's usually better if you smoke with someone the first few times, though. So they can talk you down if you start to freak out."

"What is it you like to say, Jimmy? 'It's only a bit of weed', right?"

"Do I?"

"So don't worry about me. I'm a big girl." She poked

his chest with her middle finger. "Besides, I can always phone you if I start to freak out. So long as you're not off gallivanting with thon thing from behind the bar."

"What time do you think you'll try it out?"

"It'll probably be close to midnight before I get through the list of errands our fearless leader sent me this morning."

"Sure that's loads of time, then. Even if she wants to meet me today I'll be done by twelve, no doubt. It's a school night, sure."

"Don't be too eager, Jimmy. It's a turn-off. If she gives you the number today, don't phone her until tomorrow."

"Thanks for the advice. I'll drop that in for you later. Maybe shoot you a text around midnight to see how you're getting on with it."

Grace called after him. "On my work phone? It might be off."

Jimmy turned and walked backwards for a few steps. "I'll still call you. See if I get lucky."

She watched him until he disappeared around a corner. "Will you, though?" she said.

LET HIM GO

Bridge's feet scrunched along a gravel path leading to the front door of a semi-detached house. The garden that the path cut through eschewed grass in favour of a tonne or so of small pink stones. Green and yellow weeds grew in small clusters throughout the low-maintenance patch. Some of the stones had spilled onto a tarmac driveway. A couple of them had been crushed under the tyres of the silver Mitsubishi Lancer parked there.

The DI tried the door handle before he realised it was locked. He pressed the doorbell with his thumb. Held it there for five seconds. A dog went bonkers on the other side of the door; high-pitched yelping, bouncing and scratching. Dev's own bark could be heard through the door as well.

"Charlie! Charlie! Gotobed!"

The little dog must have done as he was told. There was no sign of him when she opened the door to her superior.

"You're such an alpha bitch, Dev."

"What the fuck are you doing here?"

"I wanted to see you."

Dev looked beyond him and scanned the wide street. "Did you drive?"

"Aye. Haven't renewed the licence yet, but I took a chance in my invisible car. Should've seen the looks I got on the M2."

"How'd you get here?"

"They run buses to Antrim, Dev. It wasn't that much of a challenge."

"And why?"

"Could we talk about this inside? You're making me feel like a Jehovah's Witness here."

She didn't formally invite him across the threshold,

but she left the door open when she walked away from him. Bridge eyeballed the houses across the street from Dev's before he pushed the door closed. He followed Dev to the kitchen. She pointed at the chair she wanted him to sit on. Bridge opted for the one beside it.

"You're as awkward as a bag of shite, Bridge."

"And you're in some form. Thought you'd be all biz after lifting Clark Wallace."

"You heard, then?"

"How could I not?"

"I don't suppose you're here to congratulate me?"

"Could I have a coffee, please?"

"If you'd given me a chance I'd have offered one. And I repeat: What are you here for?"

"Would you believe me if I said it was your shiny personality?"

"I take it you don't want sugar in your coffee, you bitter cunt?"

"No. And no milk either. I want it black."

"Like your ma?"

"My ma was the Catholic one. It was my da who donned the RUC's black boots."

"Fascinating. What the fuck do you want?"

The kettle was close to boiling point. It grumbled and bubbled on the countertop. The noise made it too hard to make out Bridge's half-whispered request.

"Speak up, *boss*."

"I'm not asking you this as your DI, just as me. And I want you to consider this as if that still means something. Let Clark Wallace go."

"On your word? Just like that? Aye. No bother, Bridge. I'll phone the Super now, sure."

"I'm serious, Dev."

"Seriously behind the curve. The big fucker walked."

The kettle clicked. Bridge watched Dev's angry barista act. Boiled water sloshed in and around the French press; ground coffee splattered the Pyrex container; the plunger mashed through the whole mess much too quickly. He said nothing until after she dumped out two mugfuls of piss-weak coffee and slammed one down in front of Bridge. She left her cup, and the French press, by the kettle and sat down opposite the DI.

"Who gave the word, Dev?"

"The fucking Super. Didn't even do me the courtesy of telling me why. Just said that I had conducted myself well but he'd been under so much political pressure that the evidence wasn't strong enough to hold him. We were a couple of hours short of the standard 48 too. Clark Wallace has more get-out-of-jail-free cards than Andre fucking Shoukri."

"Do you think he's turned tout or something?"

"No way."

"Strange."

"You're strange. This is something worse." Dev remembered her coffee and crossed the kitchen to retrieve it. She sat opposite Bridge again. "So, now it's your turn. Why did you come out here to ask me to release him? As if I had the power to do so."

"You could have found a way. Especially for somebody as slippery as Wallace in the first place."

"And what about the day he dandered out of the station after your chat about his dead cousin?"

"We didn't have enough on him. Seems like he'd need to be found standing over a dead body with his gun still smoking."

"Or a pipebomb."

Bridge grunted. "Whatever the case. He'd have walked the first time as well. I'm done relying on real police work. Not like you. You're more of a cop than I'll ever be."

"Are you trying to get into my knickers again?"

"Letting me into your knickers isn't going to cure me, Dev. You're not that good."

Dev sniffed, wiped a finger across her nostrils and raised her coffee mug. "That's probably the most honest thing you've ever said to me, Bridge."

"We shouldn't have gone back in time. It's started me down a bad path."

"But the whiskey and weed was all fine and dandy?"

"I'm clean again."

Dev leaned forward. She scanned him with a cop stare, the bulk of her focus on his eyes. "It hasn't started to show yet."

"My fling with whiskey is over. I necked a couple of Diazepam before I got on the bus."

"You'd have been better off with the booze."

"Says you, Little Miss Bushmills. My drugs are prescribed now. Are yours?"

Dev flopped back in her chair. The legs squeaked across the tiles. "Now that you're back on the wagon, are you coming off the sick, then? To do this real police work?"

"I wasn't on sick. Used up some holiday time that had stacked up. But I'm not going in to the station today. It's up to you, Dev. I'm done."

"You're quitting?" Dev got off her chair. She rounded the table and sat next to her DI. Reached out to take his hand. "But you were born to be a cop. It's who you are."

Bridge snatched his hand away from Dev's loose grip. "I haven't been anything these last few years. It was all taken away from me. And you know you had a hand in that."

"I need a drink."

"Don't let me stop you."

"Not yet. I'll drive you back to your flat. I've a late shift tonight anyway. No harm in heading into Belfast a little early. Make yourself another coffee. I won't be long."

"I took the bus here. I'll get another back."

"No. I need to talk to you some more. When I interviewed Clark with Reggie, just after the arrest, he was spouting some serious shite. A lot of it about that Jimmy McAuley kid. Remember him? From the YouTube video?"

"Aye. I've seen him a few times since."

Dev stalled. She blinked and restarted her train of

thought. "You didn't tell me you'd seen him."

"We haven't been chatting much."

"But we worked the Stephen Swain case together. The crime scene was McAuley's student digs. Wallace claims he told you that, before Swain showed up dead there."

"Not that I recall."

"The big bastard really set his lips flapping. He also believes Jimmy comes from a big Republican family back in Warrenpoint. The kind that prefers the bullet to the ballot box."

"Might explain some of the kid's piss and vinegar in that video. He wished a cot death on Loyalist babies if I remember right."

"Your memory's got a bit patchy of late, though."

"Meaning?"

"That Stephen Swain *does* come from a dodgy family. And they hail from Newry. Where you had a few run-ins with Stephen senior. AKA Leafy Swain."

"This is starting to feel a little like an interview, Dev. But you're doing it wrong. You need to let me answer some of these crazy accusations."

"This isn't an interview and I'm not accusing you of anything, Bridge. I'm confused, just. And as usual, you're giving me nothing. You're as bad as Clark Wallace in that regard. He's told me so many lies that I can't separate them from the truth. I'm going on hunches here."

"I need a smoke."

"You want one of mine?" Dev left her seat and went to a kitchen drawer. She snagged a packet of Benson and Hedges and tossed them to Bridge.

He snatched the packet out of the air and laid it on the table. "Not that kind."

She placed her hands on her heavy hips. Turned her nose up. "Can't help you there."

"Go and get ready. We'll talk in the car. I'll tell you as much as you want to hear."

"Promise?"

"What are you? A child?"

"Promise me now."

"Yes, I pinky promise with a cherry on top. If I'm lying I'm dying. One hand on my heart and the other on a stack of bibles."

"Thought you were a Buddhist, though."

"Fucking go get ready. We've a fair stretch of motorway ahead of us."

Dev left the kitchen. She stopped by the door and looked at the back of Bridge's head. He'd planted his elbows on the table and was hunched over with his hands cupped over his ears. The stapled head wound that Clark Wallace had inflicted was angry and red.

"You need to take better care of yourself, Bridge."

"Go, will you?"

She clumped up the stairs without another word. Bridge reached into the breast pocket of his suit jacket and withdrew a stubby roll-up. He raised his head and yelled at the ceiling. "I'm heading out the back for a smoke."

Dev's muffled voice replied; "There's a lighter on top of the microwave. Take an extra Benny for behind your ear if you want."

Bridge rolled his hound dog eyes. The bruises around his lids and brow had faded enough so that some of the purple had given way to a dark yellow, almost a match for his brown irises. He took his own lighter from his hip pocket and stepped out through Dev's French doors. Her back garden was fenced off. A little Maltese terrier sat on a paving stone, his face to the wind. His white fur, elegantly cropped, ruffled in the breeze. He paid Bridge no attention.

"You all right, Charlie?"

The dog glanced at him, then went back to studying a little sparrow perched atop a six-foot fence.

"Well fuck you, Charlie. More weed for me."

Bridge lit his stubby joint. A peregrine's call startled the dog and the wee garden bird. The sparrow abandoned its perch and the Maltese loped towards Bridge. The cop bent at the waist to pat Charlie's little head; his hand big enough to cup the entire skull.

"Ach, all right then, wee puppy."

Bridge puff-puffed and blew a cloud of weed smoke at Charlie's face. The little dog licked its own nose then let its lower jaw hang. Bridge laughed at what looked like a goofy grin and blew more smoke in the dog's face. The dog ambled back to where it had been sitting before Bridge tried to get him high. He watched the same spot where the sparrow had been, the same steady draught of air flapping his fur.

"I don't think it's coming back, Charlie."

The dog ignored him. Bridge sighed and puffed a little more.

WHO KILLED THE VIDEO BOY?

Jimmy sat at the dresser in his hotel room. On the surface, he'd laid out his phone, the gold pen Grace had given them on their first meeting and the ingredients for a joint: weed, tobacco, papers, roach. The phone screen was lit up and an image of Squinty Steve was captured there. Jimmy tapped it and a video started to play.

Steve waved for the camera, heavy metal style, with the index and pinky fingers extended. "What up, my brethren? I've put together a wee instructional video for rolling your wacky baccy." He reached out and changed the position of the camera to show his own makings for a joint. "But first…" The sound of a lighter being struck. "I'm going to blaze one I prepared earlier. Bear with me."

"Fuck's sake, Steve." Jimmy said. He sat back in his chair and waited.

On the little phone screen, Steve blew smoke at the lens. What could be seen of the whites of his eyes was shot through with red.

Jimmy laughed. "You eejit."

He watched his friend enjoy a joint for a few more seconds before his cheeks started to twitch.

"I wish I'd made it to your funeral, mate."

Jimmy's eyes reddened without the aid of a toke. His face swelled a little before the first tear rolled. He turned off the video, swept the weed and its accoutrements from the dressing table and got out of the chair. Threw himself at the bed and buried his head under a pile of pillows.

The luxurious eiderdown barely muffled his sobs.

FROZEN

Clark Wallace shoved Freddie's face into a bucketful of ice. It hadn't defrosted enough to muffle his screams. His hands slapped at the bar the bucket rested on. He danced a clumsy jig.

"You better hope that big mouth of yours doesn't get me into trouble again, Freddie. Don't want the cops visiting this place twice in one week, do you?"

"Please, Clark. Let me go."

"Cold bothering you a bit, is it?"

Clark yanked Freddie backwards. The barman's hands went to his face and swatted away a bunch of ice cubes that had fastened onto his roaring-red cheeks.

"What do you want, Clark?"

"Two things. A shooter and an answer."

"What's the question?" Freddie's voice squeaked and quivered. His flushed face twitched.

"Who killed Caroline Andrews?"

"I thought you did."

Freddie's head went back in the bucket. He screamed. Clark pulled Freddie back out.

"Please stop, Clark."

Clark looked around and found a crumpled bar towel within reach. He jammed a corner of it into Freddie's mouth and shoved his startled face back into the ice cubes. The screaming was muted this time.

"Fuck me, that's better." Clark used his free hand to poke at one of his ear holes. He grimaced. "You scream like a wee girl, Freddie. It'd go right through you."

Clark wiped his waxy fingertip on the back of Freddie's head then grinded the barman's face against the ice. Freddie's back convulsed. Clark pulled Freddie out of the bucket and reached around to tug the towel from his mouth. A spurt of vomit landed in the bucket. Clark whistled.

"You'll not want to go back in there, will you?"

"Please, Clark. Whatever you want. Anything. Just please... leave me be."

"I've already asked for one thing and you disappointed me."

"It's just what I heard, Clark. It's why you were scooped, no? The pipebomb had your prints on it."

"It didn't, though. There was no trace of anything on it. The fucking thing blew up, like."

"Who else would want to?"

Clark lowered his head so that his mouth was just half an inch from Freddie's ear. He screamed at the top of his lungs. "I don't fucking know! That's why I'm asking *you*, dickhead!"

Freddie recoiled like he'd been punched in the side of the head. He almost slipped out of Clark's grip. The bigger man wedged a hand under Freddie's armpit and hauled him upright. He squeezed tighter on the back of Freddie's neck.

"You're choking me, Clark."

"If you can talk, you can breathe."

"I can't."

"Fuck you up."

Clark shoved his head into the puke and ice. Freddie had given up on screaming. He burbled and puked instead. Clark punched his liver for good measure. Freddie's knees buckled. Clark stuck his knee between Freddie's legs to prevent the barman slumping to the ground. The fight faded from him steadily. Clark gritted his teeth. Held him in the pukey water for a couple more beats. Then he pulled Freddie's head out of the bucket and tossed him over the bar like he weighed nothing.

"You're a useless fucker, Freddie." Clark exited the bar through the raised flap. "This is the place where all the rumours fly and you're giving me yesterday's news. I was released for a reason, you know."

Freddie sniggered. A mucus bubble grew from one of his nostrils and popped. "They say it's because you've turned tout. That arrest and release will be the death of you. You've to answer for Caroline and the rest to the boys now."

"I didn't kill her."

"Nobody else has claimed it. Nobody else had a reason."

"I'd no reason. Sure I was buckin' her."

"Either way. I can't help you, Clark. Somebody else's filled your shoes. I pay Barney Jenkins protection now. And he cleared the guns out. The place isn't safe enough now that you drew the cops here."

"It was you that fucking called them, Freddie."

"I never did. And you can't kill me. Jenkins will have you. So just leave now and we'll call it square, Clark. Okay?"

"You think I'm worried about wee Rubble Jenkins? I'll crush him."

Freddie propped himself up with his elbows. He coughed and sprayed a mouthful of bile onto his own chest. "Sorry, Clark. I don't answer to you any more."

"What good are you to me, then?" Clark reached over the bar and swept his arm back and forth. "Ah. There it is."

"Clark, don't."

Clark slammed the business end of Freddie's baseball bat into his palm. "Just try and stop me, Freddie."

THE PICKUP

Jimmy tapped the luxurious dashboard before he reached for the door handle. "Thanks, Max. Appreciate the lift, man."

Max nodded.

"I won't be long, mate. If you swing this big machine around the block a few times I'll come out and meet you when I've collected my shit. Can't wait to change out of these jeans."

"The parking here's nearly as bad as New York's."

"I know, man. Between the students and the staff at the uni it's a real pain in the hole on a weekday."

"I'll text you if I end up parked in another street."

"Did I give you my number?"

"I got it, kid."

Jimmy bounced out of the car and hopped along to nine Palestine Street. He tried a key but it didn't work. A couple more jiggles with another key and he gave up. He rattled the letterbox flap against the frame. The door opened almost instantly. Mickey Walsh sneered at him.

"Where the fuck have you been?"

"No hello, Mickey?"

"I thought you were dead."

"Wise up. I've just been busy. Why'd you change the locks?"

"Well, you know, after your fucking weed dealer ended up dead in a bed I felt a wee bit unsafe."

Jimmy blessed himself. "Can I come in? I want to pick some shit up."

"There's rent due at the end of the month. You signed a lease. I'm not covering your share."

"Chill out, man. I'll sort that all out. I've got this new job and the money's pretty sweet."

"Lucky for you. There's letters here from the uni as well." Mickey backed away from the doorway to let Jimmy past. "They look important. I left them in your room."

"Cheers, boy."

Jimmy tried to ease the door shut. It swung open and knocked him backwards. His feet tangled up and he landed on his arse. Mickey spun on his heel and got an eyeful of Clark Wallace in the doorway. The uninvited guest carried a baseball bat, the fat end resting on one of his broad shoulders.

"Knew you'd show up here sooner or later, you wee shite." Clark slammed the door shut.

"What the fuck is going on here, Jimmy? What have you got caught up in?"

Jimmy scuttled backwards and almost bowled Mickey over. "Move, Mickey. Out the back."

"And go where? The fucking yard's locked."

"Looks like you're shit out of luck, wee lads," Clark said. He pointed the bat at Mickey. "This one of your wee dissident pals? Am I getting two for the price of one today?"

Jimmy scrabbled to his feet. He tried to push Mickey down the hall, towards the kitchen. "Get a knife or something. Come on."

Mickey didn't move. Jimmy shoved him to the side and moved on. "Come on, Mickey."

"Stay where you are, wee lad," Clark said. "It'll go easier for you."

Mickey started to cry. Clark smirked and raised the baseball bat in the air. He brought it down and connected with the top of Mickey's head. Jimmy's housemate hit the deck. Hard. Clark stepped over him without a second glance.

"I'm coming for you, Jimmy."

Jimmy's voice carried from the kitchen. "What the fuck for? I did nothing to you."

"You killed my cousin, ballbag."

"I never killed anybody."

"You say that now. I'll not put you out of your misery

before you admit it, though. And beg me for forgiveness."

Clark entered the kitchen. Jimmy stood near the backdoor. He had a mop in one hand and a serrated bread knife in the other. His knees wobbled.

"Get out of here. I'll stab you, so I will."

"At least you've a bit more fight in you than that Chink-eyed stoner I strangled the last time I was here." Clark winked at Jimmy. "But good luck with that. There's no point on your blade, dickhead."

"*You* killed him?"

"Aye. When I saw the lights on I was hoping it was you. I got a wee bit carried away when he wouldn't tell me where to find you."

"He didn't know where I was!"

Clark shrugged one shoulder. "It happens."

Jimmy looked at his poorly-chosen weapons. "I'll slice your throat."

"Aye? You'll need to get very close to me. Come on and have a go, sure."

"I got this, Jimmy."

The interruption came in the form of a thick New York accent. Clark Wallace turned to face Max Mason. Soap's bodyguard clutched a large hunting knife in his bulky fist.

"This blade suit you all right, douche-bag?"

"Who the fuck are you?"

"That's not important. Your next decision is. I'll give you five seconds to make it. Get out of here and live. Stay here and bleed out."

Jimmy tried to creep a little closer to Clark's unprotected back. Clark sensed him and spoke up.

"Don't even think about it, wee lad."

"It's okay, Jimmy." Mason's voice was deep and steady. "You don't need to get involved here." He tapped his wristwatch with the flat of his blade. "Five seconds up, sir. Are you going to leave?"

"No fucking chance. Sure this'll be fun."

Clark swung the bat. Mason skipped backwards and the bat knocked a lump of plaster from the patch of wall he'd been standing next to. He lunged in and slashed out. Clark raised his shoulder to protect his neck. The hunting knife cut through trackie top and flesh.

"Ach, ye cunt ye."

Clark chalked up another swing and a miss. Mason's boxing footwork had carried him out of harm's way again. Clark chased him into the hallway, his bat held out like a jousting stick. Mason stumbled over one of Mickey's stray legs. He kept his balance but dropped his blade. Clark was on top of him before he could retrieve it. The butt of the bat sank into Mason's stomach. He huffed a lungful and bent at the waist. Clark landed a hammerfist on the back of Mason's head. The New Yorker shook it off and shot forward. He wrapped his arms around Clark's waist and picked him up. Slammed him down on the laminate floor.

Mason postured up and rained fists down on Clark. The Belfast boy tried to defend against the ground and pound by slapping Mason's arms to the side. He checked less than half the punches and ate the rest. The damage started to show immediately: a broken nose and split skin above his left eye. Clark changed tactics and reached out to grab Mason by his buzz-cut. He pulled his opponent's head closer. Close enough to kiss him. Then he sank his teeth into his ear.

The bodyguard roared and jerked his head backwards out of harm's way. Clark had hair in his fist and flesh in his mouth. He spat the chunk of ear at Mason and scrabbled backwards. Got to his feet.

Jimmy cracked Clark on the back of the head with the mop handle. The move bought Mason a couple of seconds to retrieve his knife. Clark turned to deal with Jimmy. Mason sank the knife into Clark's back. Once. Twice. Three times.

"You dirty bastard," Clark said.

He pitched forward. Landed face-first at Jimmy's feet.

SOAP ON A ROPE

Joe Soap's image smiled on Grace's laptop screen. She smiled back. He fixed his hair onscreen. His greeting was tinny through the small speakers on Grace's computer.

"I don't have a hell of a lot of time here, Grace. An early version of our little documentary got leaked. This rough cut has been… less than flattering toward The Agency. We'll need to get a lot of positive media lined up to bury this."

"I'll help you with that, Joe. But first I have to ask you for a favour. It's not much, though."

"What can I do for you?"

"I can't get that cop out of my mind. Inspector Bridge. He makes me nervous. So I really just want an update on him. What's Max found out so far?"

"Quite a bit. And I believe he's only just scratched the surface. It's probably too much to pass on right now, but if you want to meet up later, I could fill you in. Jimmy too, if he can make it. I think it's safe to say that you should both be very careful around him."

"Is he dirty?"

"It's suspected that he was, and he's made some major fuck ups in his time. He's been a troubled man since his daughter killed herself."

"Jesus."

"Yes. She was only fifteen. Unfortunately, one of far too many kids to have taken her life in the last few years. It's been like a plague in certain parts of Belfast."

"I know. It's terrible. I've covered quite a few of them in my time."

"What is it they say? Suicide is a permanent solution to a temporary problem, right?" Soap ran his fingers through his hair. "At first I thought I might have a place for DI Bridge on my team. Even if the PSNI had burned him out with one too many demands, we could have had him do some talks on the subject of social order at schools in the worst areas. Maybe recruit some fresh agents. Unfortunately, it seems like he isn't quite stable enough."

"How do you know?"

"Throw enough money around and you can find out anything, really. His psychologist, for instance, isn't the most ethical I've ever encountered. Quite a charming lady by all accounts, though. Max was quite taken with her."

"And this is only scratching the surface?"

"My dear, the stories will curl your toes. We'll meet in the hotel lobby tonight. Around nine. If Jimmy's made it back from his parents' house by then, we'll make it a threesome."

"Foursome, counting Max."

"He won't need to be there. He already knows everything about the good inspector." Soap leaned forward. His arm reached out to hit a key on his own laptop. "Look after yourself, Grace. See you tonight."

Grace watched Soap's image disappear from the screen. She took a few seconds to breathe before she flipped the lid closed.

STUCK PIG

Jimmy, eyes wide and shining, looked on as Mason checked Clark for a pulse.

"He's still alive," Mason said.

"But there's so much blood."

"Even so, he's still ticking."

"What about Mickey?"

Mason softened his face as best he could; his damaged, bleeding ear didn't help. "I'm sorry. He's gone. You want to finish this punk off?"

"What do you mean? Where's Mickey?"

Mason stood up, rounded the seepage from Clark's still form, and held firm to Jimmy's shoulders. He lowered his head and looked Jimmy in the eye. Jimmy fastened onto Mason's stare. His shoulders straightened but it was unclear as to whether Mason's grip had a hand in it or if it was all Jimmy.

"Oh," Jimmy said. "Mickey's dead."

Mason nodded oh-so slightly.

"And you're offering me a chance at revenge." Jimmy's voice rose a little at the end of the sentence.

Mason understood rhetorical shock. He remained silent. Dabbed at his bitten ear with a handful of toilet roll. Barely hissed.

"What's the point, Max?"

"That's a good question, Jimmy."

"Are you going to call the cops or will I?"

Mason let go of Jimmy's shoulders. He backed away, again mindful of Clark's flowing blood on the floor. "There was me beginning to think you'd learned something from all of this." He tapped his forehead with a thick finger. "Maybe see you around, Jimmy."

"You're leaving?"

"You should too. If you think that limp-wristed daddy's boy will stand by you through this, you're kidding yourself. I've got an overseas appointment with Soap senior."

"Wait. You have to tell me more than that."

"I've done enough for you, kid." Mason cast his gaze on Clark and his wounds one last time. "If you want an instruction manual, get religion."

And the bodyguard was gone.

SMOKE AND FLY

Dev drove angry. Anything that came out of her mouth was directed at the other road users. Even the meek ones she felt the need to overtake or cut off on the four lanes of M2 that she'd commandeered. Bridge snapped his seatbelt in place and reached for the radio.

"I'm listening to that, dickhead," Dev said.

"At last, she actually talks to the passenger."

"You're lucky I didn't rear-end somebody when I realised you weren't wearing your seatbelt. Touch my radio and I *will* break your arm."

"You had me at dickhead, my not-so-little princess."

Dev turned the radio up. BBC Radio Ulster flooded the car with country music.

"Ach, Dev. A smile won't break your face. I'm only slegging, like."

"You're not funny, Bridge. You're just high."

"Ah. So that's it." Bridge raised his hands over his head. His fingertips brushed the upholstered ceiling. "You caught me bang-to-rights, high as an eagle eye."

On the radio, a newsreader with a nasal voice informed the country that disturbances had broken out across Belfast in the wake of the release of a prominent Loyalist paramilitary leader and the leak of a controversial video on YouTube. The newsreader sounded confused as she tried to explain the origins and impact of the video. Dev lowered the volume. She muttered incoherently for a couple of seconds before starting on Bridge.

"Bad enough you tried to sell me the lie that you were clean. But that wasn't enough for you, was it?" Dev jinked into a tight space in the lane to her right. "You had to smoke it in my fucking garden."

"I didn't tell you that I was off the weed, Dev. Just the

whiskey."

"You said you were clean."

"And I am. Weed's practically a vegetable, sure. A side dish to my medication."

"Grown by scumbags, gangsters and paramilitaries."

"Farmers never get it easy in this country, do they?"

"SHUT THE FUCK UP!"

Dev tried to nudge her car into a space on the far right. A white van attempted to block her and she turned their interaction into a game of bilateral chicken. The van hit the brakes before they collided with each other.

"Dev, come on. Chill."

"Did I tell you to open your mouth?"

"Do I need to remind you who's the boss here? It's been a while since you called me that, now that I think about it. Did shagging change our dynamic again?"

"You're a bent cop. That makes me the real superior officer in this car, whatever fucking way you choose to cut it. Now shut your hole until I ask you a direct question."

Bridge mimed a zipper across his lips. He couldn't contain one last titter with the imaginary fastener, but the disrespect was minimal enough for Dev to keep her voice at a steady level.

"You've been playing me for a few weeks now. Maybe even months. And I know you blame me for breaking up your family, but surely even a bitter, twisted, fucked up weasel like you can understand that you're kicking me while I'm down at this stage, right?" She held her hand up to shush Bridge. "That one was rhetorical. Just listen for now."

Dev gave him a couple of seconds to interject. He chose to hold his tongue for the time being.

"You knew who Stephen Swain was before I told you, didn't you?"

"His friends call him Squinty Steve."

"You want to take down Clark Wallace because of what he did to your daughter, right?"

"Him and Vic both."

"Did you kill Vic?"

"Do you think you can get a confession out of me that easily?"

"That was just as good, Bridge. We'll figure out the details later."

"Fuck you, Dev."

"Wait for the questions."

The white van Dev had almost wrote off caught up with her. She glanced out the side window at him. The driver had taken the lane on the left. His window was down. White van man leaned on his horn.

"Who's this dickhead?" Dev asked.

"No idea. Why don't you flash your ID card? Put some manners on him."

"I'd rather he was humiliated by a woman than a cop."

Dev edged her car towards the van.

"Dev?"

"Keep your mouth shut."

"Dev."

"Shush."

And he did. Dev edged towards the side of the van again. The driver's face showed confusion for a second, then anger. Fear took over in time for him to find his brake. Dev took his lane and slowed her car at a steady pace. The white van man tried to bully her into picking up speed by riding her bumper. Dev eased off on the accelerator a little more, one hand on the wheel, the other on the gear stick.

"You'll kill us."

"Suddenly worried about me, Bridge? That's cute."

The van ripped out onto the left lane. Dev's engine and reactions were more responsive. She cut him off before he could get even close to overtaking her on the inside. Horns and headlights. Dev flicked her gaze from mirror to mirror. Dropped her speed again. The van attempted to get around her twice more. Dev repeated her ice-cold manoeuvres each time. White van man faked mechanical trouble. He popped on his hazard lights and veered toward a stretch of hard shoulder. Dev pushed the Lancer's speedometer needle back up to seventy mph.

"Feel better?"

"I'm still asking the questions, Bridge."

She gave him a few seconds to remember the rules. His silence proved that he was back in the game.

"Now, Stephen Swain senior. AKA Leafy. Not just a weed dealer, but also the father of Squinty. Do you think he would have sired some other waste of space with a Disney dwarf's name if not for his tragic demise?"

"Is that a serious question?"

"No, it's not. But the next one is. How come you weren't at young Stephen's funeral?"

"I didn't know him."

"You knew Leafy, though, and not just from school. You were still friends when he dropped out at the ripe old age of sixteen to help raise junior. Leafy was hurt when he found out that you couldn't make it to your godson's funeral." Dev rolled her window down and spat at the motorway. "Yes, I know Stephen, or Squinty, or whatever you want to call him is your godson. Leafy told me at the funeral. He got pretty vocal about your lack of sympathy. 'Not even a fuckin' mass card,' was the driving point behind his rage. Or as close to rage as a burned-out stoner with a broken heart can manage."

Dev paused to allow Bridge an opportunity to speak up.

"I'm waiting for the next question, Dev."

"Isn't this a fun game?"

"No."

"Wait until I start asking about Jimmy McAuley."

Bridge reached into his inner breast pocket.

"What are you doing?"

"Relax, Dev. Just my phone. My gun's at home."

"I didn't think you were going for your hardware, like," but she looked relieved. "Now's not the time for a game of Candy Crush or whatever shitty app has you hooked this month."

"I just want to turn off the buzzer. It's been going a dinger in my pocket for the last five minutes."

"How long does it take to do that? Hurry up."

"Oh, fuck."

"What is it?"

"Nothing."

"Aye, right. What's the story?"

Bridge clacked his teeth together for a few beats. He was stalling. "You want to know about Jimmy? Maybe you should meet him."

"I'll bite. Now reel me in."

Bridge held up his phone so Dev could read the screen. She checked her mirrors and her blind spots first, then looked at the text message.

Inspector Bridge? At 9 Pal St. Can you answer ur phone or call me back? I know I have the right number. I still have ur card. Help. Please? I'm in trouble. Can't call 999. Jimmy M.

"Is that for real?" Dev asked.

"I think so. Only one way to find out."

"Call him."

Bridge nodded and thumbed the screen.

"No, wait." Dev said. "Hook your Bluetooth up to my radio and put him on speaker phone."

YOUR CALL IS IMPORTANT TO US

Jimmy's phone displayed a YouTube video. A woman knelt over a seemingly unconscious man who was on his side. Jimmy put the phone down and tried to move Clark onto his side. His slender hands couldn't get a good grip on the blood-soaked tracksuit top. He let go and rubbed his palms on the front of his own T-shirt, staining the light blue cotton.

"Ah fuck."

He slipped his hands under one of Clark's shoulders. Managed to raise him a little before allowing him to flop back down face-first.

One more try, this time with an aggressive growl, and Jimmy managed to roll the hulking frame onto its side. Then he pulled one of Clark's knees toward him so that it acted like a kickstand and prevented Clark's body from flopping back into place. He took a few seconds to catch his breath before wiping his hands on his T-shirt again and picking up his phone. The video had run on and Jimmy wound it back. On the screen, the lady showed Jimmy that the airways needed to be cleared. Aping the actions shown in the video, Jimmy tilted Clark's chin upwards and leant forward to listen to his breathing. After a few seconds, Jimmy was satisfied and he scuttled back to sit on the floor with his back propped against the wall.

The phone rang just as Jimmy's lids started to close.

"Bridge! Thank Christ it's you. I'm freaking the fuck out here."

INFOMERCIAL

A band of cops, dressed in their riot blues, huddled around a smartphone. Onscreen, a YouTube video played. Joe Soap's face took up the majority of the frame. His smile gleamed. The armoured Land Rover the cops travelled in jostled them, but they were too experienced to lose balance. Constable Greene, his nose taped at the sides to guide its repair, snorted and then winced. Constable McAllister looked at him. Greene read her unspoken question from her facial expression.

"I'm fine. A wee bit sore, just."

"You should be at home, then."

"And miss out on that overtime? Fuck no. Sure if this Soap wingnut gets his way there'll be no need for any of us at these things. It'll be dial-a-mob to the rescue."

"It'll never happen," McAllister said.

"Says you. I'm going to pull as many shifts as I can until I hear otherwise, though."

Most of the other cops mumbled agreement with Greene.

"Or maybe I'll apply for a job there," Greene said. "Money's probably going to be better than a public sector salary."

The mumbled agreement lost some of its enthusiasm.

Soap's voice cut through the roar of the Land Rover's engine. Even through the tinny phone speaker he commanded a presence. But the video sound levels were all over the place. Grace Doran's interjections throughout Soap's spiel were inaudible.

"We've crunched the numbers already, Grace. The Agency will be able to provide support at riots for a fraction of the price it'd take to pay the danger money that PSNI officers have been conditioned to expect. Recreational rioting is one of the biggest drains on the Northern Irish economy. And here's the rub. Until the rioting is curtailed, through attacking issues such as poverty and a lack of education, they'll continue to suck money from the taxpayer. Let my company handle it and reroute the money to welfare and education."

Grace prompted him in some way.

"Yes, right." He waited two seconds. "Let my company handle it and use that surplus to improve the *benefits* system and education." Another few seconds passed. "You can fix that in post, right? Cool."

Grace fed him another unheard question.

"Really? The fucking Catholic versus Protestant thing again? Jesus, when will you guys get over the whole... Jesus thing?"

Grace's face filled the screen. She'd lost her usual TV smile. Her lips moved quickly.

"The Agency is an equal opportunities employer. My comments in the past were attempts at humour that were taken out of context. We only hire agents with a clean criminal record, and there are no allowances made for those released under the Good Friday Agreement. Our strenuous background checks and psychological testing will route out anybody who can't be trusted with this sort of power."

"No way you're getting a job then, Greene," McAllister said.

Greene sucked air through his teeth. "Bitch."

Onscreen, Grace relaxed her scornful expression. Asked another question with the professional grin back in place.

"Have you looked at the statistics recently?" Soap said. "This is a dangerous place."

The video cut to a scene on the Lower Falls Road. The long wall of murals gave away the location before the graphics revealed it in white letters on the bottom left corner of the screen. A jerky video, shot in portrait, showed a bunch of mischievous kids messing with a camera crew. The crew were irritated but seemed to be in no real danger.

Another scene overlapped this one. Bored kids wearing blue football jerseys and waving Union Jack flags played about on a footpath. One strayed out onto a busy road. A car performed a textbook emergency stop. The young boy gave the driver the finger and jumped back over the red, white and blue painted kerb. His companions applauded him.

This scene gave way to another and soon a montage of clips featuring a mix of similar situations played out, the only discernable difference between each clip boiled down to colour combinations. Green, white and gold or red, white and blue. Catholic or Protestant.

"What a load of shite," Constable Greene said.

All of the riot cops laughed. Some of them a little more enthusiastically than the comment merited. Suited up in riot gear, they were on their way to meet more kids like the ones portrayed in the video. Their shenanigans would seem a little less wholesome than the poorly put together video might suggest.

"Throw in a Van Morrison song and we're halfway to convincing the civilians that this place is lovely, though," McAllister said. "And the higher-ups could easily get sucked in."

The laughter faded.

"Thanks, McAllister," Greene said. "Fucking *craic* vacuum. Typical woman."

The only other female cop piped up before McAllister could. "Watch your mouth Greene or you'll be crying for your mummy when we get through with you."

The men jeered and whistled, not quite in support of the women. McAllister traded exasperated looks with her ally. Their silence marked them as 'good sports'.

On the smartphone screen, the video displayed a clash between two bands of teenagers, the divide obvious from the conveniently coloured battle garb. Pushing and shoving gave way to chaotic violence. Real danger. Punches, kicks and Belfast bricks.

A message flashed up in white text on the screen.
Joe Soap pays kids to organise riots.
"Did that say…?" McAllister said.

The question didn't require an answer. They'd all seen it.

Soap's American accent rang out again, voiced-over the violence. "Poverty, a lack of education, bad influence. We can turn this around. And we're open to applications from the community leaders who give their time so generously to attempt to bring order to their neighbourhoods. Provided they can make it through our rigorous selection process, they'll actually get paid to risk their necks for peace. There's a lot less baggage attached to The Agency than there is to the PSNI."

A new face filled the screen. Most of the cops didn't need to read the typo-ridden text displayed in the left corner of the shot to recognise this kid. 'Jommy McxAuley' cleared his throat.

"I was wrong to say what I did in that video. I wasn't myself. I'd just been glassed, like. Might have even been concussed, because I barely remember saying half of that shite. Sorry." A pause. Jimmy's lips moved through a silent three-count. "Might have even been concussed, because I barely remember saying half of that stuff."

One of the cops, his voice as gruff as his countenance, spoke up. "Turn that fucking thing off before I wing it out the winday."

"The windows don't open in the back," Greene said. "The brainiacs who designed these motors found it was easier to contain the ne'er-do-wells that way."

"So I'll shove it up your hole, then."

The Land Rover juddered to a halt.

"I'm only putting it away because we're here already, Mackin," Greene said.

The gruff Mackin didn't respond. He was busy fastening his helmet.

"What's your problem, anyway?" Greene asked Mackin. "We might be able to make a few quid from The Agency."

"Did you learn nothing from that video? It's a fly-by-night operation if I ever saw one. But feel free to walk away from a real organisation for a few shekels. Fellahs like you don't have what it takes anyway."

"Fellahs like me?" Greene narrowed his eyes. "Fenians like me, do you mean?"

"Fuck me, there he goes again," Mackin said. "You'd need to get that chip surgically removed from your shoulder. I'm questioning your loyalty, not your religion."

"Loyalty? There's an Orange Order sentiment if I ever heard one."

"Boys," McAllister said. "Play nice. The real fight's out there." She pointed at the back door of the Land Rover.

"Tell your boyfriend to toe the line," Mackin said. "It's him starting this shite."

Greene held his hands up. "Sorry, Mackin. Maybe I'm a bit touchy."

"A bit touched in the head, more like," Mackin said.

"Look after each other out there," McAllister said.

"We don't need a pep-talk, doll," Mackin said. "Looking out for each other goes without saying."

Greene offered McAllister a fist-bump. She bounced her gloved knuckles off his and then pushed open the armoured door. The hellish soundtrack of chaos filled the back of the Land Rover. The riot cops spilled out to join their brethren.

Us against them.

Same old story.

"Jimmy, you're on speaker phone. My colleague, DS Devenney, can hear you. But talk freely. You can trust her."

"Right, okay. Em… Hi, DS Devenney."

"All right, Jimmy?" Dev said.

"No. Not one bit. Can you come to my house on Palestine Street?"

"We're on our way into Belfast now, Jimmy," Bridge said. "What's wrong?"

"The big bastard from the riot – the one who I identified at the hospital – he came here. My friend got in the way. He's…"

"Where's Clark now, Jimmy?"

"Right in front of me."

"Can he hear us talking?"

"No." Jimmy paused. His breath was the only sound running through Dev's stereo speakers. On his fourth exaggerated inhalation, Jimmy squeaked. "Clark got hurt too. Stabbed in the back. He's alive, but *I* think he might be on his way out."

"Did you stab him?" Dev asked.

"No. Somebody I work with did it."

"Is this person still with you, Jimmy?"

"No. He ran away. Told me I should do the same, but I couldn't, you know?"

"Good man, Jimmy," Bridge said. "Just sit tight. I'd say we're fifteen minutes away."

"That's forever. He'll be dead by then."

"Ring an ambulance, Jimmy," Dev said. "I bet I can get there before it arrives, but better to be safe."

"What if they think I stabbed him?"

"Don't worry about that, Jimmy," Dev said. "If you're innocent, the forensics team will be able to prove it."

"Will I call the police as well?" Jimmy asked.

Dev said yes and Bridge said no at the same time. Bridge held up his hand at Dev's questioning look. Mouthed the words, "Trust me."

"We'll call it in from our end, Jimmy," Bridge said.

"And we'll be there in six minutes," Dev said. "DI Bridge doesn't know how fast I can drive."

Bridge ended the call. He disconnected his phone from the radio and tucked it away.

"Are you phoning it in, then?" Dev asked.

"No."

"Why the fuck not?"

"I want to make sure we get there first."

"What's the point in that? You know I'm not going to let you do anything dodgy. We're going by the book. No Charles Bronson shite."

"Can you really get us there in six minutes?"

"Ten, maybe fifteen. Was just trying to keep the wee lad calm. But that gives you time to explain something Clark said about Jimmy McAuley when I interviewed him."

"Ask away. No point trying to hide anything from you now."

"Phone it in, first."

"Fuck's sake. Fine. Just a second." Bridge took his phone back out of his pocket, fiddled with the screen then pressed it to his right ear. "Cecil! Quick on the draw as usual. Aye, Bridge here. Can you send some uniforms to nine Palestine Street, please? I'm on my way there with DS Devenney." He nodded along to whatever was going on at the other side. "Aye, I'm meant to be off, but what can you do? Too important to get a whole week to myself, y'know?" He mimed a flapping beak with his left hand for Dev's benefit. "I know. Complete piss-take." He forced a laugh. "Aye, later, mate."

Bridge ended the call.

"You were awful chatty, Bridge."

"Ach, you know what Cecil's like."

"I do. But I know what you're like too. Never heard

you say a nice thing to him in my life."

"Right."

"And I thought he was on leave this week as well."

"Fuck's sake, Dev! Do you want me to phone him back through the loudspeaker, or do you want to quiz me about Jimmy instead?"

Dev checked her speed and the time on the dashboard clock. There was very little traffic build-up at the end of the M2. She decided.

"Fine, Bridge. One thing at a time, then. Why did you tell Clark that Jimmy's family has a republican background?"

"I was just trying to get him to lose his temper. You've used that technique before."

"Not by throwing a random innocent under the bus, though."

"Is that another question? What else do you want me to say?"

"Why would you take such a big risk?"

"It didn't seem like a risk at the time. I'd no idea that Clark would, or could, track him down. I mean, it's taken me this long to track down Wallace himself."

"But you knew Clark had the phone. And that the phone had a picture of Jimmy outside his house on Palestine Street. You also actually had Jimmy's phone for a while too, right?"

Bridge shifted slightly to look out the passenger side window before answering. "What of it?"

"I think you were going to use it to frame Clark. But that plan went to shit after Clark waltzed into your apartment to nick it back off you. You see, Clark may be paranoid, but he's very much right about the fact that you're out to get him."

"He *told* you that he broke into my place."

"Like I said, his lips were flapping. And I've just found another thread of truth, haven't I?"

"Fuck's sake. And what do you think I was going to frame Clark Wallace for?"

"I haven't got that far yet, but let's speculate, shall we? Three deaths recently that have your little tiff with the Wallaces written all over it. Vic Wallace, Stephen Swain and Caroline Andrews. Vic's murder, you got away with clean thanks to the riot and a shoddy investigation that you were able to influence even though you weren't on the case."

"What actual proof do you have of that?"

"None. Yet."

"So this is Jackanory time?"

"All the best stories have a grain of fact in them. Now, the second murder... maybe I'm wrong, but I hope even *you* wouldn't kill your godson, so let's pin that on Clark for now. I practically got that out of him anyway. Before the Super set him free, that is."

"Did you have evidence for him?"

"Aye. But stop trying to derail me. Because there's still the case of Caroline Andrews; the signature pipebomb was good. And it's a pity Clark nicked Jimmy's phone back off you, because a phone that could be traced back to the murderer... Sure wouldn't that be the icing on the cake? Especially since you knew the shrapnel would have been devoid of DNA evidence. Unfortunately, Clark had the same idea and he planted it at Steve's murder to frame Jimmy."

"And your sure Jimmy couldn't have killed Steve?"

"No. Sure look at the cut of him, with those narrow shoulders and piano-player fingers. He couldn't strangle a wee girl. Also, Clark was smart enough to wipe his prints from the phone before he planted it. He wasn't smart enough to wipe the numbers that he'd dialled from the call log, though. No reason in the world for Jimmy McAuley to phone Clark's aunt Aggie, like. Looked like you were fly enough to only phone the numbers already in Jimmy's contact list. Like Jimmy's weed dealers."

"You always were a good detective, Dev. You've connected the dots rightly."

"So I'm right?"

"Please, Dev. You always say a career criminal knows

his rights better than his lawyer does, don't you?"

"Think I got it off a TV show or something, but aye, it's true."

"Well, a cop knows them even better. I'm not answering any incriminating questions until you've arrested me and my solicitor is with me."

"Dirty cops are particularly clued in, right enough."

"Oh, fuck you, Dev."

"No, fuck you. And don't think I won't put a bullet in your head if you come at me."

"Just get us to the Holylands. We'll figure the rest out later."

SOAPY DODGER

Jimmy held a folded tea towel against Clark's wounds. The white cotton was heavily blood-stained. Another towel, almost entirely drenched in the same shade of red, was balled up on the floor beside them. Thuds at the door made Jimmy jerk to attention. He hesitated for a second, not sure what to do with the towel clenched in his fist, then draped it over Clark's upper arm and stood up.

On his way down the hall, Jimmy turned his head away from Mickey's lifeless body. He dry retched before he opened the door. Soap and Grace waited for him on the doorstep.

"What the fuck is going on?" Soap asked.

"Come in," Jimmy said.

"Sorry it took us so long, Jimmy," Grace said. "Joe couldn't track down Mason so I had to drive. There's riots brewing around the city again. Traffic's a nightmare."

"This one's dead." Soap said. He'd bent at the waist to check Mickey's pulse.

"There's another guy dying in the kitchen."

"Oh, fuck you, Jimmy. Fuck you for dragging me into this. We have enough on our plate already!"

"I'm glad to see you're okay, Jimmy," Grace said. "Isn't that a good thing, Joe?"

"Nothing's good about this almighty fuck-up. Come on. We have to leave."

"I called that cop as well, Joe," Jimmy said. "Inspector Bridge. He's on his way."

Soap raised his hands to his head. Buried his fingers in his blond hair. "You did what?"

"I didn't know if you guys were going to make it, and the big guy was going to die. What else could I do?"

"It's okay, Jimmy," Grace said.

"It fucking isn't," Soap said. He'd taken his hands from his hair but it hadn't flopped back in place as it usually would. Sweat from his palms had left it tousled. "But we'll fix it. Come on. We need to leave."

"But the cop said to wait."

"Did you phone the police direct, or did you contact Bridge on his own phone?" Grace asked.

"His phone."

"Okay, then. That's not so bad. I looked into Bridge. He's got a bad record and he's recently been on long-term sick leave. For mental health issues. And now that you know, Jimmy, you can't be faulted for leaving the scene of the crime."

"How did you get that info?" Soap asked. "I didn't give it to you. Do you have a source in the PSNI?"

"Did you forget I'm a journalist, Joe? I have sources everywhere."

"You dig for shit on everybody you meet?"

"Just when they seem off, Joe. Why? You got something to hide too?"

"Now's not the time for jokes, Grace."

Grace wasn't smiling. "Let's get Jimmy out of here, then."

KEYSTONE

Disorder.
The crowd roars.
Noise.
It crackles and fizzles like a radio between stations.
Violence.

A troop of civilians moves as one. There's a savage beauty to this chaos. It tumbles like the tide. Crashes into riot shields. Seeks a break in the seal.

It's relentless.
Disorder.

DS Mackin flipped his visor up and broke away from the frontline. Another riot cop took his place before anybody could breach the plastic force-field. Mackin sucked as much air out of the violent atmosphere as he could, an easier task since he'd opted to leave his balaclava out of his riot ensemble. He holstered his baton to allow himself more freedom to rotate his shoulder, and his mouth flopped open to release an inaudible moan.

DS Greene approached Mackin. The white bandages supporting his healing nose had turned red from the reopened wounds in his nostrils. He raised his visor and pulled down his balaclava to wipe away a coating of blood from the lower half of his face. They yelled at each other to be heard above the clamour.

"You take another smack in the face?" Mackin asked.

"No, big man. It just started bleeding. Maybe it's my blood pressure."

"Young pup like you? Hardly. My heart's going a dinger, though. I think I need a beta blocker or something."

"Maybe nick a spliff from one of those wee scumbags over there."

"Wouldn't touch that junk."

"I'm just joking, like."

"Not everybody gets your jokes."

"Jesus Christ. You're minus *craic*, mate."

"Why do you Catholics love to take the Lord's name in vain, *mate?*"

Greene poked Mackin with his baton. "I *knew* you were a sectarian bastard."

"Ach, dry your eyes. I was trying to make a wee joke too, just."

"My hole. Hope your ticker loses its tock, you wanker."

"No need for that, Greene."

"Is there not?"

"You're not doing my heart-rate much good here, Greene. Would you kindly get lost?"

"No worries. But don't call my name if you get yourself in trouble. Deal?"

"Just dander on, wee lad."

Greene forced a savage smile and backed away a few steps. Then he paused and swapped his baton into his shield hand. He raised a finger in the air, Columbo style.

"But here, Jesus can suck the back of my balls."

By some miracle, the words made their way to Mackin's ears. He watched Greene turn on his heel, and then Mackin drew his baton. The older cop darted forward and clunked the back of Greene's helmet. And Greene toppled like timber.

DS McAllister had been given a break from the onslaught. She stood close enough to see Mackin attack Greene; too far away to prevent it. But she snapped into action when her colleague hit the deck. Intercepted Mackin before he could do any further damage to her fallen comrade.

"Stop it, Mackin! Are you nuts?"

"You didn't hear what that turncoat said to me."

"What he *said* to you? Grow up."

"You'd need to watch your lip and all, *girl*."

"We're in this together!"

"Not Greene," Mackin said. "He'll sell himself off to

the highest bidder."

Greene climbed to his feet using his baton and shield as makeshift rungs. He wheeled on Mackin but held back on the attack his body language telegraphed. McAllister would have been sandwiched in a head-on collision. Then Mackin swatted McAllister to the side. Her light frame bowled into a small group of recovering riot cops. Mackin pointed at Greene.

"You should have stayed down, wee lad."

"And let you off with a dirty Joe attack? No chance, woman beater."

"Aye? 'mon then."

In perfect synchronicity, they dropped their batons and shields, pushed down their visors and ran at each other like duelling stags. Clashed. They became a jumble of limbs, desperate for the upper hand.

A group of battle-weary cops were alerted to the tussle. They drew closer, like a small band of lion tamers with little confidence in their training. The bravest of the bunch acted first. Three of them abandoned their shields and batons. Their gloved hands worked to separate the wrestlers.

And they got sucked into the bedlam.

Now five men had been enlisted in the battle royale. A circle gathered around the spectacle. The older officers had gravitated towards one side. And the younger generation unconsciously bunched together. They all called for blood.

On the outskirts of the human ring, McAllister screamed until her voice cracked:

"STOP THEM. STOP THEM. STOP…"

Her breath was wasted.

And then came the chanting.

"S-S. R-U-C. S-S. R-U-C. S-S. R-U-C."

The younger spectators banged their batons against their shields. They were the PSNI generation. The elders had roots in the old RUC. And so the old school returned fire with:

"P-S-N. I-R-A. P-S-N. I-R-A. P-S-N. I-R-A."

The skeleton crew of riot cops left behind to hold the

line lost their battle. Protestors swarmed the previously enclosed battleground. And toppled over each other. They struggled to make sense of the situation playing out in front of them. But they wouldn't be outdone on the chant-off.

"U-V-F."

"U-F-F."

"Up-the-hoods."

The intermingled syllables mashed together; the human pressure cooker imploded. Every man and woman for themselves.

DS Greene dragged himself towards DS McAllister. She'd been knocked unconscious. Greene lay across her prone body while the storm raged around them. He closed his eyes and waited for it to end.

Violence.

Chaos.

Disorder.

PUSH ME

Dev got a parking space a few doors down from nine Palestine Street. Bridge tapped the face of the digital clock mounted in the Lancer's dashboard.

"That was some ten minutes, Dev."

"I didn't know we'd hit a fucking roadblock. Did you?"

"Looks like we got here before the ambulance, though."

"Big surprise. They'll be as stretched as we are by these rioting bastards."

"Come on."

Bridge was the first out of the car and the first to get to the door. He hammered the panelled wood with a fist. Wound back to kick it. Dev collared him.

"Bridge. Give the lad a chance to answer."

"He must have split."

"Count to ten."

He raced through the numbers. "Can we break it down now?"

Dev looked up and down the street. No sign of interest in their activities. "Go ahead."

Bridge took a step back and launched his shoulder into the sweet spot just below the night latch. The door juddered open.

"Some security," Dev said.

Bridge didn't seem to hear her. He was already in the hallway. Dev followed him.

"There's the housemate," Bridge said. He knelt to check Mickey's pulse. "Poor fucker. Didn't do anything but cross the wrong path."

"He's gone, then?"

Bridge nodded. He led the way to the kitchen. They both stood over Clark for a few seconds. There was no obvious sign of life.

"Maybe Jimmy freaked out because the big man clocked his card," Dev said.

"No. He can't be dead. Not yet." Bridge didn't kneel to check the pulse this time. He hunkered at the edge of Clark's pool of crimson to keep his trousers dry. Stretched out to place his fingers on the side of his throat.

"Well?"

"Still alive. All this blood and the fucker hung on."

"Looks like Jimmy helped him out a bit before he split." Dev indicated the bloody towels with a tilt of her head. "We may wait until the ambulance comes."

"Thought you were on duty."

"I've got a little more time before the shift starts yet, Bridge. And even if I didn't, I wouldn't leave you alone with him."

"If you knew the whole story, you would."

"Try me."

Bridge straightened up. He backed away from Clark *and* leaned against the kitchen worktop. Folded his arms.

"It's his fault that my little girl died."

"Come on, Bridge. We've talked about this before. Suicide is a big problem here. Your Lily was knocking about with the wrong crowd. I don't think sleeping with Clark Wallace would have been enough to tip her over the edge. Like I said before, if you go down that route, you may as well blame me too."

"I probably should. But not as much as I do Clark *and* his runty wee cousin." Bridge looked down at the barely-living but still remaining Wallace. "When Clark was finished with her, he passed her on to Vic. Like she was a hand-me-down. One of them – and I don't think they even knew which one it was for sure – got her pregnant."

"Bridge..."

He held his hand up, the speed of his movement lending violent intent to it. "Let me finish." His hand curled into a fist, but he let it drop to his side. "Rather than face up to the fact that one of them would be a parent, Clark told Vic to sort it out. Even lent him a little money, because that's what a good cousin does. Vic paid for two tickets to England and took her to an abortion clinic. On the face of it, it was a couple of kids heading to London for a wee city break. Lily had turned sixteen by then, so she was legal and nobody batted an eyelid at the fact that she was with a man just a few years older than her. Not that Vic had waited until she turned sixteen or anything. No, she'd gotten pregnant before that."

"It happens, Bridge."

"But not every father has to listen to the cunts who raped his daughter boast about it."

"Rape?"

"She was fifteen and off her head. Statutory at the very least, Dev."

Dev didn't challenge him on it.

"Every time I went near either of the Wallaces they'd remind me that Lily had been with them. It only stopped after she hanged herself. The note said she couldn't handle the guilt of the abortion. Her mother's obsession with raising her Catholic didn't help." Bridge stared hard at Dev. "So, you see, Dev, we all deserve to shoulder some of the blame. Me, you, Lily, her own mother. But two people in particular have more to answer for. One's dead and the other's dying."

Dev swallowed before she spoke. When she did, her voice was soft. "Why didn't you tell me all this before?"

"I didn't want you to stop me."

And then Bridge darted forward. Yelled at Clark. "Wake up, you bastard!"

He kicked Clark's head like it was a football. Wound back to do it again. Dev pulled her Glock from under her jacket. Closed in on Bridge. Pushed the muzzle into the side of his head. Bridge almost fell over. He abandoned the second kick in favour of keeping his balance.

"Don't make me shoot you, Bridge."

"If you kill me, it's on you, not me."

"That's why I don't want to do it. But I will. I can't let you murder somebody in front of me."

"Even though you know what he did?"

"We can add statutory rape charges to the growing list. Maybe we can get Billy Andrews to support your statement. He might be the one person who hates Clark as much as you do."

"That won't be enough."

"So we track down this Jimmy McAuley lad. He'll be another nail in the coffin, won't he?"

"Clark'll get away again. The fucker always gets away. It's up to me to end this."

"It's not, and you know it."

The sound of a siren carried through the house.

"That'll be the ambulance," Dev said. "Can I put the gun away?"

Bridge moved backwards. Slowly. Dev waited until he was leaning against the countertop again before she holstered her piece. By the time they'd settled into their respective nonchalant poses, the sound of the siren had swollen to a near unbearable level and then stopped abruptly. The ambulance was on Palestine Street.

"Do you know where we can find Jimmy?" Dev asked.

Bridge nodded. "He'll be with Joe Soap, I imagine. The great American hope that's all over the papers these days. Jimmy's so-called boss and a sleekit wee shite by the looks of him. They've an office on the Dublin Road."

"We'll pay him a visit when Clark's been carted off and we've reported to the uniforms, all right? It's on the way to the station anyway."

Seconds later there was a knock on the busted-open door. A male voice called through to them. "Hello? Paramedic. Did somebody call an ambulance?"

"I'm DS Devenney." She pulled her PSNI ID and marched into the hall. "Everything is secure. Come on through to the kitchen."

KEEP IT CLEAN

"Where the fuck is Mason?" Soap had patted down the wild strands of hair, but his usually calm face had morphed into a sweaty, wide-eyed mess. "He's not answering his phone."

"The way he was talking, I'm pretty sure he's done a runner, Joe," Jimmy said. "He's probably across the border by now."

They were in Soap's office at the top of the Dublin Road building. Soap sat in his chair and Jimmy and Grace were at the other side of his desk, on their feet and hunched like two kids called in by their school principal.

"He wouldn't do that to me. We've worked together for years. I pay his salary."

"I'm just telling you what I took from his last words to me."

"Which were?"

"Something like, 'Don't expect Mister Soap to stand by you,' I think."

"You think or you know?"

Jimmy shrugged. "I'm not sure about the exact words, but that's definitely what he meant."

"Did you believe him?"

"I'm here, aren't I?"

Joe looked at Grace. She'd snaked her phone out of her bag during the exchange with Jimmy and was reading from the screen.

"Am I keeping you from something, Grace?"

"Sorry, Joe. Just trying to stay on top of things. It's work related."

"I don't care what it's related to. Pay attention."

She put her phone on the table, screen facing up.

Soap alternated his death-stare from Grace to Jimmy

and back. "Doesn't anybody in this country respect authority?"

"I thought a minarchist like you would appreciate that, Joe." Grace said.

Soap's death-stare settled on Grace and intensified. "I don't remember telling you about my political background."

"Anti-political, surely. And no, you didn't tell me about your somewhat militant past. It wasn't that easy to dig up either. What with you doing your best to bury it down deep."

"What are you talking about, Grace?" Jimmy asked.

"It's old news, Jimmy," Soap said. "Dig about in anybody's past and you'll find something embarrassing. No matter how many times they change their name."

"I don't even know what a minarchist is," Jimmy said.

"A bit like an anarchist," Grace said. "But they think that law and order should be in the hands of a very small government."

"A bit of a simplification, but she's close enough, Jimmy."

"Doesn't sound so bad to me."

"Joe probably felt the same, Jimmy. Until he was beaten by police at an Occupy Wall Street rally. I imagine he might have switched to anarcho-capitalism after that."

"Replacing the government with corporations?"

"That's close enough for government work, Jimmy. You're not always as stupid as you act. Not sure how satisfying the philosophy behind it has been for Joe's daddy, though. He's an old school capitalist with a long list of political back-scratchers."

"Let's not worry about labels, people." Soap's easy smile was back on his face. His game face. "Surely my father's philosophical differences can be no real surprise, Grace. Remember my unofficial mission statement? Fuck the politicians—"

Grace cut in. "Fuck the government, blah-blah-blah. I get it."

"So... why bring it up?"

"It's an observation, Joe."

"Do you have other observations you'd like to share?"

"Tonnes. Will we start with the fact that you stole your father's nickname to use as your surname? That's weird. Soap Cope. Why couldn't you have been Joe Cope? It's a cool name. I'm guessing you have serious daddy issues. And how about I show Jimmy a picture of you when you were going through your dreadlock and bandana phase…?"

Grace reached for her phone. The landline on Soap's desk bleated at the same time. Soap pressed a button and a hurried female voice shot from a tinny loudspeaker.

"I'm sorry, Mister Soap."

Soap held a finger up for the benefit of Jimmy and Grace. "What's wrong, Jenny?"

"There are two police officers on their way up to see you. I told them you were in a meeting, but they just ignored me."

"I'm sure it'll be fine, Jenny. Thanks for trying."

Soap pressed the button again and silenced Jenny in the middle of another apology. He pulled open his drawer and took out a mirror. Adjusted his hair, the knot of his tie and dabbed his face with a red cloth handkerchief that he carried in his breast pocket.

"You guys just follow my lead with the cops. When they're gone, I'll put any concerns you have to bed, Grace. Be cool, Jimmy."

Neither Grace nor Jimmy had time to reassure their boss. The lift pinged open and revealed their visitors.

Dev elbowed Bridge's ribs. "That's Grace Doran."

"So it is," Bridge said. He rubbed the spot Dev had sunk her elbow into. "And there's Jimmy McAuley and Joe Soap."

Joe got out of his seat and crossed the room, his hand extended. He shook with Dev first and then Bridge. "You're both detectives, right?"

"I'm Detective Sergeant Devenney and this is Detective Inspector Bridge."

"Are you here for another application form, Inspector

Bridge?" Soap asked. "You're dogged. I'll give you that."

"No, no. Judging by the press you're getting recently, there'll be no jobs to apply for soon enough." Bridge said. "Seems as if the PSNI might be more secure than your security firm. Is that irony?"

"You're a funny guy." Soap patted Bridge's shoulder. "I'm sure you'd have been a lot of fun, if not for the whole mental illness thing."

Bridge didn't acknowledge the remark. He walked past Soap to get to Jimmy. Dev smiled apologetically at Soap but followed her colleague.

"What happened, Jimmy? We asked you to wait at the house."

"I… uh…"

"He was going to, I can assure you."

Bridge turned to look at Soap. "I'm talking to Jimmy."

"The kid's in shock. I'm just helping him out."

"Are you his lawyer as well as his employer?"

"Heaven forbid." Soap let loose a measured laugh. Crisp and spontaneous. His practiced smile took over where the chuckle left off. "I'm many things, inspector, but please don't accuse me of that."

"There'll be plenty of other things to accuse you of in due course, I'm sure."

"What do you mean by that, Inspector Bridge?" Soap's smile had gone the way of the dodo.

"Call it a hunch."

"I'm not satisfied with that explanation."

"And I'm not satisfied with the explanation you shared on Jimmy's behalf."

"Did you set Grace on my trail? I doubt that'd be above board."

"I looked into your past off my own bat, Joe," Grace said. "It was journalistic curiosity at first. Now it's car crash fascination."

"I knew the atmosphere in here was a little off," Dev

said. "Maybe you and I should chat, Grace."

"Sounds good to me."

"I haven't done anything illegal," Soap said.

Dev looked at the unoccupied office space. "And yet your office looks like a front for something very dodgy."

"It's just a start," Soap said. "In the next few months, maybe a year, the whole building will be full of gainfully employed citizens. It'll rival any police station in Belfast."

"And what about the real Agency stations?" Grace asked. "Or does Big Daddy Soap not let you play about with the profitable ones?"

"This is *my* business, Grace. Not my father's."

"Daddy's backing you, though. Isn't he? Couldn't trust you to run anything too high risk, what with your flaky past as a political activist and all."

"I think the officers are here to see Jimmy, Grace. Not me. Let's get out of their way."

"I'd like you all to stick around a little longer, Mister Soap," Dev said.

"I'm a busy man."

"We're all busy, Mister Soap." Dev dropped her good-cop face. "You can't be ignorant to the fact that there are riots going off all over the city right now. A riot that your so-called security company had a hand in starting with that fucking infomercial, or whatever you'd call it. No doubt I could be put to use out there, but instead I've had to track you down after you helped Mister McAuley leave the scene of a crime."

"He was in fear of his personal safety. There was no need for him to stay there."

"Apart from the fact that he was the witness to a murder and an attempted murder?"

"Precisely because of that."

"When my colleague spoke to him on the phone Jimmy reported that one of your other employees fled the scene. Have you heard from Mister Mason?"

"I can't get in touch with him."

"Is that unusual?"

"Perhaps I need to call my lawyer?"

"Probably. But you're not under arrest just yet." Dev looked to Grace. "A colleague of mine may want to chat to you, Grace. Any problem with that?"

"Not at all."

"Good. His name is Detective Constable Reggie Prescott. Check his ID just in case. I think he could well be a fan of yours, but I'll ask him to be professional."

"Not a problem."

"So if you want to leave me a business card or something, you can be on your way."

"Oh." Grace looked at Jimmy. "I'll wait for you in the car park."

"No need," Dev said. "We'll give him a lift to the station. He's going to have to provide us with a statement."

"It's okay, Grace." Jimmy smiled at her with the good side of his face.

Grace leaned forward and kissed Jimmy's undamaged cheek. "Call me when you can."

"Call her on her private number, Jimmy," Soap said. "She's no longer an employee. I'll be striking her from the phone contract and everything else."

"Fire her and you may fire me."

"That's sweet, Jimmy," Grace said. "But I'd have quit anyway. If there was an actual job to leave, that is. He'd have run this business into the ground, just like the other trust fund investments before them. Then he'd feed us to the auditors while he moved on to the next gig."

"That's defamation," Soap said. "You heard her, officers. Defamation."

"I didn't hear anything," Bridge said. He'd drifted towards Soap's desk while Dev had held centre stage. His fingers tapped at the keyboard. "There's fuck all on this except for funding applications."

"Get away from my computer, Bridge," Soap said. "I

have rights. The PSNI have no right to investigate my property without a warrant."

"This machine wasn't password protected and I have reason to believe you're part of a terrorist conspiracy."

"Laying it on a bit thick, surely?" Soap looked to Dev. "Can't you do something about this man? He's clearly unhinged."

"Now, I heard *that* little bit of defamation," Bridge said.

"Please don't leave the city, Mister Soap," Dev said. "We'll need you to help us with some enquiries."

NOBODY'S BUSINESS

Dev held the back door to her Lancer open and waited for Jimmy to settle into his seat. She closed the door and spoke to Bridge over the top of the car.

"Wait. Don't get in just yet, Bridge."

"What is it?"

"Did you put Grace Doran onto this Soap character?"

"I might have suggested it. Grace had already started her investigation, though. For a story."

"Why?"

"She figured he was too sweet to be wholesome, just. He didn't seem natural when I met him either."

"He's American. Dyed hair, polished teeth, bullshit charm. Pretty standard, like."

"Tactful as always, Dev." He shook his head, but his hound dog eyes had a little extra puppy love in them. "It was more than that. A slight stiffness that crept up on him when he realised he could smell bacon."

"Like any other criminal."

Bridge shrugged. "More of a compulsive liar than a criminal, really."

"I don't get that vibe off you, though. Is there hope for you?"

Bridge shook his head. "But I won't make it easy for you to nail me."

"Can you get home all right on your own?"

"From here? Piece of piss."

"Sorry. I'd drop you off on the way to the station but I should really see if I can get a lead on this Mason character. I'll call Reggie now and see if he can meet Jimmy somewhere nearby."

"No sweat, Dev. Stay safe."

270

"Stay in the city, Tommy."

"Touché, *Patricia*."

Bridge headed off in the direction of an alley that led to the Europa Bus Station. Dev watched him until he was out of sight. He didn't look back. Dev opened the back door.

"Come on up front like a big boy, Jimmy."

Jimmy treated her to a half-smile. "Is Inspector Bridge not coming?"

"He's got somewhere else to be."

"Bit scary, isn't he?"

"Ach, he's got a lot on his mind."

They got into the car and buckled up. Dev pulled out onto the Dublin Road.

"I'll drop you at the station, Jimmy, but you'll be chatting to my colleague, Constable Prescott."

"You off duty now too?"

"No, my shift started half an hour ago. But I've somewhere else to be."

"Ah right. One of the riots?"

"This whole city's a riot."

PAGING DOCTOR BRIDGE

Bridge used his PSNI ID to silence the protesting ward sister.

"I don't give a damn about his recuperation. Clark Wallace killed a man today and I have questions for him. If he's conscious, I demand to speak to him."

Her hatchet face sharpened. "Please don't use abusive language."

Bridge thought for a few seconds. "Damn?"

The sister rested her hands on her bony hips. "We operate a zero tolerance policy to verbal abuse."

"It wasn't even directed at you."

"Policy is policy."

"I suppose it is. I officially retract my offensive language. Will you lead me to Clark Wallace's bed?"

"Yes, I will, constable...?"

Bridge held his ID closer to the sister's squinting eyes. "Inspector, actually. Detective Inspector Bridge."

"Right this way, Inspector Bridge."

She led him through the ward on heels that clacked off the wipe-clean floor like drumsticks on a snare. A pair of nurses shuffled some paper at a station, afraid to look at each other in her oncoming presence. She stopped in front of the station and rapped the countertop with a tight little fist.

"This is Inspector Bridge. I've given him permission to visit with Mister Clark Wallace. Just so you know not to chase him out."

They nodded agreement.

The sister looked at Bridge, pride of position blunting the hatchet slightly. "My team is very conscientious, you see. No sense in you waving your badge at every nurse you see."

"I thought the PSNI had ID cards," one of the nurses said.

The sister attempted to wither her with a look. Bridge was a little friendlier.

"Aye, the aul' ID card is as close to that sheriff's badge as I could get when I grew up. Always wished it looked more like a gold star, though. Even the Lone Ranger's silver star would have done the job."

"Mister Wallace is over here, Inspector. Follow me."

The nurses shared a sneaky smile with Bridge when he saluted the sister behind her back. Then he trotted to catch up with her. They passed a couple of filled bays before they got to a door.

"He got his own room?" Bridge asked.

"His injuries were very serious. He's lucky to be out of ICU. Probably wouldn't be only we're preparing for more casualties tonight."

"Ah, riot season. You have to love it."

"Quite." She checked the watch pinned to her tunic. "You can use the call button if you require anything. I have tasks to attend to, Inspector Bridge."

"Thank you, sister."

His use of her professional title earned him a tight little nod and something that would one day evolve into a smile. Bridge took a few seconds to breathe before he opened the door to Clark's private hospital room.

"Ach, fuck me," Clark said.

"Good to see you too, mate." Bridge sniffed the air. "You're looking well."

"Wanker."

Clark had a broken nose and two black eyes. The purple bruises were all the more ugly against the background of his paper-white skin. He looked smaller, curled up on the bed. Tubes ran from his wrist to an IV drip, one a bag of blood, the other something clear. His breathing was assisted by more tubes hooked to his nose and a ventilator. He lay on his side and didn't attempt to sit up to greet his visitor.

"I always said you'd be stabbed in the back one day.

Thought it would have been one of your Loyalist buddies, but I was half right at least."

"I bet you were devastated when you found out."

"Only because I thought I'd been robbed of the chance of doing it myself."

Clark double-blinked. "Did you not set the big bastard on me?"

"No, Clarky boy. Pure bad luck on our part. Getting a hard-on for the only student in Belfast with a bodyguard, like."

"I was blaming you in the wrong, then."

"Well, I'm not totally innocent. You can thank me for the reconstructive surgery." Bridge indicated his own eyes and nose. "I got a wee boot in after I found you."

"You always were a sleekit shite."

"I know. That's how you fight the big boys."

"Vic wasn't much bigger than you. You still needed a hit squad to hold his arms when you cut his throat, though."

"You know?"

"Sammy visited me earlier. Brought me some grapes, underwear and a story. Bit fucking late, but still. Think he realised I'll be going nowhere any time soon. Trying to get into my good graces again before I remove Rubble Jenkins from my territory."

"You just can't buy silence in this country anymore. Everybody's lips have been flapping since the Good Friday Agreement, especially on your side. Should have paid the extra for a bunch of Republican dissidents. They're the only ones keeping it old school. Did Sammy tell you he was one of the hit squad?"

"Aye. Said you blackmailed him into it, though. And you threatened his kids too. How did that new low feel?"

"Will those things exonerate him?"

"You wha'?"

"Will you go easier on him because of the threats and blackmail?"

"No. Sammy's as dead as Rubble. They just don't know

it yet." He said it without a second thought.

"Probably for the best. I didn't blackmail him, I paid him."

"Aye? What about his wee ones."

"That, I'm guilty of."

After a few seconds of eyeballing Bridge, Clark said, "Speaking of kids, Vic really loved your wee girl, you know. He didn't deserve that. Her topping herself was punishment enough. He was a drugged-out mess after."

"Boo hoo. He took my daughter from me."

"That wasn't his idea. It was all mine."

"And here was me thinking you'd tell me you loved her too."

"Nah. She was just another skank to me. A little more memorable because she was a cop's daughter, but still a skank."

Bridge breathed deep.

"If she'd been raised better it might have been different," Clark said.

"I can't wait to snuff you out, big lad."

"You going to strangle me?"

Bridge shrugged out of his suit jacket and tossed it towards a plastic chair. Missed. The expensive material landed in a heap on the floor. He wore a brown leather shoulder holster over his black shirt.

"I'll probably use a pillow." Bridge started to roll up his shirt sleeves. The tattoos on his right arm looked more colourful than ever under the hospital fluorescents. "A cliché as far as hospital deaths go, I know, but I wasn't confident that I'd get a pipebomb in here."

"Caroline definitely didn't deserve that."

"Matter of opinion. She definitely deserved it more than Steve Swain or Mickey Walsh."

"Did that other wee lad die, then? Looks like I'm in the lead."

"You can take that victory to the grave."

"I'll call for a nurse. You won't get away with it."

"They look pretty short-staffed out there." Bridge drew his gun from his shoulder holster. The standard Glock 17. "And then there's this. I'd rather you went quietly, so I can escape, but I'll do time in a pinch."

"Dirty as you are? I bet you'll fit right in. Come on, then."

"Dignity? I'm disappointed. I might have to stretch this out. See if I can break you a little more. Took a lot of effort to find you. No point rushing the fun bit."

The door opened. Bridge tucked his gun away before he turned to face the newcomer. It was Dev. She had her own gun drawn.

"Dev. Let me have this, will you?"

"I nearly did. But I've been talking to the Super. That's why I wasn't here before you, like I'd hoped."

"Did the Super tell you to leave Mason and tail me instead, then?"

"That was the whitest lie ever told compared to some of the shit you've been spinning for me."

"Good to see you, big girl," Clark said. "You going to arrest this prick or what?"

"He's not doing anything illegal," Dev said.

"There's a gun in his pocket, he's not just happy to see you."

"No doubt it's for personal protection. Totally legit, Clark."

"Is that why you've whipped yours out?"

"No, I just knew I'd feel under-equipped around you dick-swingers." She waggled her Glock. "This is a comfort to me."

"What did the Super say?" Bridge asked.

"Clark's getting scooped on a much bigger charge than either me or you could lay at his feet. The higher-ups had caught wind of our Clark's ejection from his band of merry men. And now the touts are lining up to put the boot in. It'll be like the super-grass trial all over again, except Clark Wallace is the star of the show."

"What charges?"

"Racketeering, sex trafficking and drug dealing. The Loyalist classics. The Super's confident that murder'll get thrown into the mix too. Stephen Swain will top that list."

"It's not good enough."

"Catch yourself on, Bridge. This is a dream come true."

"No. It won't do. I've gotten this far." Bridge's hand inched toward his chest. He was going for his gun, slowly but surely.

"Don't do it, Bridge. This could be your happy ending."

"I don't deserve that, and neither does he."

"He's going to jail."

"Where he can bulk up on steroids, get off his tits on whatever else he can get his hands on and shoot the shit with his mates? I don't fucking think so."

"Ach, come on, Bridge. You know it's not really like that."

"It kind of is, though," Clark said. "I'd miss bucking birds, like, but any hole when the lights are out, what?"

"You're not helping, dickhead," Dev said.

Bridge's hand had made its way under his jacket. Dev raised her gun and pointed it at his head. He turned away from her. Faced Clark on his deathbed.

"Bridge, don't." She was close enough now to press her gun against his temple.

"*Déjà vu*, Dev."

"Please, Bridge."

"Listen to the big dyke, Bridge. You're done."

"Shut the fuck up, Clark," Dev said. "Why don't you do something useful and hit the call button?"

"Fuck that. I want to see how this pans out."

Bridge eased his gun from its shoulder holster. His finger was outside the trigger-guard and the gun was pointed away from Clark, but it was out in the open now.

"Bridge, ignore him. Listen to me. Don't make me do

this to you and I'll forget all that shit I figured out. Nobody cares enough about Vic to look into it properly."

"Hello?" Clark said.

"Nobody that matters," Dev said. "And they'll probably let Caroline's death go if they don't manage to pin it on this lump of shite. You were careful enough, Bridge. And you weren't in your right mind. Maybe you're still out of it, but there's a part of you left in there, isn't there? A little bit that wants the real Bridge back. And I'll be here with you to welcome him home. But you have to meet me halfway. You have to let this go, Bridge. Do that much for me, and I'll know there's hope for you. Just put the gun away. Even if I *could* let you kill this ballbag in front of me, there is no way we could sell it as anything but cold-blooded murder. He's unarmed and in a hospital bed, for fuck's sake. Tommy, *please*."

"I never really blamed you, Patricia," Bridge said. "Can I call you that?"

"Only if we're fucking."

Bridge huffed a half-formed laugh through his nose. "Nobody ever tickled my funny bone like you, Dev. And I really did love you. Maybe you never felt it, but it was there. When I lost Lily, you were all I had. But I didn't deserve you. I couldn't protect my own child. What good was I to anybody else? I couldn't drag you down with me. So I pushed you away. All the shitty things I did. Freezing you out, swiping the promotion out from under you, joining in with the station meatheads when they came to the conclusion that you'd turned gay."

"Fuck you very much for that one."

"I know. It's obvious to me now. I wasn't protecting you from my shitty karma. I tortured you. No wonder you thought I blamed you. But I never did, Dev. And it's important that you know that. You're a good person. A great detective. And I'm so sorry I have to put this on you."

And he went for it.

Dev had a head start but Bridge was faster.

Both guns went off. Dev had whipped hers downwards

to aim for Bridge's leg. A non-fatal shot. And it hit him just above the knee. Bridge continued to pump his trigger on the way down. The bullets from his gun punched Clark's chest, once, twice, three times. Two more bullets went wild, one smashing the only window in the room, the other puncturing the IV bag of clear liquid hanging above Clark's bed. Bridge was on his backside in the middle of the floor. Blood oozed from his leg at an alarming rate. Dev holstered her gun and fumbled with her belt buckle.

"Fuck's sake, Bridge!" Dev's loud voice cracked. "Hold your fire. You'll bleed out if I don't strap your leg."

"Just one more," Bridge said.

"No. Stop! You got him."

Bridge jammed his Glock into the soft underside of his jaw.

Dev screamed.

He pulled the trigger.

The bullet tore through his skull. Lifted his crown. Bridge toppled back from his sitting position and Dev fell to the ground by his side. Lay across his chest. He was silent, she wailed like a banshee. And when she gasped for a breath to start again, Clark Wallace spluttered a mouthful of blood.

"I didn't tell you what kind of underwear Sammy brought me, Bridge. Fucking bulletproof vest, like. Yeeeooo!"

Then his laughter filled the space between Dev's shrieks.

BURN

The coffin rolled into the crematorium. Grace, Jimmy and Dev blessed themselves then shared a conspiratorial smirk. It was as far from a Catholic burial as you could get, but old habits died hard. They edged in a little closer to each other as the door slammed shut, cutting them away from their dearly beloved. The hum of the machinery got louder as it worked to burn every trace of DI Tommy Bridge. Reducing him to ash.

Jimmy spoke first. "I thought it would smell worse."

Grace looked at him, her eyes on stalks.

"They've got special filters and all that," Dev said. "Keeps it civilised."

"Are we supposed to stay until it's finished?" Jimmy asked.

"I don't think so," Grace said.

Neither Jimmy nor Grace made any sign of movement.

"Is it wrong that I just want to go outside and smoke?" Dev asked.

Jimmy and Grace tried not to smile, but the struggle was obvious on their faces. Dev tipped them a wink and they took that as permission to indulge their graveyard humour just a little.

"I think I'd like a cigarette too," Grace said.

"A big joint would do me better," Jimmy said. Then he caught sight of Dev's suddenly less playful expression. "Pity it's against the law, like."

Dev led them to the grounds outside.

"There's a wee bench around the corner, just."

And there was.

"You've been here before, then," Grace said.

Dev lit her coffin nail. "Occupational hazard." She held the lighter out for Grace, the flame still burning. "You not having one, Jimmy?"

"You got a spare at all?"

Grace was the first one to produce a cigarette for him. Dev lit it.

"Nothing like a brush with death to put a craving on you, like," Jimmy said. "Probably not the kind of habit I should pick up without a job, though. Can't even apply for a student loan since they kicked me out of uni."

"What are you going to do with yourself, then?" Dev asked.

"I haven't a fucking clue. No hope for the future at all. Maybe the cancer sticks aren't such a bad idea after all."

Dev and Grace simply nodded and smoked.

Jimmy tried to get the chatter going again.

"That was some feature you did on aul' Joe Soap for the Irish News, Grace."

She let him have a smile in lieu of words of gratitude. Wisps of blue smoke escaped her nostrils.

"My mum was all biz when she saw my name in there. You made me look really good. Like a private investigator or something. I didn't even do all that much."

"*De nada*," Grace said. She sucked on her cigarette. Inhaled. Exhaled. Sighed.

"Maybe I should look into joining the PSNI," Jimmy said.

Neither of his companions commented.

Jimmy accepted the conversational dead-end and focussed on Dev. "You think Soap's going to go down?"

Dev nodded. "Aye. And even though the case fell into my lap, thanks to Grace, I'm getting all the kudos. I wanted to hand the whole mess over to Reggie, like, but the daft fucker's too loyal. He's just letting things tick over until I get back from my leave. The yank prick's going nowhere either. Until his da' figures out a way to buy him out of trouble, anyway. But a result's a result. Looks like I might be offered a promotion off the back of it."

"Congratulations," Grace said.

"I appreciate the sentiment, but save your congratulations for another occasion. It's unlikely I'll accept."

"Why?" Jimmy asked, before Grace had a chance to shush him.

"I was due a promotion years ago. Worked my arse off for it. Bridge got it instead. Look how things turned out for him."

"But Bridge was…" Jimmy held his hand up as if he could pluck the end of his sentence from thin air. "Well, he was Bridge, wasn't he? He had troubles."

"And now I do too, thanks to him."

"Don't make any decisions yet," Grace said. "See what happens when you get back from your leave. You've been through hell and back, but time's a great healer. Take as long as you need. Just don't write yourself off yet."

"We'll see." Dev reached into her bag and plucked her mobile phone from it. She lit up the screen and opened a text. Held it up for Grace and Jimmy to see. "It's another 'wear blues' message. Somebody at the station's putting me on riot duty by mistake. They keep sending these even though I keep replying to tell them I'm on leave. And every time I get one, I think of Bridge and his wee blue suits. I swear he had one in every shade except for riot gear blue."

"It must be so hard," Grace said.

Dev nodded and looked up at the grey clouds over Roselawn Cemetery. Thunder rumbled. "Settle down, Tommy. I'm not mad at you. Just saying."

It started to rain. Dev raised her face and let the falling drops join her tears.

"Maybe *he's* pissed at *you*, though?" Jimmy said.

Grace thumped his arm, but Dev didn't seem that bothered.

"Chances are you're right, Jimmy. But if aul' Buddha can be believed, Bridge is going to swing by this world again. And maybe he will forgive me. In time."

EPILOGUE: NO ESCAPE

Clark had the best seat in the lounge. His own armchair. Right in front of the TV. He was thinner and paler, but the marks on his face had faded, and his red and blue striped polo shirt hid the scars inflicted by Mason and Bridge. His nose had been reset so that only a small kink remained as proof that it had been broken. He was on the mend. And without a baseball cap to cover the fresh snow in his widow's peak, he could have passed for a slightly wiser man too.

Other prisoners were sprawled out on a cluster of sofas and armchairs. The news was on. Coverage of a riot in the city centre. It was impossible to hear the newscaster over the noise of the prisoners' chit-chat and speculation.

"They say they're going to call in the British Army to sort it out," a ratty teenager said to Clark.

"Sure they always say that, wee Ali. When it goes on for more than a few weeks, it's just one of those catchphrases they use to make people think something'll be done. And it's a scare tactic for the rioters too. But it'll keep going on, you know? There's no stopping it really. Not when so many people are so pissed off. The Army won't ever step in. They were as relieved as the Taigs when they got out of this shithole."

Ali looked over his shoulder before he allowed himself to laugh at Clark's last remark. "Good one, mate."

"You're looking well, Clark."

Clark closed his eyes for a few seconds at the sound of the voice. He mouthed a silent, "Fuck." Then he used the arms of the chair to push down on and help raise his arse off the worn cushion.

"All right, Billy?"

"I'm not at my best, no."

Clark turned to face Billy Andrews. The smaller man

was gaunt and twitchy, his pallor the same shade as cigarette ash. But beyond that, he looked dangerous. Some prisoners picked up on his vibe immediately and left the lounge right away. They started a chain reaction that led to a mass exodus. Ali was the last one to move away, and even then it was only when Clark gave him the nod.

"Sorry, big man," Ali said.

"No worries, kid. This isn't your fight."

When it was just Clark, Billy and the news, Billy produced a shiv. A flat piece of metal with a handle made from insulating tape. The product of abused prison privileges.

"I've prayed for this, Clark."

"Weird wish for God to grant, do you not think?"

"I don't care if it was him or the man downstairs. I'm just happy that I've been given this chance."

"You sure you want to do this? I might be a wee bit under the weather still, but I've fight left in me."

"If you could have, you'd have taken me out by now."

"Fair enough."

"Good to see the colour back in your cheeks, though."

"Aye?"

"Aye. Means there's more blood in there for me to spill."

"You doing this for Caroline, then?"

"Who the fuck else?"

"You really think I killed her?"

"Aye."

"Come on to fuck, then. Take your best shot, Billy."

The smaller man didn't hesitate. He bowled into Clark, shoulder first. When the big man hit the deck like a stone, Billy was all over him. He scrambled to mount Clark's body and brought the shiv down in an arc that started behind his head. Metal punched through flesh. Clark jerked, convulsed and sighed. Billy pulled the makeshift dagger from his enemy's chest. Hammered it downwards again. This time Clark barely reacted. Blood foamed at the corners of his lips.

"This is for you, Caroline," Billy said.

A little spurt of blood shot from Clark's mouth and landed on Billy's T-shirt. Stained it just above his heart. Clark coughed and cleared more bloody sputum from his throat. The bigger expulsion missed Billy. A laugh followed that cough, though, and it hit the mark. Billy went into a frenzy and didn't stop until well after Clark had stopped laughing.

On the television a politician in her best business suit was being interviewed. In the background, a pair of water canons hosed rioters into submission. The politician glared through the screen into hundreds of thousands of homes. Her makeup was severe, red lips and black, angry eyebrows. She scowled and said:

"We won't put up with this any longer. Something must be done."

ACKNOWLEDGMENTS

Thanks to David Torrans, bookseller, festival stalwart, and now publisher, along with Claudia and all the staff at No Alibis, where my crime fiction education began.

My most important novel to date would not exist without Andrew Pepper and Dominique Jeannerod. I'm eternally grateful for all your advice, support and patience during the PhD years.